## Praise for Ann Pearlma _____ ..kie Club
## Se

### A GIFT FOR MY SISTER

"This is a fast-paced novel, full of a varied cast of characters. There are no easy answers but lots of soul searching and heart-racing action." *Booklist*

"Poignant….This is a story about love, loss, embracing second chances, and finding the courage to move forward…." *Publishers Weekly*

"An eloquent and moving novel." *Minding Spot*

"A moving, deeply resonant novel…Pearlman skillfully evokes empathy on both sides." *Shelf Awareness*

"Ann Pearlman tells an effortless story. You're halfway through the book before you even know you're hooked… …" *The Cairns Post, Australia*

"A Gift for My Sister leaves you emotionally raw and rips your heart to shreds…before putting I back together in such a way that you'll never be the same again…This is the contemporary read I recommend everyone read at least once in their lives." *The Bawdy Book Blog*

### THE CHRISTMAS COOKIE CLUB

"Pearlman has delivered a passionate and heartfelt story of women's friendships and their importance with *The Christmas Cookie Club…The Christmas Cookie Club* would the perfect gift for girlfriends of all ages this holiday season." *Las Vegas Review-Journal.*

"Readers with large groups of friends will love this story of women who support each other through tough times." *Book Page*

"Ms. Pearlman has written a book filled with love, friendship and heartache. Besides offering an entertaining storyline, the author also shares cookie recipes. A Wonderful holiday book!" *The Romance Readers Connection.*

ALSO BY ANN PEARLMAN

*Keep the Home Fires Burning*

*Infidelity: A Love Story*

*Inside the Crips: Life Inside L.A.'s Most Notorious Gang*

*The Christmas Cookie Club*

*The Christmas Cookie Cookbook*

*A Gift for My Sister*

*His Eye is On The Sparrow*

*Other Lives*

*Angels*

# THE LOTTERY

a novel

## Ann Pearlman

Dancing Books Press
Ann Arbor, MI.
2015

# *The Lottery*

Disclaimer: This is a work of fiction. Names, characters, places and incidents are products of the author's imagination or the author has used them fictitiously. Any resemblance to actual persons, living or dead, events or locales is entirely coincidental.

Cover design by Ann Pearlman

## Dedication

To people who appreciate the joys as well as the limits of money.

# Cast of Characters

*Players:*

Jeannie----- Mark
      (Sara)
      parents: Jack and Frances

Marnie ----- Jim
      Sky
      (Rachel)
      Tara----Aaron
      (Levy and Hannah)

Juliet------- Dan and Tom
      Brother: Joey, Larry
      Mom:

Rosie-------- Kevin
      (Ben)

Taylor-------Rick
      (Buzz and Nicole)

Sissy
      Aaron---Tara
      (Levy and Hannah)

Chandra----- Tony

Vera-------- Flynn


*Non –Players:*
Allie
Alice
Tracy --------Silver
Charlene

# One

*Moses used a lottery to decide who among his flock would win a plot of land by the river Jordan.*

*THERE IS NO PAST, it's never gone. It determines how you view the future. And life exists only in your mind. It is how you see it,* Jeannie thinks, standing on Juliet's porch just before she rings the bell. The thought, with its smidge of pessimism, comes as a surprise since she is nothing but excited and happy to be at this gathering.

Sure enough, Juliet opens the door with a hug, her laughter erasing the thought. "This is going to be so much fun. We'll win the lottery. I know we will." After she hangs Jeannie's coat in the entry closet, slides the door closed, it's as if Jeannie were never outside in the gusting snow, her breath never visible in the air.

Juliet's house is perfect. Evidence of the holidays has vanished except for miniature lights embellishing a six-foot tall ficus tree in the corner of a mostly white living room. Pale maple floors, smooth and gently satin, surround Turkish rugs. Classical music plays on the stereo. A cello piece, sounds like Yo-Yo Ma playing Gershwin.

Juliet pulls Jeannie to her kitchen--black granite, maple cabinets, and stainless appliances. Cabinets closed. No mixers, coffee makers, dirty dishes in evidence as though the food was magically prepared, and proof of toil and dirt erased. Rosie is already there, usually the hfirst to arrive anywhere, and Chandra. Rosie is slicing a piece of Juliet's Amaretto chocolate torte, knife in hand.

Chandra grins, "You have to get some cake. It's fabulous. Chocolate! Almonds! Alcohol!"

Just then Vera enters along with Sissy and Marnie who have driven together. They hug and kiss each other, this throng of good friends, who celebrate throughout the year, ending with a Christmas cookie club.  Spirits are high in the warmth, bright colors and boundless love, a welcome refuge from dark and bitter snow. Each of them has brought a bottle of wine.

Rosie hands a plate of cake to Vera, "So. Is this the best cake ever, or what? Wait till you taste it."

"This is better than sex," Chandra's teeth gleam white in her brown face.

"Nothing's better than sex," Juliet says.

"Sex? What's that?" Sissy jokes.

"I'm here. Sorry I'm late." Taylor calls, stomping her boots in the entry.

"We're all here!"  Juliet announces. "All who want to play."

There're twelve members of the cookie party. At the last cookie club, Sissy announced she won ten grand playing the lottery. They decided to form a lottery club and play together.

"So there'll be only eight of us," Marnie says.

"This is going to be soooo much fun." Rosie's voice trills.

"Maybe we'll win enough we could all take a trip together. Chicago."

"Chicago? Let's go someplace warm in February," Juliet says. "The Caribbean."

"Maybe even Paris," Rosie squeals.

"Or Barcelona."

"China."

"Brazil."

They throw in dream vacations, the places they haven't been.

"We might be able to win the whole thing. Even more. Maybe a million!"

"God! What would I do if I won a million?" Jeannie muses.

"We all dream that," Juliet says. "It's everyone's dream: winning the lottery."

"Say 'fuck you' to Rick," Taylor blurts out. "Who *still* hasn't paid child support and his latest settlement offer is shit. That's what I'd do. Sign his damn papers and be done with him."

"I'd buy a house with Jim and help Sky start her law practice." Marnie's voice is wistful.

"Quit my job," Chandra says.

"Buy that empty building on Stadium that would be soooooo perfect for yoga," Jeannie says. "I can just see it with a few studios, maybe a massage room. A comfortable waiting room. Sauna. Showers. Or maybe an entire wellness center."

"Pay off my kids' college loans," adds Chandra.

"Get a face lift!" Vera says.

"Start a foundation!" says Sissy. "Urban farming for Detroit," Sissy adds.

They spill out wishes, fast and furious, dreams toppling on other dreams, overlapping, fighting for first place in a hierarchy. What they'd do if they won a million dollars. All those unlived lives. Shopping sprees, houses, trips, boats, helping kids and family, donating to a charity, starting businesses. The excitement of owning unlimited beautiful, thrilling things spills out. Security at last. Security and freedom.

"The more numbers we have the greater our chance for winning!" Juliet sings, swaying her hips and doing a little dance, as she pours white wine.

"But the more we have to split the loot!" Chandra chortles.

"It is what it is. And if we want four more numbers we can get easy picks," Sissy wears the multicolored scarf she bought with her lucky ten thousand.

3

"What's that?" Taylor says. "I've never done this before."

"Let the computer pick numbers for us."

By now, the cake is almost devoured, only a few stray almonds lie on the plate. The friends move to the living room, glasses in hand. Juliet totes the basket of tangerines, and Vera the wine bottles, and places them on the Noguchi glass coffee table.

Jeannie sits on the sofa and pulls a cream-colored cashmere throw over her legs. Outside it's thick night, Juliet has no blinds so the winter dark is like dead eyes. A stray flake falls and it looks lonesome, as if a fleck from the white walls, or the white sofa, or the chairs had sparked to the outside.

"We're going to play the Mega Millions, yes? The Power Ball?" Juliet asks.

"I thought so. Right?" Chandra scans the room waiting for nods.

"It's on Tuesday night, so we buy the tickets by Tuesday."

"How do we want to do it?" Marnie asks.

"I thought we'd each pick a set of numbers and play all of them. We'll have eight chances to win each week," Juliet says.

Everyone nods. "That way each of us would play her own and everyone else's favorite numbers."

"But we won't change the numbers. They'll be our magical numbers," Jeannie says.

"Well, who is going to do it? Are we going to take turns?" Juliet asks.

"How 'bout one person buys the numbers for a month and then we rotate the next month."

"We'll meet every month to change the buyer? Let's meet at the buyer's house." Jeannie wants to make sure they keep meeting. "I'll do it next month."

4

The truth is, she's not doing this for money. She likes the idea of *all* of them meeting every month and is aware of the absent cookie club bitches. Yeah, money would be nice, who wouldn't want to win a million bucks, but if someone said, do you want to meet every month and discuss books, or the stock market, -- hell, even shoes, Tupperware, or the dog park (and she doesn't even have a dog) she'd sign up. She wants the camaraderie. Jeannie still misses the closeness she once shared with Rosie and Sue when they were the three musketeers. Then Sue started an affair with Jeannie's father and told Rosie. Rosie kept the secret, but Jeannie found out. Her two best friends, and her father betrayed her. She shakes away the memory. *Enjoy this!* She reminds herself.

Yes, she wants to be with Rosie in spite of the tarnished friendship. All weekend, she smiled when she thought of this night, cherishing and anticipating the joy. The laughter. The crazy fun of playing the lottery.

"Okay. So we'll each have our numbers in play, and one person will buy for an entire month." Marnie summarizes. "Whatever we win we'll split up evenly, right? Regardless of whose number it is, or who actually bought the ticket, right? We pay in evenly and split evenly."

"Of course." Everyone says.

"That goes without saying,"

"I picked up some Mega Million tickets." Juliet passes papers with red numbers from one to fifty-six in five panels, each divided by yellow bars, numbers for the easy pick options at the bottom. On the right side, it says *Mega Millions* in blue. On the left, *insert face up*. Jeannie has never seen one before. Each slip, about a quarter of page in size, has the option of five bets. The panels are divided in two. "I don't get this," she turns to Sissy figuring she's the expert. She won.

"The top part is for the five numbers, called white balls, and for the bottom half, you pick one number, and that's called the power ball. If all six numbers hit, you win it all. Millions usually. If you match five, you win $200,000. I matched four," Sissy picks up a tickets and points to the top panel. "Four of these, and the power ball. I used my dream book and won with 12, 10, 17, 20, which were for babies, tree, laughter and green. She points to the bottom part, "My power ball was 14 for cook, 'cause I sure was cooking up those cookies." Sissy laughs.

"How do you know which numbers go with which dreams?" Vera asks.

"From this." Sissy holds up a tattered pamphlet, the red in the picture rubbed to pink, the black ink rubbed away in spots. The title, *Aunt Sally's Policy Players Dream Book,* worn to grey. "It was my mother's. That's how old it is!" She smiles at it, lovingly.

"It worked!" Rosie says.

"A little bit of magic," Juliet says.

"Superstition." Chandra says. "Numbers are about probabilities." Chandra teaches math in high school.

"Or getting in the groove of the vibe of the universe," Jeannie suggests.

"Let's face it, we can't predict the numbers and the odds are way against us." Marnie says.

"Well, we're gambling."

"We're not gamblers. We're dreamers. We're optimistic dreamers." Marnie's platinum hair is striking even in this mostly white room.

Sissy laughs, "That's me. Always the dreamer, always believing the dream can come true. And you know what?" She nods her head. "Sometime it does. Look at our Aaron and Tara." Sissy looks at Marnie. Aaron is Sissy's son, and Tara is Marnie's daughter, married with a little boy and a baby on the way. "They're just kids who followed their dream and now have a number three hit song. That dream came true with work and talent. Sometimes dreams come true with luck, like my win. But was it luck? Or was I prescient with the numbers and is this old dream book more than it seems?"

"Dreams are messages from our unconscious." Juliet reaches for a tangerine and peels it. The vibrant rind is a splotch of color against her white pants and sweater, her silvered nails.

"Maybe messages from the universe if you interpret them correctly," Jeannie says.

"Or random firings of our brains discharging the day's events." Chandra adds.

"I hope there's some justice in who wins because I can't tell you how much I *need* money." Vera shudders and pulls her shoulders closer. She sits on a white leather chair and her urgent delivery rivets everyone's attention. "I lie awake at night trying to figure out how to juggle accounts and bills. Each month I rotate which bills to pay. Ever since my cancer when we had to use credit to pay bills. So," she turns up a palm, "I borrow money on my house to pay my credit card." She turns up her left hand, "Thank God we got a line of credit before the housing crash and haven't used it all up. Then, I pay some of that with a different credit card," She presses both palms together in prayer, "and *hope* my commission check comes in on time. Every month I hold my breath praying I can get through without nasty calls. When I can't sleep, I sit at the computer checking my balances, as though I've hidden money in an account or the interest has made some huge difference." She draws in air through her teeth.

*That explains the circles under Vera's eyes, and the weight loss*, Jeannie thinks.

"I thought that was my routine," Taylor says. "Every month, a different anxiety dance. I don't want to pick up

7

my own the mail. When the phone rings, I check to see who's calling, scared it's a bill collector. Then around the first, I wonder, will I make it? What won't I pay? So what's my dream? To have no debt. To pay my bills. To stay away from the abyss," she shrugs. "That's all." Her eyes fill. "I've already accepted that I won't be able to help my kids go to college. Buzz will probably join the military. And Nicole?" She shrugs.

"Yeah, I don't get it. The stock market is doing great, but most of us still struggle. Even American cars have bounced back. But everyone I know..." Vera's voice trails off.

They sit on the sofa and turn toward each other. Vera grabs Taylor's hand and squeezes it.

"It's going great for the rich again. In fact they're richer than ever. Just not the rest of us," Sissy says.

They're talking about something they never discuss. Money. A secret they keep from each other. One of those unpeeled layers of secret shame and pride. Vera doesn't go out to dinner with them anymore. When they go, they split an entrée and don't order wine. Most of them no longer get their nails done, and see movies at a matinee or on discount Tuesdays. They borrow books free from the library or exchange them in book trades. These aren't big deals, just little extras. The recession still hits them all one way or another. But Taylor and Vera are in real financial trouble. Jeannie looks around at her other friends and wonders about them.

"Tell me about it," Marnie utters one of those I'm-going-to-joke-about-it-because-that's-the-only-way-I-can-even-tell-you laughs that sound bitter and sarcastic. "I've had a thirty thousand dollar income cut every year since this recession started. My house is *still* underwater."

*We're naming figures. We never discuss income,* Jeannie thinks. They talk freely about problems with kids, or partners, infidelity on the part of a husband, or lovers, even how often they have sex, - or don't have sex-- but never before have they mentioned income. Jeannie has no idea how much her friends make. She assumes they're in the same general class. They manage to *appear* as if they are by their houses, clothes, cars. But some of us buy used clothes at Lemon Tree.

Then Taylor says what Jeannie is thinking. "People never talk about money. We're afraid to."

"Afraid?" Juliet asks.

"Yes. If you're poor, you think *you're* responsible. Not a good person." Her voice trembles. "Being lazy. Or a shopaholic or stupid." She clears her throat and almost shouts. "Or unlucky! And unlucky means you're not favored by God. If you have money, God has made it happen because you're a good person." Her eyes are shellacked with tears. "Poverty drives you to do things you can't believe. That you can't even imagine doing and then there you are, picking up throw-a-ways from the street." Taylor clenches her eyes and bows her head as her voice drifts away.

Marnie's brows are lifted, her lips open. "I didn't have any idea."

"I *feel* like there's something *wrong* with *me*." Taylor points to herself, poking her chest with her index finger. "I'm supposed to pull myself up by my bootstraps."

"It's not you, it was never you. It's the economy," Marnie says.

"That and a rotten husband," Vera adds. "And Pfizer closing."

"People *are* judged by their money. You don't know that unless you've been poor," Juliet whispers these words. The tangerine peel lies curled into itself like a nautilus shell seeking its own beginning. Then she inhales sharply. "I've been poor," she announces almost as if she's confessing adultery.

"You?" Taylor asks.

"I grew up in a trailer park. White trailer trash." She shoots a look at Marnie. "Remember?"

Marnie presses her lips to a sad and empathetic smile. "I remember how you didn't ever get the minis of the school picture to pass out and always pretended."

Juliet blinks and then looks around her elegant house.

"Well. You don't have to pretend anymore," Taylor says. "You're safe. And secure."

Vera says, "I've been poor, too. And crawled out only to be back in it now."

"My worst fear," Juliet says softly, staring at Vera. "Being a homeless shopping bag lady."

"That's your worst fear?" Taylor says. "Mine, too."

"Me, too!" Marnie, Vera, and Rosie add.

"All of us?" I ask. "We're all haunted by the same homeless bag lady?"

"Yep. That and being raped." Chandra says.

"Ohmygod. Yes. That's why I won't park in a structure. About ten years ago that perv was grabbing women in them, remember?" Marnie says.

"Of course," Rosie says. "One was down the street from our office."

"Let's not even go there. I don't even want to think about it," Chandra says.

"So we agree. Everyone's wish: winning the lottery. Everyone's fears: Being raped now and being a homeless bag lady when we're old," Sissy says.

"Don't you get it? The lottery maintains the dream of American capitalism... anyone can be rich. It's the modern version of the Horatio Alger myth," Juliet says.

*They don't know, but I've been poor too. Temporarily poor, but poor. Does temporarily poor count?* Jeannie thinks.

This is what happened.    Mark and she were both working in the admissions department at Michigan State the summer before their senior year when they fell in love. It was one of those sudden, can't think about anything else, stomach flipping, mad loves as though they found missing pieces of themselves in the other.  Twin souls, they called their relationship. Mark and she rented an apartment and Jeannie called to tell her parents.

"What?  You're living with a boy? A boy we haven't even met?"

"He's a man, Dad. A man. And his name is Mark."

"And you're not married. Not even engaged?"

"I just met him two months ago.  I mean, we know this is right. We're in love, but we're not ready to get engaged."

Jeannie heard her mother scream on the other side of the phone. *She's moving in with some boy? A boy. Who?*

"You're sure enough to LIVE with him, but not sure enough to MARRY him."  Dad yelled, "Are you out of your mind?"

"It's not the 1950's anymore," Jeannie shot back to my father. "It's 1989!"

"Honey," he inhaled. "The year is unimportant. These things are universal. You should marry him first, believe me." A tinge of fear trembled his pleading, his slow, thought-out words.  "You have to make sure he respects you.  You have to make sure you're safe."

"What are you talking about, Dad? Sex? Or living with him?

He didn't answer. Jeannie had crossed a line she didn't know existed.  Beyond the window of her dorm room, the grass had already turned brown. Beyond the field was the street for the highway home.

"You're certainly not going to say he won't buy the cow if he gets the milk for free, are you?"

Dad didn't answer. Jeannie imagined his face red with rage, imagined him pacing as far as the telephone cord allowed. She wrapped the cord around her wrist, chaining herself to the phone as though she could never leave her father, while their conversation disintegrated into stereotype.

She looked out at West 43, the highway home. "Maybe I should bring him home to meet you and Mom." Once he met Mark-- smart, handsome, poised, personable-- they wouldn't have any objections.

"He might be a fine young man. I assume he is if you've fallen in love with him," he said as though Mark's and her love was commonplace and ordinary instead of once in a lifetime, and unique with a rare connection and passion. "But that doesn't matter." He stopped a beat. "What. You. Are. Doing. Is. Unacceptable," he said as if she were a five year old and he was telling her she should never cross the street without looking both ways. "I'll be glad to meet him. But you need to know if you're living with a man then *he* can support you. Not me." He stopped for a minute for emphasis. "That means no tuition. No room and board. No allowance. No dealership cars. You're on your own. You and your boy friend."

She hadn't anticipated that. Mark and Jeannie had counted on Dad giving her what he had paid the previous year.

Now, Jeannie realizes he was trying to protect her from men like himself, from what he did to Sue and others. She doesn't know how many others. He drank the milk and let the cows roam.

"Okay, Dad."

"Here's your mother," but the receiver was already on the way to its cradle.

So that's how she became poor. Jeannie parlayed her full time summer job to part time for the school year. Three nights a week, she worked as a waitress in the Peanut Barrel Restaurant. She earned less than minimum wage plus tips, and, since most of the customers were students, tips were meager. Some Saturday nights, she brought home thirty dollars. Her grades fell, but she graduated on time. The next year, Mark was in law school in Detroit and she worked for minimum wage, $3.35 an hour. She hunted for a higher paying job. After all Jeannie was a college graduate with a new shiny degree in sociology. But it merely bestowed bragging rights that couldn't be parlayed into cash.

For four years, she didn't buy clothes, not even a new bra. Not even a tube of lipstick. She learned to cook beans and rice. She learned to stretch a chicken and eat thighs, not breasts. She fried smelts. Then sardines. Baked bean and hot dog casserole was a Saturday night treat. She lost weight and walked two miles to work. They didn't own a car. They lived on minimum wage and used loans for Mark's tuition.

But they were blissful. It was a creative challenge figuring out how to make a home without buying things. Jeannie picked up furniture from the streets and Goodwill and repainted. She made a quilt from old dresses and scraps on sale at Jo Ann's.

They made love every night.

Every dollar was precious, every single one meant so much. Was it just inflation? Or was it working so hard?

Jeannie and Mark watched TV on a twelve-inch television Mom and Dad gave her for her sixteenth birthday, and listened to music on a radio alarm clock. For four years, they lived below the poverty line. There it was, the poverty line in black and white: 8300 dollars for two people. Jeannie earned 7000.

"Well, at least our taxes are low," they'd joke.

Then, in the middle of Mark's final year of law school, she got a raise to $5.00 an hour. "Hey. Now it's ten thousand. We're no longer poor," they laughed.

Is temporary poverty, poverty? Poverty that's self-induced for a specific purpose? Poverty you know will end? Was she playing at poverty?

Vera and Taylor don't know if it will ever end... a daily, yearly grind of sinking incomes and used up resources from better times.

When Jeannie got her raise, she bought new underwear and a bra and a tube of lipstick at Kmart. The first things for herself she purchased in over three years. That's not an exaggeration for emphasis, or to convince. When she got a raise to $5 an hour, she bought mushrooms and steak on sale and a bottle of wine to celebrate. She remembers thinking, *if I could have mushrooms and wine at dinner, I'd feel rich.* Now, they do that. In fact, they take it for granted.

Then Mark graduated, got a job in Ann Arbor making $25,000 a year. They paid off his $25,000 for law school debt. And got married. Jeannie wouldn't let her parents pay for their wedding, but did resume working at her father's dealership.

She's been rich and poor. She was as happy as she'd ever been when she was poor, but proud of how far they've come. Then, she and Mark had hope, now they have security.

"Well. I've worked all my life. We push the negative away so deeply, we forget the pride of the redemption, the amazing achievement when we crawl out," Jeannie says. " She looks around at her dear friends. "We all have."

"The trick to money is living on less than you make. Then you have enough," Sissy says.

"Unless your income sinks so low you can't." Vera reminds us. They're back where they started.

"Tell me about it." Marnie laughs her bitter chortle. "When we win, we'll get rid of our debts, have security and freedom, and learn to live on less than we have."

"Back to picking numbers... And playing these dreams of ours. How else can we figure which ones to play beside that book?" Juliet points to Sissy's dream book.

"Birthdates," Jeannie suggests.

"Give a number to each letter in a name and add it up, and if it's too high, -- the numbers have to be under 56, and the Powerball under 46,-- collapse it by adding the digits together." Sissy suggests.

"I'm going to do that," Marnie pulls out pencil and paper from her purse, prepared as always.

Jeannie fishes around in her purse, and recovers a pen, but no paper.

" I'm making the Powerball my lucky number. Five," Marnie continues.

"Why five?"

"Because there're five kids in my family. It's always been my lucky number."

Juliet stands, opens a drawer in her sideboard and tosses pencils and paper on the coffee table.

First, Jeannie writes her birth date, then Mark's. They were born the same year. Their daughter Sara and she were both born in June. So she uses 6, Sara's and her birth month, as the Powerball. She adds up Mark's and her birth year, 68 together to get 5. And those are her numbers. 7 5 11 26 31 6. *Do they hold magic, our birthdates all jumbled up like that? My family. What would it mean if we won?* Jeannie wonders.

*We're a winning family? Special? The universe recognizes our bond, our unification. Or is it all random luck?*

There's quiet as everyone works out her numbers. Marnie's head is down, her platinum hair hides her face. Rosie sits back, legs crossed, wearing black leggings, a grey cami and a flowing shawl in fuchsia. Her tongue wets her upper lip as she writes. A gesture that indicates she's thinking. "I'm turning everyone's names into numbers."

Okay, so that will be her, Kevin, Ben. Who are the other three? Her mom and dad? Sue? Probably. Jeannie's left out.

Vera and Taylor thumb through Sissy's dream book.

As each one finishes, she hands the list to Juliet. Jeannie presses a copy into her purse.

"Hey. We're all done." Juliet sits back. "Here're our magic numbers," she grins as she waves the papers. "I'll email the numbers to everyone so we can check and see if we've won."

"Not if. When," Marnie corrects her and then laughs.

Jeannie grabs a tangerine. She's been working on advanced variations of the firefly pose and feels tenderness in her biceps as she zips away the rind and draws in the fresh citrus aroma.

"Okay. Now the money."

"Are we going to do easy picks, too?" Marnie asks. 'What do you think?"

"It just costs a dollar to play. That's five dollars a month from each of us. Think we can make it ten?" Rosie asks.

Vera looks away and Taylor hunts in her purse. Silence lasts a beat too long. Taylor lifts her head and glances at each of them.

In the uncomfortable indecision, Marnie says, "Well, in the months there're only four Tuesdays, we'll have eight extra dollars and can play the easy picks with that. Cool?"

"Why don't we each put in 6 dollars a month?" Jeannie suggests. "Then we'll be able to have one easy pick each week and the last Tuesday of the month blow whatever's left on them. How's that?" She checks Taylor and Vera's faces and they're both smiling.

"Cool."

"All agreed?"

"Yep."

"You have to play in cash. So each of you divvy up 6 dollars." Juliet waves her fingers toward herself. "Gimme the money. Gimme the money," she chants.

They laugh as they start the required change making gymnastics so that each puts in six dollars. Jeannie throws in ten and pulls out four one-dollar bills and ends up giving some to Taylor and Rosie. All the money, bills and change, lands in a messy pile. Juliet immediately stacks the bills and sorts the change, puts it all in an envelope and in a large loopy letters, writes *C3 Lottery!!!!*

"At least the money will help support the schools. We're not giving it away to some casino," Chandra says. "It's doing a little good."

Taylor grabs the envelope and draws caricatures of each of them grinning with a banner pronouncing, **WE WON THE MEGA MILLIONS** above their cartoon heads. "This will make it happen," she says with a nod.

"This is sooo much fun. I can't wait till we WIN," Rosie's eyes shine.

"We're going to be rich and happy," Taylor laughs.

Juliet raises her glass.

"What fun!" Chandra says.

They say it in unison as their glasses create a chorus of crystal pings.

17

"To winning!" they all say.

## Two
*More than half of all Americans play the lottery.*

JULIET DANCES AS she folds and drapes the afghan over the back of the sofa, fluffs the cushions. The warmth of her friends, the dream of winning the lottery spread to her steps. She swings her hips as she picks up the plates and glasses from the coffee table, sings while loading them in the dishwasher, and spins while returning the bowl of tangerines to the granite counter. She leaves the entry light on for Dan, skips to the office, forms an email group of the lottery players, sends off a list of numbers, prints a copy for herself, and places it in her purse.

Dan arrives as she's massaging her face with lotion.

"How's the great lottery group going?" Dan purposefully uses alliteration when he can. It used to charm her, proving his wit and intelligence. Now it seems pretty perfectly predictable.

"Fun." She wipes creamy fingers on her neck careful not to smear her flannel pajamas.

He slides his tie out of its knot.

"I'll buy the tickets tomorrow."

"Your mom will be happy. She thinks everybody should love playing."

"Mom has been pushing everyone in the family to pool their money for decades."

"She and your brothers play together." Dan stands before his closet, hanging up his suit.

"They do? How do you know?" Juliet walks toward their bed.

"I heard them talking about it at the July 4th party."

19

Juliet rolls her eyes. The party was one of those family gatherings she forced herself to attend. That one was burnt chicken with too sweet sauce.  One brother, Larry, drunk by noon, made comments about Juliet's body.

"You need some meat on that ass, Juju... Dan's getting to be an old dude, he needs something to hold on to." Larry laughed.  It was his way of being friendly, calling her the family nickname and joking about something personal to remind her they once lived together, slept in the same bed, wore each other's clothes, knew each other's history.  Now, he was divorced. His two daughters, teens with pierced noses and Monroes by their lips to mimic Marilyn's mole, lounged in jean shorts and camis.

Her other brother, Joey, complained about a summer cold.  But he sniffled year round. He never married, never had children, not that he knew, he routinely quipped.  Joey still lived with their mom.  He had a girlfriend for a few years, but that ended a decade ago.  Juliet asked him once -- in a rare moment of closeness, of feeling sorry for him instead of disappointed in him -- if he were seeing anyone.

Joey had swilled his beer and said, "Nah.  Don't want to catch any feelings. Don't want to get hurt.  You can't get hurt if you don't feel, and you can't be sleeping with anyone more than a few times without catching feelings."

Juliet thought about his phrase, catching feelings, as though love were a contagious disease resulting from the exchange of bodily fluids. Maybe it was. "Yes, you sure can get hurt once you care about someone.  But isn't that part of the point?" she asked, but Joey had looked away.

Neither of her brothers tried to escape the trailer park.

"Family is more important to us than to you," Joey commented once. "You wanted a better life," his fingers drew imaginary quotation marks,  "while we wanted to enjoy the love, live in the moment. Ain't no better life, isn't that what it is really about?  A string of moments?"

"You should have been a philosophy professor," she shot back at him.

"But then I wouldn't have these moments." He held his head back and laughed. "They'd be all used up in meetings, papers, and lectures."

She turned to him, "Come on, you're smarter than that. Those are still moments strung together. Just different ones."

"You got me, Juju." Joey nodded and swilled his beer. "I just like this better." Maybe he was trying to get close to her. Usually, she sensed a sad tenderness beneath his joking and easygoing wisecracks.

Mom sat on an aluminum chair with blue and white webbing staring at the parked cars, a diet coke in one hand, and a cigarette in the other.  She and Joey lived in the same trailer Juliet grew up in.  Now Juliet paid their lot rent and utilities.


SO WHAT DID you do tonight?" Juliet asks Dan as she sits on their bed.

"Worked late on that new account. Ordered from *Seoul Corner*. Went for a drink with Dave."  Only the slight hesitation between Dan's sentences indicates his lies. Juliet doesn't know why she asked the question when she doesn't care about the answer.  Simply doing the marital routine, she guesses.

"Well, tomorrow night you're on your own too." She pulls the quilt up and turns on her side, facing the window that looks out into forest and night sky, purple from reflected city lights, a crescent moon its only ornament. "I have that usual staff dinner meeting.  I'll buy the lottery ticket on the way to work," she says with a tinge of annoyance to portray her busy, busy day.

That's her lie, too. She's visiting the apartment and secret life she has maintained for over a decade with Tom, a married doctor she met at the hospital. Long ago they arranged their schedules to spend a few hours during a weekday and an evening at their apartment. Sometimes Saturday for afternoon delight. Sometimes, they managed to go to "business conferences" now routine and plausible to their respective spouses. Juliet is so practiced at lying, her voice doesn't even change. So good at telling tales and making up quick stories that she does it in mid-gesture. So adept at switching from compartment to compartment in her life it's as easy as walking into another room.

What would she and Tom do tomorrow night? She'll probably pick up some salmon, a bag salad, and a bottle of wine. She'll crawl in bed with him nude, the smooth joy of his skin next to hers. Perhaps they'll fall asleep holding each other, her head on his shoulder, her leg thrown over his body. They'll cuddle under the quilt of Monet water lilies they picked when they furnished the apartment. Then, they imagined they were starting a new life together. It didn't turn out that way. Instead, they created a hide-out cloistered from the rest of their lives: the bustling downtown area outside, their separate jobs at the hospital, their separate children, their separate spouses, their separate homes, their separate luxurious vacations, their separate retirement funds and investments, their separate closets.

They tell themselves their love isn't sullied by day-to-day practicalities or logistics and remains totally focused on each other. But is it? It's as carefully orchestrated as staff meetings, mammograms, kids' sports games, and hospital fundraisers.

Who started telling the lies first? Those habitual lies she and Dan tell, lies that each accepts as the fantasy they've created to coast in a smooth, seamless life together.

Sometimes she goes around in circles thinking about it.  Does Dan know I'm lying?  Men seem so poor at noticing small signs of deceit or reading emotions. Does he know I know he's lying? Or do I need to imagine his dishonesty in order to rationalize my guilt? Maybe he really was working on taxes for that new account, maybe he and Dave really did go to the Sportscaster for a drink.  Or maybe he, too, has a secret love nest. Maybe in his parallel nest, they cook together, and laugh together, dance to music billowing from the stereo they bought together. Sleep under sheets they picked out together. All the things that Tom and I do that Dan was too busy, too uninvolved to do with me.  Do each of us do with our lovers what we don't do (but wish we had) together?

The bottom line: neither one of us really wants to know the other. Not me and Dan.  Not me and Tom. Not Tom and his wife.

And then right before Juliet falls asleep, she thinks, It's easy to skate on the surface, to move from one to another carefully crafted self, the middle class professional who came from trailer park trash, the wife my husband sees, to the persona my lover sees. Ironically, Tom started as a way out of this isolation, a man who understood her background.  Now he simply gets another version, a nude version, but a version nonetheless.

THE NEXT MORNING she stops at Wolverine Party Store.  A young man, tall, well built, and brown skinned with dark brown hair, stands behind the counter.

"I want to play the lottery," she tells him.

"Which game?"  He has a slight accent.

23

For a moment she's startled, she didn't realize there were other games. "This is my first time." she says and smiles, puts her hand in her purse. "I'm a lottery virgin."

"Really? Most people play."

"Most?" Her eyes widen. She only knows her mom and brothers play, but maybe people don't talk about it like everything else about money.

"Yep. More than half of all Americans. But there're different games. Keno, Daily 3 or 4, Classic. Instant. We've got a new instant game every week."

"Mega Millions?" He didn't say that in his list.

"Yep. Mega Millions and Powerball."

"I thought Mega Millions *was* Powerball," she says.

"Nope. Powerball is a bunch of states together. Forty-one states, I think. But they're played the same way. Better chance of winning a prize in Powerball, but less of a chance to win the jackpot."

"The Mega Millions then," Juliet unfolds her printed email. She purposely did not list which friend offered which numbers to avoid any problems if the woman who suggested the winning numbers thought she deserved more.

She hands him the paper. He pulls out a Mega Millions ticket and ticks off the numbers on her list. When he bends over, she notices the beginning of a bald spot. He presses the pencil so firmly the tips of his fingers whiten. She waits while he carefully completes her ticket. The store smells vaguely of cleaning fluid. *Mr. Clean,* Juliet thinks.

A woman and a toddler stand behind her. The woman juggles cartons of milk and orange juice in one arm, Cheerios in the other.

The clerk diagonally slashes the numbers, glancing back and forth from Juliet's typed list to the red and yellow panels.

The woman shifts from one foot to another. The toddler walks to the candy shelves seductively placed near the register and grabs M&Ms and Gummi snakes. "No. Come back here," the mom demands.

Juliet wishes the man would hurry, but she appreciates his careful checking. She takes a credit card out of her wallet, taps it on the counter.

He looks at her and says, "Cash only". She knew that. She pulls out a ten-dollar bill.

"Any Easy Picks?"

She hesitates, how many was she supposed to buy?

"Then the computer makes the decision."

Juliet looks back at the ten dollars.

The toddler, his hair sticking out from a knitted cap and bundled in a down jacket with mittens clipped to his sleeves, grabs a Reese's Cup and darts pleading eyes and sad lips at his mom. "Just one?"

"Three easy picks." Juliet hands the clerk the bill.

"Okay. One. Pick one. Only one." The mom has been worn down by waiting, needing the toddler to behave, not willing to give him candy when she's just bought breakfast, but knowing the store has provoked the situation with its beckoning sweets. "But you can't eat it until snack time." Her voice is firm.

The clerk grins easily, unperturbed by the waiting woman with the nagging child. A man joins the line holding a 40 in the crook of his arm. The clerk strides to a machine, inserts the red and white tickets and pushes levers.

"Here you go." He hands her two receipts labeled Mega Millions, with a list of the numbers and the date. "Good luck." His eyes meet hers as she slides the papers from his fingertips.

These must be her tickets. She has to hold onto them.

"Don't lose those. You can check online to see how you've done." When he grins again his eyes gleam. "And remember me when you win." His eyebrows rise slightly, his fingertips rest on his counter.

"I will." *He likes being part of customers' wishes and dreams.* Juliet places the receipts and the carefully slashed tickets in the envelope and returns it to her purse. "I'll keep my fingers crossed that I hit it," she laughs and walks away. Her long wool coat flaps with her motions. She pulls her hood up, but a blast of wind from the force of opening the door blows it back down and silvery snow embellishes her curly hair.

She starts the car and waits for it to blow warm air. The receipt says: *Players are winning big by playing Lucky Lines. 115 players have won $5000 or more by playing. Buy your Lucky Line ticket today!!* The state advertises just like any other big business.

And then she crosses her fingers and closes her eyes. She inhales the warm air. *Please please please* win. She glances at the ticket and searches her own numbers, the amalgam of dreams from Sissy's book. But not sleep dreams, the dreams she wishes about her life. Laughter. Health. Her mom living in a condo. Just one love, one man who knows her completely, loves and accepts her. Wants only her. Intimacy. Why does she long for more money? To get her mom out of that trailer park. Not her brothers, but her mom. And her cookie club friends need it.

She glances at her dream numbers and says again *Please.*

### Three

*During the New Guinea Kula Ring, ornamental objects are given away. By the act of giving, the giver is of higher status than the receiver. Giving displays the greatness of the giver.*

JEANNIE FLOATS IN *Savasana*, corpse pose, feeling limitless space and time, aware that she breathes in the universe, and exhales the glories of her own body. Then Molly, the leader, rings tinkling chimes and asks the class to wiggle fingers and toes, but Jeannie lies still, resisting the release of the mindless eternity of drifting.

She doesn't want to go outside into the shredding cold, but wishes she could stay here where tides wave through her. Then she remembers, *Tonight is the lottery group meeting at my house. My friends.*

She rolls up her mat, and wraps her cardigan shawl closer. She thanks Molly who congratulates her on her improvement in firefly pose. "You're ready for the next level of certification," she smiles, eyes twinkling. "You've come a long way from when you started, what was it? Four years ago? Not just in your *asanas.*"

Pride and gratification surge. "I've quit trying to change what I can't change."

"There's a workshop in April in Chicago, we can go together." Molly braids her dark hair in two plaits that reach her breasts. Sometimes Jeannie watches them whip

27

around her head as she flows from cobra to down dog and twists into wild animal.

"I'd love to."  Jeannie has been working for this certification to give her additional cachet with her students.

She slides her arms into her down coat, and her feet into furry boots, ties a wool scarf around her neck, pulls a knit cap over still damp hair, and enters snow-flecked air.

Yesterday, she straightened the house for the lottery meeting.  As soon as she gets in her car, her phone rings.

"Hi, Vera.  Can't wait to see you tonight!"

"That's what I'm calling about.  I'm not coming."

"Oh?  You have a cold?  You sound like you're sick."

"I'm sick, but it's not that."

"You okay? You want me to come over?"

"My cancer is back."  She says it just like that. Straight out as though she's telling herself, too.

"Oh, Vera. When did you find out?"

"My colonoscopy last week.  My doctor said, 'We're 90% sure your cancer has returned.'  That's what she said the first time, too.  I didn't make my five years."

"You want me to come over?" Jeannie asks again.

"Flynn's here. We have a bunch of appointments today at the hospital with the oncologist and the surgeon. Well, I have, and Flynn'll be with me." She catches her breath and Jeannie hears tears stuck in Vera's throat.  "I guess I'm having more surgery and then another round of chemo and radiation."  Her words are flat as though she's rehearsed what she'll tell people.  Jeannie remembers how sunken Vera eyes were and how thin she was at the cookie party, as though the cancer had already started its march.

"You should come anyway. You'll be able to bask in all our love."

"I don't know if they'll be able to undo my colectomy this time, like they did before," she sobs. "But I don't want to play the lottery." She catches her breath in between her cries. "I feel like I've already lost the big one."

"Come on. You've beaten this before. You can do it again!"

"All we did this month is lose. I checked every single week. The most we got was four out of all those ten numbers... not even two balls or one Mega Millions number. It's just more depressing shit," Vera spits.

"We've only tried ten different combinations, three times. That's just the beginning. Besides, being together is fun." Jeannie tells her the reason she's playing.

"I know the odds." The way she hisses out the words Jeannie knows she's not talking about the lottery. "Almost impossible," Vera whispers.

"Maybe we won't win. But it'll be fun and it's another excuse to party. We want you with us." Now tears fill Jeannie's eyes, salty and warm. She sits in her car, still in the yoga studio's parking lot. Finally, warm air blows on her. She unwraps the strangling scarf. "Vera, you're going to be okay. I can feel it." Jeannie gives her hope. "But what a struggle." She remembers how sick Vera was the last time, her hands and feet cracked and sore. "Hey. You didn't even lose your hair," Jeannie reminds her.

"This time I probably will."

The air freshener, *New Car*, plugged into the heating vent scents the car with expectation. "Please come tonight. Scoop up all our love and concern. Please keep playing with us."

She doesn't respond, just sniffles on the phone, wipes her nose and then blows it. Then Flynn calls, "We gotta get going, Hon. You ready?"

"Well, maybe," Vera says to appease Jeannie. "But I've definitely decided not to play anymore. I don't know if I want to tell everyone about my illness."

29

"Can I call you later on this afternoon? What time will you be home?"

"Probably by four."

"Okay. I'll talk to you then, Vera. I'll be thinking about you."

VERA DOESN'T ANSWER her phone when Jeannie calls.

Jeannie arranges red and white tulips bought on sale.

She tries Vera again and picks up Sara from her play rehearsal at Young People's Theatre.

When Sara got the part, eyes wide, she said, " I'm only thirteen and some of the other kids are like fifteen!"

"Thirteen! A teenager," Jeannie replied. "Already!"

Now, she bakes a rum cake. Sara helps and, when the cake is in the oven, licks the rubber spatula and mixer bowl.

Jeannie emails Vera.

It's cold and windy outside; cream of mushroom soup simmers on the stove.

Again Jeannie calls. Still no answer. Mark is playing basketball and will be home later. Sara and she eat the soup, bread, and salad for dinner.

Jeannie texts Vera's cell phone. *How did it go? What did the Drs. say?*

She sets up the coffee, and pulls out wine glasses. She still prepares for eight. And eight mugs for the coffee. And eight plates and forks.

When she checks her cell, there's no return text.

*Are you coming tonight? Please come.*

Then the doorbell rings. And simultaneously the ping ping of a text.

*I'll talk to you in a few days.* Vera's text says.

Rosie and Chandra bear bottles of wine and lipsticked smiles. Rosie hugs Sara and tells her how

30

beautiful she is, becoming a gorgeous woman. "My how you've grown, you're almost as tall as your mom." It's a comment on their diminished friendship that Rosie hasn't seen Sara in several years. Jeannie realizes that Sara, too, has lost by the conflict. Rosie (and Sue) used to attend all her soccer and field hockey games. Of course, now Rosie has a baby of her own, Ben. "You look more and more like your mom, with your dad's hair. Do you know that?"

Sara touches her hair, curly and dark like Mark's. "I wish it were straight."

Rosie laughs, "When it comes to hair, we all want what we don't have."

Ping Ping. Another text. *Thanks for understanding.*

Sissy arrives, "The highway was slow going. I almost turned back. Ann Arbor seems far away from Detroit in the snow."

"Spend the night. Drive home in the morning." Jeannie hugs her.

"I might take you up on that," Sissy says.

Marnie, Juliet, and Taylor enter, stomping off snow and hanging their coats in the closet. Marnie hugs Sara and shakes her head at how beautiful she is. "I hear you're in a play now."

Sara beams, "Yep, I'm Lucy in *The Lion, The Witch and the Wardrobe.*"

"Wow, that means you're going to be Queen Lucy the Valiant," Marnie laughs.

"At the end."

"You like babysitting? Sky is always looking for help with Rachel," Marnie asks. "You could play with her while Sky cooks dinner, works on a case, or cleans the house."

Sara's eyes widen. "For money?"

"Of course," Marnie says.

"Sure." Sara beams at the thought of a job and then she adds, "If I'm not rehearsing. But next year, I'll be old enough to officially babysit. Alone." Sara slices herself a piece of cake.

Everyone has arrived. All who are coming.

They hang out in Jeannie's kitchen, sit around the table scooping up soup and eating slices of cake.

"Well, I have a test tomorrow." Sara waves, a plate in her hand as she leaves.

"Aren't we missing someone?" Rosie looks around the room, her dark hair gleaming with bouncing lights. Jeannie thinks, *I still notice her, notice her clothes... the simple black cashmere sweater. (Only Rosie has a long enough neck to carry off a turtleneck.) And blue jeans. Gold stars in her ears. Her nails smoothly manicured. I wonder if Sue still wears the turquoise my father loves so much.* Then Jeannie reminds herself to inhale and exhale. All this happens in a flash.

"Where's Vera?" Chandra asks.

Napkins in hand, Jeannie walks from the kitchen toward them. "She's not playing any more." She places the napkins on the table. "She's had bad news. Her cancer has returned and they're scheduling her for surgery, chemo, and then radiation."

"She could still do this... We'd be there for her," Juliet's blue eyes meet Jeannie's. Juliet's hair, a light mane of loose waves, catches the spotlight.

"I suggested that," Jeannie says.

"She called me late this afternoon about work," Marnie says.

Vera is part of Marnie's sales force.

"She'll be enduring a battle with this treatment with only the energy to focus on getting well, and continue to work a bit. Some weeks she probably won't be able do more than a few hours. She doesn't want other obligations."

32

"Are we going to continue to play her numbers?" Taylor asks. "What are we going to do? We can't just forget her, not now, when she's so ill."

They look at each other, checking emotions.

"We could play her numbers instead of the easy pick," Sissy suggests.

"Let's think this through," Rosie walks to the counter, grabs a bottle of red wine. "We should respect her decision and not play her numbers. It might create confusion if we pay for them, and they win. Would we cut her in even though she didn't play?"

"Well, we could."

"What about the rest of the cookie bitches? Cut her in and not the others? " Rosie asks.

Marnie says, "It's easier making up rules about cookies than this. But we get to drop out, quit paying, and playing. Anyone could decide to do that and the rest would keep going."

"Anyone in the cookie club who hasn't joined could, right? When she feels better, Vera could rejoin?" Taylor asks.

Again, they glance at each other.

"Yes. And if they join then they divvy up and divide equally," Chandra says. "From that month on. And if they quit, they quit. No pay and no pay-off."

"But then what about the rest of us who've been playing for months? Isn't there some cumulative, I don't know, membership?" Taylor asks.

"It's the lottery," Sissy says. "You pay a dollar and take your chance. You don't get a thing if last week's numbers win this week."

"Well, okay," Taylor says, smoothing her pant leg, "We can join or drop out. We're full members as soon as we join and our numbers are erased when we drop out."

When she says it like that it sounds as though the person is erased too. Juliet and Taylor's mouths both turn down.

"But only the cookie club members, okay?" This is selfish of Jeannie. She wants this to be a comfy gathering of friends.

"Okay," Marnie pulls back her shoulders. "We're in agreement. Anyone can drop out at anytime, and her number is no longer played. She has no obligations or rewards. Any of our other cookie bitches can join and is a full member starting that month. Right? We all agree?" she glances at each of them and they nod. "No one sees any possible downsides that'll haunt us?"

"But you have to play for at least a month, and start at the beginning of it. Otherwise it'll be too complicated," Chandra adds.

"Yes."

"It's decided," Rosie says. "Should we write our rules down?"

"Do we need, too? " Jeannie doesn't believe they'll win. Not big anyway.

"But we haven't talked about the most important thing," Sissy says. "How are we going to help Vera?"

They brainstorm ideas... of course they'll take turns cooking food so she doesn't have to do that, knowing that she may be on a special diet. Marnie says she'll take charge of organizing the cooking. Rosie offers to help her get back and forth to the hospital for her treatments when Flynn can't. Taylor is going to create a playlist of healing, soothing meditative songs. Jeannie offers to do restorative and healing yoga sessions with her.

Then they get to business. They cross Vera's numbers from the list. They talk about the disappointment that they didn't win anything, not even seven dollars, or one dollar.

34

"That doesn't mean we picked bad numbers. It just means they didn't work this month," Sissy says.

"There's a way to study the numbers and see which fall more often since the balls themselves are slightly different and come through the shoot faster," Chandra says. "I found a book on how to predict the balls, but only if you play the three number Lotto, not the Mega Millions or the Powerball."

"Did you know there was a difference?"

"Yep," Juliet says. "The Powerball is on Wednesday and you win more, but have a harder time winning. 200,000,000 maybe. There're lots of states involved in that one. The Mega Millions is on Tuesday, is just Michigan, and you win less."

"I like that it's just Michigan. Our schools need all the help they can get," Chandra says.

"You see all the advertisements on TV for this? I wonder how much actually gets to our schools. And besides, when you play the Powerball does the money played in Michigan stay here?" Rosie glances around the room as they shrug or shake heads. No one has a clue.

"Let's talk about this next month. We've had enough for tonight," Marnie reaches into her wallet for her money.

"Whose house in March?" Jeannie asks.

"Me," Rosie volunteers, handing Jeannie her money.

Jeannie stacks the bills in a pile as if they were cards. Juliet hands her the silly envelope with the grinning faces that Taylor drew. Jeannie notices the receipts are in it and a bunch of Mega Millions tickets as she stuffs the envelope with playing money.

"I'll do April," Sissy says. "We can enjoy Motown. Maybe even go to a casino."

THE SNOW HAS stopped, and Sissy leaves as Mark returns home. "How're the roads?" she asks him.

"Okay. At least here. Everything has been plowed. Oh, and the highway is good, too."

"Great," she says.

One by one the friends depart.

Mark snags the last of the cake, and a glass of wine. They bring each other up on the day's events, that easy exchange of witnessing that they do.

"How's Rosie?" He's really asking, *How are you and Rosie?* hopeful the tension between them has faded. If Jeannie asked whether her father is still seeing Sue, Rosie would tell her. But Jeannie doesn't, and Rosie never volunteers.

"We're politely cordial," is what Jeannie answers.

"I saw Kevin at lunch today. He's looking forward to retirement."

"Ben has to grow up first," Jeannie says. She knows that Kevin wasn't interested in being a father again and did it because of his love for Rosie. She loads the last of the wine glasses in the dishwasher. And thinks, who knows, really knows what goes on in someone else's marriage? It's hard enough to understand your own. Marriages that work are unusual; marriages in which both people are truly happy after twenty years are rare. Who knows what goes on under the covers of social appearance?

We live such lush lives, so comfortable. Our friendship circle is part of the richness we enjoy. She wipes the counters. At least that's how it appears. We each have different selves that we pull out contingent on the occasion, depending on the closeness and the topic, the layers of ourselves that we strip away.

I wonder how much any of us reveal, she wonders as she sweeps the floor. All the secrets we keep, even all those fleeting thoughts and forbidden wishes we barely let ourselves recognize, but instantly shove to a dark drawer in our mind. Is this what we call denial? Or is it simply the complications and build up of toxicity we ignore so we can get on with our lives? We push away the contaminations from disappointment and inevitable hurts from our partners, our children, our friends, our careers.

How do we not deny, but yet think positively?

Ah, two mutually exclusive suggestions guaranteeing a happy life. (Is that it? Or is it a fulfilled life? Or is it really unsurprised?)

And then we're told that life exists in how we view it. How do you weigh seeing things straight and thinking positively? *I should contemplate this in tree pose. It's about balance. But I might fall over.* She chuckles at herself.

The kitchen is clean. Tasks completed. She doesn't want to think about Rosie's marriage. Or her friends. Not now when she sees Mark there, in their kitchen, still damp from the exertion of the game, his curly hair clinging to the back of his powerful neck, a towel draped around his neck and another clasped around his waist. She realizes she likes him. Yes, she loves him. But she likes him, too. His earnestness, how much he cares for his clients, her, and Sara.

"Falling in love with you was the smartest decision I ever made," Jeannie says.

He grabs Jeannie close to him and holds her. "That crazy falling in love we did and smart decision don't sound like they should be in the same sentence. We were lucky, both of us, our lust turned out to also be intelligent."

Of course they make love that night-- that couple sex that's perfected by years of practice, efficient and adept at bringing them to simultaneous climax.

Right before they fall asleep entwined, Jeannie thinks how easy it is between us, this relationship dance that so many find so tricky.  Right now, right now my life is so good, as perfect as it gets.   She shudders, scared that the comfort and safety might dissipate.

Everything changes, right?

# Four

*The odds of winning the lottery are 1 chance in 54 million. There's a 1 in 3 million chance of freezing to death, and 1 in 2 million chance of getting struck by lightning.*

AFTER JEANNIE DROPS Sara at school, she stops at a party store to buy lottery tickets. She's third in line. A white woman somewhere between the ages of 40 and 55, dressed in a wool coat, skirt, shell with matching cardigan, patent leather pumps in spite of the cold and snow, holds a stack of filled out tickets. She hands her picks to the clerk who feeds them through the machine.

Jeannie has already filled out their seven plays. Seven is her lucky number and she crosses her fingers for extra luck.

The woman gives him a fifty-dollar bill and he passes her the printed receipts. *Wow. She plays fifty dollars a week?* Jeannie thinks.

A skinny black man, deep creases from his nose to the corners of his mouth, with a short braided ponytail, stands in front of Jeannie. Wearing baggy jeans and a jacket that looks too thin for the bitter cold, he hunches over, scratching off instant tickets. He shoves his receipts to the clerk and says, "Got thirty coming back at me."

The clerk counts out the bills and the man hands him a pile of hopes. The clerk passes them through the machine. "You owe me forty. Not bad, uh? Ten to keep playing."

A net loss of ten a week mounts up. Maybe that's his entertainment. Better than the fifty the previous woman played.

Jeannie never knew this separate culture of lottery players, betting in solitude, from various walks of life

39

existed. Multitudes of people with hopes of wealth. Here they are. She considers yoga, the practice and the life style that begins to accompany it, but so many are women, are into physical fitness or spiritual development, they're similar. Lottery is different. What's another hobby that creates a group from widely diverse life styles? Dog training, but they meet at the shows. This is solitary. None of them know each other. *Us.* Jeannie reminds herself. *I'm one of them now.* Smoking, maybe that's similar. People from all classes, - executives, office workers, and mailroom clerks, - huddle outside of buildings puffing away together. America is stuffed with cultural niches: Tractor pull contests, Nascar, off road racing, darts, options investment, Trekkies, swingers, Burning Man. Such a wide assortment of passions expressed by hobbies.

When it's Jeannie's turn, she hands the clerk filled tickets and ten bucks. He returns the red and white Mega Millions ticket and receipts. Jeannie turns it over and realizes she can use it again and smoothes the receipts and tickets back in the envelope.

Later that afternoon, she drives to Sara's rehearsal. In the darkened auditorium, Jeannie holds her breath anxious about how Sara will do. But she perfectly recites her lines and performs her character, Lucy's, motions. Jeannie feels Lucy's compassion and courage as she uses the magic potion to heal everyone. Even though Sara wears school clothes, -- jeans, a tee shirt and a hoody, -- her shoulder blades are on her back, her chin lifted as regal as Lucy is supposed to be. Sara's excitement and tinge of nervousness, the adrenaline from the battle that Lucy has just won roils in Jeannie's chest. Then she is crowned Queen Lucy the Valiant.

Jeannie's pride is double, both for Sara, and for herself. *How and when did Sara grow so capable in her own right and so autonomous?*

Sara recognizes the delight beaming on her mother's face, hugs her, and says as she fastens her seat belt in the car, "I'm having so much fun. I just love this."

"You are such a joy." They laugh as they pull from the parking lot to drive home.

JEANNIE IS READY for bed when she decides to check the winning lottery numbers. The computer is on, the Internet at her fingertips, so she clicks to the Michigan Lottery page to compare the winning numbers. The first one, the very first one is a 2. *We have a 2!* And then right next to it is 26. Just like the winning number. Her heart picks up its beat. They have a 31, too, but not in the same pick. Her elation evaporates as she sorts through the two last white balls neither of which they have chosen. The mega ball is 12. *We have it! Yep, right with that first number that has the 2 and 26! We won!*

She scans the descriptions of winners. Two white balls and the Mega Ball net a prize of $10.00! 1,487 other people have also won ten bucks this week, but no one has won the jackpot that is now 85 million, or matched the five white balls for 250,000. One person matched four white balls and the Mega Ball and won $10,000. And the cookie lottery club won ten bucks.

Jeannie sends an email to the lottery group:

*Hey guys! We WON!! Yep. Got two white balls and the mega ball netting us a grand total of TEN DOLLARS!! I suggest we add the ten dollars for more easy picks spread throughout the month. Is that okay? We need another rule. ☺ Add our winnings to our betting until we win $10,000?*

*Or should we divvy up at $150?*

*Let's do an email vote.*

*Let me know before next Tuesday because we're on a winning streak! ☺*

*Love Ya,*

*Jeannie*


IN THE MIDDLE of the night, the phone rings. Its bleating is morphed into a dream of flying through yoga *vinyasas* as though Jeannie is weightless, boneless, the rhythmic ringing setting a pace for her flow.

When she realizes it's the phone, she grabs it as though she's putting out a fire.

"Jeannie?"

"Mom. What's wrong?"

"Jeannie." When she utters Jeannie's name, it tilts downward, as though simply speaking it is solace. "Dad's had a stroke."

"What?"

"I'm at the hospital."

"What happened?"

"While I was sleeping something woke me up, he wasn't in bed, I didn't hear him in the house, I got up to hunt for him. He was crumpled on the bathroom floor." She stops.

"Mom?"

"And so I called 911. He was breathing okay, but he wouldn't talk to me, couldn't call my name or answer and I threw on some clothes and the ambulance came and brought me here. Us here. He's in a coma."

"Why didn't you call sooner so I could be with you?"

"I just did. As soon as I could. They're rushing to get him some medicine, special medicine that has to be given immediately. This all just happened. This is my first chance." She thinks a minute, "I didn't even think of it till now. It's so fast. All so fast. I wanted to tell you something. I didn't want to wake you up. He's getting a CT scan now, right now, to make sure what kind of stroke it is for that special medicine, but they think it's an intracerebral hemorrhage."

"From his high blood pressure?"

"Turns out he hasn't been taking his medication."

"Why wouldn't he take his medication?"

Mom doesn't answer. In the emptiness, both of them hold their breath, Jeannie knows why. Of course. Does Mom know? The medication is notorious for interfering with erections. How could he keep a young woman satisfied without erections?

He's still seeing Sue. Maybe it's for Mom, too. But Mom would just want him alive.

Why didn't he use Viagra? Maybe he uses that, too.

Jeannie grits her teeth. Damn him. Damn sex. Damn Sue. Hate rises thick and bloody, choking her.

Then she starts crying. For Dad helpless and fighting for his life. For Mom. For herself. But it snaps like a vicious switch to bitter rage, burning her with fury at Sue. At Dad. How could he do this, risk this for himself? For all of them? "Is he going to be okay?" but as soon as Jeannie asks she realizes what a silly question. Maybe she's really asking, *Am I going to be okay? Are you, Mom, going to be okay?* She clutches the phone between her ear and shoulder as she slides on jeans and a tee shirt.

"After the CT scan, they'll give him the special medicine, I forget the name, to diminish the bleed. Then, maybe, he'll come out of his coma. They don't know."

"What's happened?" Mark is awake now.

Jeannie covers the receiver. "Dad's had a stroke. I'm going to the hospital."

"Want me to come?"

"Take care of Sara. I'll call when we know anything."

Jeannie walks downstairs as Mom continues, "They can't tell me much. Not yet. 'Time will tell', the doctor said. Maybe, they can help. Maybe not." Her voice is a whispery

43

monotone laced with confusion. "They just know he's had a stroke. They don't know the life and death answers. Or predict his future functioning," she's quoting the doctor.

Jeannie slides on her coat, wraps her neck with a scarf, hunts up keys and purse and pushes the remote control starter.

"They answer with statistics and probabilities and sometimes and maybes. If he lives the next few days, then the next few months, he'll be out of the woods for awhile."

"I'm on my way, Mom. I'll be right there."

Jeannie shuts the door and feels she's saying goodbye, but doesn't know to what. The house? A certain illusion of innocence?    Those almost smug, almost arrogant self-congratulations that her life was okay, more than just okay, terrific?   Her pride at Sara's abilities and her luck winning a bit at the lottery?

## Five

*Money Magazine revealed that states with lotteries collect more in taxes and spend less on schools than states without lotteries.*

JEANNIE STANDS AT his door and sees Sue bent over her father's body, the sheets smoothing the edges of him so he seems small and winsome. Her heart sinks. She hoped Mom would be here, but she's not. Jeannie watches Sue with her gleaming cap of hair, lift her face from his chest. Trace his eyebrow with one finger, smooth a few stray strands of hair from his forehead. Her gesture, Sue's gesture, so tender, so loving and so sad that Jeannie senses the trembles of Sue's hand, the sorrow in her own.

His eyes slide to Sue.

They can't see Jeannie standing in the doorway. Watching, swallowing a lump of her own dismay stuck in her throat.

He tries a smile, but it's a lopsided grimace with only a twitch on one side of his mouth. Sue's hand goes to his lips, the side that is immobile.

*How long should I watch them, this intimate moment between them, portraying their love and the sadness?*

*Am I witnessing their goodbye? Or merely another pledge of continued lust and collusion to diminish the importance and primacy of my mother and our family?*

As Jeannie shifts her weight, Sue flinches, a blush waves over her features from the base of her neck to her forehead. Her mouth opens. "Jeannie. I....I thought you'd be at Rosie's for the lottery meeting."

Jeannie strides in, leans over to kiss her father. He moves his head toward his daughter and jerks the fingers of one hand in an attempt at a wave. Jeannie ignores Sue and steps in front of her as though she's not there.

Dad's eyes move from his daughter to his mistress and back to his daughter.

"Well, I just stopped in to see how your Dad was doing…." Sue's voice trails as though she is merely one of his salespeople and this is merely a courteous professional call.

"Cut the shit."

She wears a hunk of turquoise on her index finger and has polished her nails the same shade. Jeannie smells Sue's *Obsession* over the hospital ammonia.

Mom enters, carrying a tote bag. "Oh." She stops, looking at both of them and then, as though ignorant of any other possibility asks, "Did you two stop in together? How nice."

"No. I was merely letting Mr. Jeffries know that everything was okay at the dealership. He shouldn't worry for one minute about it right now. It will all be waiting for him when he feels like returning." Sue slides her palms down her thighs, straightening her navy pencil skirt.

Her words seem so out of place, with him immobile, unable to walk, to speak while Sue behaves as if this is a temporary inconvenience like a flat tire, or a broken leg. *Well, maybe it is. I hope it is.*

"Well no. He shouldn't. Shouldn't even be thinking about work." Mom glances at Jeannie, takes off her coat, places it on a hook on the wall and moves toward him. "Here, Jack, I brought you your favorite chicken soup, it'll be easy for you to swallow." Mom slides his dinner tray over his bed and pulls a Tupperware container from her bag, flips open the lid, and sits in the chair Sue vacated. Her back is toward the other women.

*Is Mom's attention to Dad her way of claiming position and territory? Or maybe she's solely intent on taking care of the man she loves. She's secure in her role in his life. Now she has dominion over him,* Jeannie thinks.

"I'll be going, then," Sue watches Mom tuck a napkin under Dad's chin and scoop up the steaming soup.

"Here you go, darling. I know how you love it. Something better than that hospital food."

Dad watches Sue walk away.

"I'll show Sue out," Jeannie calls over her shoulder as though she's at home and seeing a friend to the door.

She closes the door and turns to face Sue.

"I had to see him," she says, wetting her lips with her tongue. "I didn't mean to intrude."

Jeannie crosses her arms, shaking her head "How could you bring your affair right in front of my mom? Throw it in her face."

"I checked to make sure that she wasn't visiting before I stepped in." Sue meets Jeannie's eyes and Jeannie is aware of how green Sue's are with their yellow flecks. The darker hair with its reddish tinge brings out their colors, now shimmering with tears. "I miss him."

Jeannie's nostrils expand with shaking rage. "How could you? How could you be so selfish? How could you let him stop taking his medicine so this would even happen?"

"What are you talking about?" Sue narrows her brows.

"His blood pressure medicine. He stopped taking it so he could BE with you."

Sue blinks, then looks away.

He never told her. Never told her that he maintained at all cost the illusion of himself as the ever potent, charming, delightful alpha male.

"You never knew him. Never even knew him," Jeannie says so softly it's almost a whisper.

Shockwaves cross Sue's face. She glances downward as she consumes this information. Jeannie's comment surprised her. Jeannie answered a question Sue hadn't asked anyone but herself. She didn't know. What?

That he was even on blood pressure meds? She swallows and says, "Jeannie. I miss you, too. You know that? But this, him having this stroke, it's like I lost him."

"Lost him? He was *never* yours. He's Mom's." Jeannie spits the word, her anger for sleeping with her father when Sue was her best friend, her double betrayal. His betrayal of Mom, her, their family, hits Jeannie fresh. Now, he forfeited himself and all of them to have sex with Sue.

"It's a crisis for me, too." Tears slide down Sue's cheeks that she wipes with the back of her hand. "We've never talked about it, not you and I, not in all these years, but he is, your father is, the love of my life. My soul mate. I'll never belong to another like I fit with him." She looks at her shoes. Then meets Jeannie's eyes again. "Maybe I shouldn't be telling you this...but maybe it's time that you know. We didn't go into this lightly. We felt terrible about you and your Mom, but we couldn't betray ourselves. That seemed a worse crime."

"Yeeaaah. I just bet you'd be there by his side taking care of him now. No. That's up to my Mom and me, and you'll skate away." A cart rattles as it's pushed down the corridor.

Sue tilts back slightly on her heels and shakes her head. "You're wrong. So wrong. I envy Frances because *she* gets to feed him, *she* gets to bathe him, *she*'s the one who is beside him encouraging and applauding his recovery."

Jeannie narrows her eyes, not buying for a minute this show of devotion and unbounded love. Jeannie resents Sue calling Mom by her first name, *Frances,* as though she's a friend, a peer. *Sue will probably cry for a few months and then try to figure out what to do with her career, derailed without my father's protection. Figure out what man will be next and dye her hair to please him. Change her turquoise for garnets, or plain gold.*

"I don't hope or expect your forgiveness. But I hope someday you'll understand."

Sue seems diminished, as though somehow the last few years, how long has she been involved with Dad now? Five years? Looks like it's been ten, and Jeannie notices the sagging lines around Sue's mouth, the creases in her very knuckles as though holding herself together has taken a toll.

"If you need anything from me, anything, either to help Jack or Frances, let me know. Okay?" Sue pleads. "If you need anything at the dealership, right now I'm acting as the manager, waiting for him to return, but if you or Frances need anything, just tell me."

"I only need you to stay away from him."

She turns and walks away.


WHEN JEANNIE ENTERS her father's room again, Mom is dabbing his lips. The smell of basil has wafted over remnants of Sue's musk and mandarin. There's a greasy stain of soup on the napkin.

"That was so sweet of Sue to drop by." Mom's voice is distracted.

Jeannie moves the IV pole back toward the wall. *Should I tell her? Does she need to know now before she takes care of his shell in her commitment and boundless love for him (a commitment that is not returned) (a commitment predicated and shored by deceit) sacrificing the rest of her life to that task? Or would the knowledge only serve to destroy her sense of their marriage, her life, herself?*

"She's such a good employee. Your father did a good job of hiring loyal workers. She could have been out doing something much more exciting, I know, than visiting a sick old man like Jack. It's poignant really, isn't it? Your father stimulates such passion and loyalty that his young employees sacrifice for him and the dealership. I've seen it happen over and over. One after another." Mom shakes her head, then picks up his hand and kisses it. "I'm glad you and Sue are such good friends."

Jeannie doesn't reply, just watches the tenderness and concern with which her mom bathes her father. She wonders if he realizes how much he is loved even in his diminished state, and if Mom knew all along that the young women who seemed so devoted to the dealership were having affairs with Dad. If she did, she also knew she'd be the one by his side. The victor in the long run. If this is indeed victory.

Jeannie remembers the fight with her father long ago when she started living with Mark. Even then, he indulged this stream of adoring, young women. His fear was that his daughter would become one of these-- a dalliance for another man. A diversion. But he was unwilling to stop his onslaught. Now he is weak, undone by his own vanity and, as heartbroken as Jeannie feels, there's also a sense of retribution. A retribution taken from her mother's and her hides.

And then Mom asks, almost as an afterthought, "Did Sue go with you to Sara's dress rehearsal?"

"No," Jeannie answers with the realization that in the old days Sue would be applauding Sara almost as passionately as Jeannie.

"When's the play again? I wouldn't want to miss it."

# Six

*Every year in America:*
*$7 billion is spent on movie tickets*
*$16 billion is spent on sports tickets*
*$24 billion is spent on books*
*$62 billion is spent on lottery tickets*

ROSIE WASHES HER face, smears cream over it, flosses and brushes her teeth.  Kevin is propped in bed reading files, a pencil in one hand. His tan skin contrasts with the pale sheets and a gold cross on his chest that his mother gave him when his sixteenth birthday fell on Good Friday. Rose starts to crawl into bed with him when she remembers the lottery and gets the envelope with the ticket she bought that morning. *Jeannie still hasn't come by with her six bucks,* Rosie thinks as she walks to the computer, opens her bookmarks, and hits the one named *Michigan Mega Millions.*  Gold coins twinkle promises on a tree. The webpage says *Tue. 3/8. Numbers drawn* and lists the numbers with the power ball in red. It's a 6. *Isn't one of our Powerballs a 6?*  The next drawing is Fri. 3/11.  The estimated jackpot is 125 million.

Rosie pulls the receipt from the *We Won the Mega Millions* envelope, now folded, one corner tattered. She remembered correctly, there is a 6 in the power ball, in fact there are two. One is an easy pick.  She checks the first drawn number: 5. Yep, there's a 5 on the computer.  It's Jeannie's numbers. And right next to it is 7. Lucky 7. And sure enough 7 is one of the drawn numbers. Two white balls plus the Mega Ball, they got that before. It's ten dollars. The next number is 11. It, too, is on her receipt.

Rosie's heart starts pounding.

*Hold on,* she tells herself. *That's just three numbers and the mega ball. $150, not that big of a deal.* She places her fingertips on her chest.

The next number is 26.

It's there, too, in Jeannie's list. Now they've won $10,000. Wow. That's over 1400 bucks each. What would she do with it? A new stove? A long weekend vacation, just her and Kevin, to a bed and breakfast at a ski resort? The next number is 31. She closes her eyes and says *please please please.* Opens her eyes, checks her computer screen.

Holy shit.

They won.

They won!

Her heart throbs in her ears.

She can't believe it! She checks again. 5 7 11 26 31 and 6 for the Mega Ball. She bounces in her chair, and shrieks over and over, "Ohmigod, Ohmifuckinggod! Kevin," she yells. "Kevin. My god. We won the Mega Millions. I can't believe it. Am I seeing this right? Make sure I'm seeing this right. Ohmigod."

Kevin runs down the stairs tying a fleece bathrobe.

Rosie bounds out of her chair, jumps up and down. Laughing and crying. Still shrieking, "Ohmigod, Ohmigod," and gasping for breath.

"What is it? What is it?" Kevin can't decipher whether she's thrilled or terrified. His eyes are wide, mouth open. He places his palms on her shoulders. "What is it? What's happened?"

"We won. I think we won," she takes a deep breath. "Look. Look." Rosie points to the computer screen, hopping up and down. She hands him the ticket, fingers trembling. "Am I doing this right? Is this right? I can't believe it. I can't fucking believe it."

Kevin quickly scans the numbers on the ticket.

52

"It's this one here," Rosie points to the third list of numbers. Jeannie's numbers.

He glances between the receipt and the computer list. "5, 5, 7, 7. 11, 11. 26. 26, 31, yep 31, 6, 6. Yes." He turns to her, color drained from his face. "It says there's 1 winner. That's this ticket." He shakes it.

"I'm going to faint. I need some water," Rosie says.

"You won. Wow. We won." He stands up and holds her. "My God."

They hold each other their hearts filling their ears, the room, both gasping for breath.

"125 million," he whispers.

"125 million," they say simultaneously.

Rosie tries to imagine that amount, but she can't. "How much would it be? What would we get, you and I?"

Kevin types in megamillions.com and the site pops up. There's a picture of a woman jumping, hair flying, holding a glowing ticket with the question, *You won, now what?!* Above that it says, estimated jackpot 125 million. Cash option: $80,000,000. "There's your answer. The club gets 80 million. How many are playing?"

"Seven."

"Divided by 7." He opens the calculator and punches in the numbers. Each would get $11,428,571. But don't forget they will withhold 25 percent for federal taxes and 4.35% for state. That's 29.35% off the top. Which means each of us will get $8,085,714 million. We may have to pay additional taxes on that." He stares at the monitor, Rosie leans over him. "Eight million," he whispers. "We'll have eight million."

He looks at her, a shocked frozen expression on his face. Then he shuts his eyes, clamps his lips shut and shakes his head.

"Our lives have just changed," Rosie whispers.

"I'm free. We're free." His eyes glance upward.

"That's enough for forever."

They gaze at the flashing stars on the website, *Your dream here,* it says.

"We're rich. This means we're rich," Rosie says. "Maybe we'll be one percenters. Are we?"

"As long as we're not stupid. And we won't be stupid. We'll be safe. No more worries about getting enough clients to pay that monthly nut.  I can just take the cases I want," he shakes his head, trying to comprehend the change.

"You can hire an office administrator.  I can stay home with Ben."

"I can hire Sky." He swallows, then, voice filled with awe, he says, "Or I can quit. Sell the practice. I can retire."

"It's Jeannie's numbers."

"That doesn't matter. It's all of yours. You agreed to contribute and split equally, right?"

"Yes."

"You have to keep it that way."

"I have to tell everybody." She checks her watch. It's after midnight.

"Let's wait until tomorrow. Let's have this night for us," Kevin says. "Let's dream our dream before it gets crazy."

"I'll email them!"  She hits *compose mail,* and loads the lottery group in the *To:* box.  For the Subject: she types, WE WON!!!! And in the body of the letter she wrote *We won 125 million. Yes! 125 million dollars.*"

"Tell them there'll be a meeting at our house day after tomorrow. Thursday. We need to figure out what to do next!"

"I love how you're always so practical and efficient." She types: *We need to figure out what we're going to do. Take it all in a lump sum which should be, after initial taxes, $8.085,714 for EACH of us?  Have the annuity? Can you believe it???? Bring your spouses! That way we'll have two*

54

*lawyers. And an accountant. Ha. Ha. See you Thursday at 7. My house. Oh, I'll call you tomorrow, but I couldn't wait to tell you tonight! Love love love. I still can't believe it. This must be a dream!!!!! We're sooooooo fuckin' lucky! Rosie.*

She hesitates before she pushes *send,* wanting to savor the win all by herself. Just herself. For a minute she imagines having 125 million. Then they wouldn't even need to be smart. Her selfishness doesn't surprise her. If she had the entire amount, been the only winner, she'd be special. So special. So unique. She considers not telling them and lying. 80 million dollars is enough for generations to come. Ben's great grandchildren. A dynasty from her genes and her money comforting, protecting, assuring eons into the future. She, Rosie, would be immortal.

That's what she wants. Permanent, immortal specialness. Immense wealth buys that.

Then she remembers, they know the numbers, too, and some of them might check. She looks at Kevin, her finger poised.

"Now, is our time," Kevin says. "Let's enjoy this while we still can."

Rosie pushes *send.*

There's a bottle of champagne left over from the lottery meeting and Kevin pops it open, fills two glasses and says, "To having more fun." They sit on the sofa in the living room close to each other. Arms touching. They dream where they want to go on vacation, maybe take a cruise around the world, maybe even bring a nanny so they're free to explore. How about buying a condo on a beach somewhere? Or a small island. Or better yet a huge a boat. He's always wanted to spend months on a boat. That's what he wants. Just to float around the world on a boat. No responsibilities except finding the next port. Kevin points out the legal ramifications, the media learning that a Christmas cookie exchange won the big one, and the negative side of the publicity, their lives exposed to the public.

It may be best to form a company to collect the money and disburse it, he suggests. It's best to decide how they're going to handle the money within the group before they receive it. "I'll work with Mark. We'll figure out a way to keep us protected and minimize the taxes. Of course, he'll be at the meeting."

Rosie doesn't pay attention. Kevin's arm is warm on her shoulder. "Jeannie still hasn't brought over her cash, but it's her numbers that won," she whispers.

"Don't complicate things," Kevin kisses her forehead. "There's enough for everyone and everything is good. Let it go."

"You're always so forgiving and generous."

Kevin throws his head back, eyes on the ceiling. "How far I've come," his voice is husky. "I never would have anticipated this when I was a boy in Puerto Rico, scared to even come here. All this was enough," he nods at the house, and fireplace sending warm flames, " And now...we can be extravagant."

"Really extravagant." Rosie leans her head on his shoulder.


THE MORNING AFTER the lottery meeting, before the lottery drawing, Taylor opens the latest ridiculous version of Rick's settlement and presses the pages flat. Three forms, one for Rick, one for the court, and one for her. After she drops the kids at school, she stops at the bank. The notary is a plump, middle-aged woman wearing a periwinkle cardigan set. Taylor holds the bank's ballpoint between her fingers, starts to write her name and stops. She meets the woman's brown eyes, shakes her head and says, "I don't know if I'm doing the right thing for my children, but I'm doing the right thing for me by finally finishing with this bastard." She presses her name so fiercely on the line, that it embosses the pad on the desk.

"If you do the right thing for you, you're doing the right thing for your kids. We women do what we have to for our kids regardless." The notary nods then clamps the papers with her seal and stamps each one with the date in red ink. More embossing. Legality leaves bumps, Taylor thinks. Sometimes visible and sometimes invisible. She slides a set of the documents into the envelope, shakes it down to the bottom, licks the flap and presses it. At the post office's automated service center, she arranges for it to be sent priority with certificate of receipt.

She returns to her car and fastens her seat belt. Then, she dials Rick's number. She knows he won't answer. When it reaches his voice mail, she says, "You got your wish. I signed your grossly unfair and irresponsible settlement offer and it's in the mail to you. This afternoon, I'll file it at the courthouse. Our divorce is final. So Rick. Fuck you. We are now officially free of each other."

She clicks off the phone and sings, at the top of her lungs, *I'm a Woman,* and *Let the Good Times Roll* until she arrives at the library for her part time minimum wage job with no benefits in the stacks, damp, exhausted, but proud.

She stops at the courthouse and officially files the papers. She watches as they stamp the papers with the date and thinks, *Rick is over. Finally.*

Later that night, Buzz and Nicole are sound asleep in their room, though Taylor knows she needs to move to a three-bedroom apartment. Or maybe she should share with Nicole and let Buzz have the smaller room. They're getting too old to divide one room. At least they're not homeless. Now they both sprawl in their own beds. She pulls the covers over Buzz and kisses Nicole who wipes away the wet kiss.  Taylor tosses a load of laundry in the apartment sized washer, throws in grains of detergent, pushes the button and hears the familiar sound of rushing water.

She sits in front of the computer to check if they won. This routine, this dream for security salves her sorrowful disappointment.  The few minutes of pleasurable anticipation has lured her since the beginning of the lottery club. How many times? Twelve times now.  She coasts as the dream lulls her, relieves her. And opens the website.

125 million.

One winner.

And the winner is from Ann Arbor.

Taylor grows alert, her comfort intensifies to excitement.

Wow. We got one number.

Two. Three.

Four. Five. Oooooooo. And the Mega Ball.

We won. Fuck. We won!!!

Her heart slams her throat, her ears. Taylor checks the numbers again. It *is* theirs. One of their magical numbers. She doesn't know whose. She doesn't even remember which one is hers. They're no more personal to her than the easy picks.  But here they are.  On Juliet's email.

They won.

She won.

She checks again.

And again.

*It's my prize for signing that form. The universe made it right for me when Rick wouldn't.*

*Someone, somewhere looks after me, rewards me and blesses me.  I am not alone.*

*Aaaahhhh.* Tears stream down her cheeks.

She's dizzy. She might faint. Taylor walks to the kitchen, touching the walls with her fingertips, grabs a glass and fills it with tap water.

She slowly drinks, swallowing a new reality. Closes her eyes. The room spins, her excitement bounces inside her.

Clear water centers her. *I'm free. I'm safe. I'm rich. Me and the kids.*

She returns to the computer and hunts to see how much that will be, finds the Mega Millions page and realizes that the payout will be 80 million, does the division, figures 30 % for taxes and knows she'll have eight million in the bank.

Eight million.

There's no one to tell. Her parents are both dead and she hasn't talked to her brother for years. Allie. Allie would be so happy for her, for all of them. But it's too late. She's alone with joy. She's alone with relief.

Then, Taylor goes into her kids' bedroom and whispers in each of their ears. "We're going to be all right. Everything is all alright." A smile flits over Buzz's lips visible in the slight haze from the streetlight shinning through the venetian blinds. Nicole wraps her arms around Taylor's neck and pulls her close. Taylor lies down beside her, her heart still quick.

*My life is saved. All of our lives are saved.*

She matches her breath to Nicole's, trying to quiet the exhilaration flying inside her. But can't fall asleep.


TUESDAY IS A working day for Sissy and the last few months she's been a follow up nurse for sexual assault victims. Jackie's file detailing reports from rape kit and ER doctors remains unopened on Sissy's desk. Sissy wants to hear the story from Jackie, not a file.

59

Jackie walks in with a slight limp, a tall and slender woman in her mid thirties, one eye still deep purple, her forehead bandaged. Her coat wrapped tightly around her. Underneath, a turtle neck sweater reaches to Jackie's chin.

Jackie sits, unmoving, her fingers balled in her lap, her purse hanging from her shoulder. Sissy explains that her role is to set up appointments for crisis intervention and group therapy. Psychiatry if she needs it. STD and HIV tests.

Jackie watches Sissy's mouth as if her words are solely sounds.

*Still shell shocked,* Sissy thinks as she brings her a paper cup of water and sits back down. "I know it's difficult, but tell me what happened."

Jackie wets her lips, her eyes dart around the room and then settle on the balled fists in her lap.

"I know you told the police and the medical personnel in the ER, but this is the next step." Sissy waits.

Jackie sips the water. "I had just left a meeting at the high school where I teach. It was dark, after nine. My husband texted we needed milk for breakfast so I stopped at a 7-11. I was in a hurry. Such a damn hurry. Like getting milk the most important thing in the world." She shakes her head, clicks her tongue. "He must have been waiting, watching. It was dark, like I said." She continues to talk to her lap, not looking at Sissy.

Sissy leans toward her, straining to hear.

"I got back in the car and started driving down the street, and then something hard, cold pushes at my neck. A rough voice says, 'Turn this corner and park. Do what I say or I'll kill you.' I could smell him. I tried to look at him, but he was wearing a mask, a knit mask to stay warm. We were in a strip mall, the parking lot vacant." Jackie stops, her head tilts. Her eyes on Sissy's now. "He musta been hiding in the back seat, musta been waiting for me. Musta

60

watched me run to the store. I didn't lock the car, too eager to get to my husband and kiss my kids goodnight." Now Jackie shakes her head, "I should have locked the car. I should have. I know."

"It's not your fault," Sissy says.

Sissy still isn't immune to these stories, these tales of viciousness, of men who believe they have the right to women's bodies, and women trying to understand the bad luck of being in the wrong place at the wrong time. 92,000 forcible rapes each year. An ocean of horror.

Often the victim wonders what she could have done differently. Wear baggy clothes. Not park in a structure, remember to lock her car, not walk in a park, not be out after dark. Very hard that last one in the winter when dark starts at 4:30 before work ends. Sissy reaches her hands across the desk toward Jackie. "The hardest thing: there is no reason, nothing about *you* that made this happen. Crazy as it is, it's not personal. But all of us try to figure out a reason and we're willing to take the blame to regain control." Maybe it's too early to say that, Sissy thinks.

But Jackie says, "Yeah. I redo everything that happened and want to put my finger on the place where I did something wrong and my life changed." Now tears roll from Jackie's eyes. "So he ordered me out of the car, pushed me down in the snow at the edge of the parking lot. There were trees there. It was dark. So dark. Nobody else. I struggled, fought, tried to get away and run somewhere but he hit me with the thing in his hand. Flashlight, butt of a gun, don't even know. That's how I got these." She touches her eyes, her forehead, and then her chest. Her turtleneck hides the bruise or the cut on her chest. "It was dark. So dark," she says again as though that describes a mood, a new order rather than merely the night. "He wore gloves and a ski mask. I couldn't even recognize him. And what he did to me. God. Everywhere." Her eyes well with

61

tears. "Shit. Bastard. I hadn't ever done it there. In my ass. Disgusting." She looks back down at her fingers, clenches her eyes. "A phantom of horror. Every woman's worst nightmare."

"Yes." Rape. Every woman's fear. We organize our lives to avoid it. Marnie won't park in a structure -- a rapist used them as his M.O. for several years and they seem permanently foreboding. While she walks, Allie pulls the points of her keys between each finger forming a weapon if anyone should try to grab her. Tara is terrified of getting lost -- a friend got lost hunting for a gas station, stopped to look at a map and was raped by four men standing on a corner. All of us constrained by the possibility of rape.

"We can't, none of us, undo what happened to you. Hard as we may want to, we can't pretend it never happened. But there are ways to diminish the impact. Talking with other survivors, group therapy, really helps, so does individual therapy. It takes a while. The fact you're here shows your strength and determination. Healing prevents him from taking more than he has."

Jackie's terror, the reminder that life can change in a heartbeat pervades Sissy with a sense of the world wrongly tilted.

Sissy reaches her hand to cover Jackie's. "How's your husband doing with this?"

Jackie bites her lower lip and shakes her head. "He's trying to be helpful but he's so angry. Angry at himself. Angry at me."

"There's a group for partners of survivors too, so they can learn how they can help. Sometimes anger covers his sense of impotence and guilt. Like that he told you to get that milk. And then...." Sissy stops. "There's another worry and possible negative outcome. You'll need an HIV test, one today and then another one in 6 months.

It may be that you could start on a preventive regimen. Your husband will need to wear a condom."

"Oh," Jackie says as if all the air has been punched out of her. "I can't tell him that."

"I'll talk with both of you. Maybe that will help. Also, some survivors and their partners find it empowering to join a group working to change the culture of rape."

"You mean like *Take Back the Night?*"

"That's one, but there're others." Sissy hands Jackie a brochure that lists organizations striving to diminish the incidence of rape and challenge the rape culture. As well as one on HIV. "Most importantly, you're here. We'll help you heal."

Jackie studies her hands for a minute, and then reaches for the brochure. "Thank you." And they schedule her next appointments.


AFTER WORK, SISSY attends a meeting of the Urban Coalition. She hears a story of a young man, 19 years old, who was found guilty of home invasion. He and several of his friends were in a car and stopped by a girl's house. The young man waited for his friends, and, after they were gone for over an hour, he opened the front door. One of the boys had raped the girl, the other grabbed her cell phone, and then they bolted. He was charged with conspiracy to commit all those crimes and, because of a juvenile record for a marijuana possession conviction, they enhanced the time he must serve, struck him out, and sentenced him to 57 years.

His mom sits in the meeting, tears streaming down her face, "What can I do? What can I do?" she says over and over. "You're my last hope. What can I do?"

"It'll cost the taxpayers almost three million dollars," one of the attendees says and clicks his tongue. "Enough to give all the kids in Detroit school books and provide toilet paper again."

Sissy thinks about Aaron and his juvenile marijuana conviction. She knows the statistics. White suburban males use drugs at a higher rate than black men. Yet, because of the high rate of police presence in minority communities and their stop and search policies, lack of money for a lawyer, black incarcerations for drugs are seven times greater. All are measures designed to get young minority men in the system, which provides jobs for correction officers, lawyers, and judges, and money for vending machines, food service, and phone companies. It's another form of Jim Crow, another form of slavery.

Heaping punishment and tragedy on top of each other, the person is no longer eligible for federal financial aid, (a reason why more black men are in jail than college) and his family is kicked out of public housing. The Urban Coalition is raising funds to pay for an appeal, but the problem is so much broader than this one young man now doomed to an adult life in a cage. She knows all this. Everyone in the meeting knows this. They see it day after day.

Sissy arrives home to finish her day, like so many before it, aware that she's seen evil. It shrouds her, weighs her. Her woe from relentless wickedness continues in spite of her constant attempts to understand, examining events from all angles. There's not usually a vicious, bitter desire to hurt, but carelessness and cowardice. It is out there, free floating like a miasma churning all their lives.

As much as she hates the legal system with its blind destruction of so many black sons and brothers, fathers and lovers she thinks it's evil in its result, not in conception. Though sometimes momentarily persuaded, she doesn't believe it's a purposeful racist attack. There's certainly complicit desire for political advantage, but not intent.

Sissy thinks, as she glides on Shea butter warmed between her palms, then silky pajamas, *It's, perhaps, a result of not caring, not seeing people who do not look like you. Mindlessness. A turning away.*

*Is it a force in the world as a test, to prove by contrast the existence of good? Or is it a blind collusion that we each must struggle against? Many people, maybe most people, care, but are too busy or feel too powerless to make a difference. You see character when someone is tested,* Sissy muses. People are tested when their conflicting selves battle. Or like Jackie when they face trauma. *That's when we glimpse what they're made of.*

It is, in the final analysis, important only in the consequence, the outcome. But that's unpredictable. Do vicious acts create terrible outcomes? Not necessarily. Do good works yield positives? Not always. She knows from her own life that you can't predict the results of any event. Things that initially seemed like tragedies became blessings. That is what she tried to tell Jackie. In spite of her worst fear coming true, she can thrive. *All I can do is the best I can, what seems best at the time.*

To comfort herself, Sissy imagines groups of young people farming, processing the food they grow, starting grocery stores, and barber shops, and appliance stores as they rebuild Detroit. *This time we'll keep it local, a self-sustaining community. This time we'll make it ours,* she tells herself as she drifts into the dream. *This time we'll remember to glory in ourselves and each other, enjoying lives in which the goal is personal integrity and not personal toys. Who dies with the most toys isn't the winner. Who dies with the most kind acts and gratitude is.*

JULIET ROUTINELY SPENDS Tuesday evenings with Tom and tonight is no different. They don't make love, they cook together and lay next to each other, and he falls asleep. Juliet listens to his breathing and thinks about her husband knowing that, in a few hours, when she's lying next to Dan, she'll think of Tom.

The aroma of bergamot and cinnamon diffuse from the bottle next to the bed. Outside, snow hushes noise.

She fingers the scar under her breast, almost imperceptible, except she knows where it is. It's been over five years, she reminds herself. I'm safe. The dual implants and the replaced nipples give an illusion of perfect breasts. Her practiced fingers palpitate her lymph nodes in her armpits and neck. Nothing is as it seems, she thinks, and slides out of bed, leaving Tom to snore quietly as she puts on her scrubs. The snow descends heavily enough that, even with the streetlights, driving home will be difficult through the swirling white. She wiggles her feet into her boots, pulls on her hat and gloves. She doesn't disturb Tom with a kiss. She shuts the door so silently behind her that the latch hardly clicks.

When she arrives home, Dan, too, is sleeping, the snow sheeting the windows in the dark night. White flakes whirl away the world outside. The trees. The house next door. The sky. Even her own driveway. Outside, nothing is visible, but fighting, bitter flakes. She checks the lottery as she has done every Tuesday night. Since January, it's been Tom, then the lottery. Now she scans the numbers on the computer and the ones she typed up a few months ago. Her eyes move back and forth and, with a growing certitude that is neutral, neither joy nor dismay, she recognizes they've won. It'll be about 8 million dollars for her. For them, she reminds herself. Which them? Her fingers rest on the keyboard, her index fingers feel the little nipples that exist as a guide. She circles them, amazed at the numbness of her reaction. Curious about her absence of thrill.

She doesn't wake up Dan, nor call Tom. She doesn't call her children. She doesn't wake up her mom, or Larry, or Joe. She stares at the numbers, the blinking gold coins, the red Mega Ball and thinks, *This should have been their win. Larry and Joe's. All those years, decades, they've played. All those years they've soothed the press of scarcity with the dream of these riches.*

*What now for me? I can do what I want.*

*But what is that? What is that indeed?*

She waits, as if expecting a message from the little dashes under her fingertips. Images of the trailer (the messy room where the three of them slept, piles of clothes rank with the hormones of adolescence on either side of the bed, stuffed in the closet, tumbling from the hanging, broken bi fold door, the damp tattered smell of the living room furniture, the used grease of frying oil, her sense of embarrassment at school, never knowing what she'd have to hide next) slide behind her closed eyelids. *In spite of it all, I'm lucky. And don't deserve it.*

No one else would recognize or predict what I am now from the poor girl with too curly hair in the trailer park. Yet here I am the same person, living this narrative. All these different narratives.

*What's constant? Who am I under all this stuff?*

*What's me?*


WHEN JEANNIE VISITS her father, her mother is again feeding him. "You should be home with Mark and Sara," her mom comments.

Jeannie puts her hand on her mother's shoulder. Mom cooked her father's favorite pot-roast, cut it into tiny pieces; her father sucks them and slowly swallows. Swallowing is a chore.

"How was Sara's play? I feel terrible I missed it." Frances turns to Jeannie, their eyes meet and then Frances looks away. "I forgot it in all...." She rolls her hand around the air.

"That's okay, Mom." Jeannie places her hand on her Mom's shoulder. "She was great. Didn't miss a line. Marnie came and so did Allie. Sara understood that you had to be with Dad. Beside, there's a matinee this Saturday, the final day. Why don't we both go to that?"

"Oh, good." Mom wipes away a tear, "I'm so glad I'll see it." She shakes her head, "I think we have to face it," Frances says. "Your father is not going to be managing the dealership anymore." She wipes juice that dribbles from his lips to his chin. "He told me if something happened to him he wanted you to take over."

Jeannie assumed Sue would be the manager. Sue made it clear she was at the helm now. "When did he tell you this, Mom? How long ago?"

Her mom shrugs. "Must have been a month ago. Maybe two. Why?"

"Just wondering."

"He signed some papers to that effect. He said, you've worked there the longest and have been the most loyal. And you're family. The papers are somewhere. I suspect his lawyer has all that and the contracts with GM, etc. We can take care of that later."

"Do you want to do it, Mom?" Taking over the dealership would prevent Jeannie from developing the yoga studio. On the other hand, she wanted to run Dad's dealership since she was in high school.

"Me? No. I have my hands full. The doctor told me today that *maybe* he'll learn to walk with a walker, and *maybe* some of his speech will return, but. Well..." Mom stops and sighs. "He's not going to be able to manage a dealership with all the turmoil and stress in the industry and the financial markets. Not for some time. You're the one for the job. Beside, we need the money. Or, hell, let's sell it and let's be done with it. We always assumed that would bring in enough for our retirement. But who knows now? Though American cars are doing a bit better."

Mom shrugs then turns to Jeannie, eyes filled with tears and Jeannie says what she knows her Mom is thinking, "It would be such a shame if all his hard work, all our family's labor and love end like this." Then Jeannie adds, "Just think, two generations ago we were working the line, and then the dealership. Grandpa was so proud. And now?" She turns her palm up and spreads her fingers wide as though the toil and pride drifts away like sand.

Her mom whispers, "It's a new time. We have to do what's best for us in the present."

That night, Jeannie lies in bed wondering what she should do. And then she remembers that she still hasn't stopped by Rosie's with the money.

First thing tomorrow.

## Seven

*Among the Pacific Northwest Native Americans, there's a tradition of potlatch, which is a huge party during which the hosts demonstrate their wealth and prominence by giving away food and goods. Its main purpose is the re-distribution of wealth to create more equality among the tribe members. Franz Boas*

JEANNIE GETS OUT of bed, pulls on yoga pants, sport bra and tee shirt, zaps leftover coffee in the microwave, and yells to Mark, "I gotta get Rosie that lottery money. Will you make sure that Sara gets to school?" She puts on her coat, fishes out car keys, and slings her purse over her shoulder, "Okay? Don't forget to pack her some extra snacks. She's been so busy with the play."

He hasn't answered.

"Will you. Pleeeeze?"

"This early? Really? Okay," his muffled, morning voice replies.

The car is cold, she forgot to push the remote start, and shudders her shoulders together, hunching to escape the chill as she turns on the ignition, backs up and then drives to the ATM. She withdraws a hundred dollars, but it's all in twenties. Then she withdraws twenty, but gets two tens. No ones. *Well, I'll give Rosie ten.*

It's so early, she's reluctant to stop, but she has to arrive before Rosie leaves to drop off Ben and go to work, before Jeannie's early yoga class. Jeannie rings the bell, hears its Westminster chime and waits. Thick drapes prevent her from peeking movement, or lights. *Maybe they're in the back, eating breakfast.*

She knocks.

Jeannie presses her ear to the door, but hears nothing. She pushes the bell again and listens to its music.

In her car, she looks for an envelope, a piece of paper, anything, and finds the receipt from the ATM and scrambles through her purse for a pen. *Rosie, Sorry this is a day late, but it's not a dollar short. In fact it's extra. Things have been so terribly crazy. Here's ten dollars. The ATM wouldn't give me any $1s. Use the extra few bucks for easy picks. Maybe it'll help us WIN!!! Maybe something good will happen,* she writes.

She wraps the receipt around the ten dollars, folds it, and tries to wedge the papers between the door and the jam.

There's some shuffling and the door opens. Rosie wrapped in a black shawl, no makeup, blinking. "Jeannie? What are you doing?"

"I'm here to give you the lottery money. So sorry to wake you. So sorry. But with what my days have been, busy with my father, and Sara's play, and my certification and all, if I didn't drop this off early I might miss another day, and the last thing I thought before I fell asleep was that I had forgotten to give you my lottery money. So here." Jeannie jabs the bill and the note at her. "Here it is."

Rosie shakes her head with an expression on her face that shifts from bewilderment to annoyance, and then, surprisingly, fury.

"I'm sorry. I mean, I know it's late..."

"Way too late." She crosses her arms. Then exhales an exasperated sigh and moves to the side. She waves her arm, as a way of ushering Jeannie into her home and out of the cold.

In the entry, where a Queen Anne table holds a bowl of forsythia, Jeannie presents the money again. "Well, here it is anyway."

Jeannie can't decipher Rosie's expression. She's annoyed, but there's also a secret pride, like a cat that ate the cream and is casually licking her paw.

*I don't get this. I'm a day late giving her six bucks. She had to play once without my money. I woke her up, but it isn't like I've committed a crime.* "Rosie? I'm sorry I'm late, but there's lots of interest here for extra easy picks," Jeannie tries to laugh.

"So. You don't know, do you?" Rosie asks in a monotone, in bemusement.

"What's wrong?"

"You didn't read your email?"

"No. I came here early, worried you'd leave to drop Ben off before work, and I'd miss you."

But Rosie crosses her arms and lifts one eyebrow and stares at Jeannie as though she's a bug about to get squashed. "I don't know what to do. Your money wasn't part of the rest when we played yesterday. So. Does that mean you dropped out?"

"What?" Now Jeannie is getting angry. "You know I didn't drop out. The lottery group is one of the highlights of my month. Especially now." Tears fill her eyes as she thinks about her dad. "I can't believe you're making such a big deal out of lending me six bucks for one day." Hunting in her wallet shaking her head, she pulls out a twenty. "I was already giving you, well, us some extra. Here's some more, Rosie. I don't get this." Jeannie attempts to keep her voice modulated. "What's the big deal? Is it about Sue? I saw her visiting my father and was pissed. Are you angry I said something to her, is that it? Instead of pretending everything is hunky dory like I usually do, I confronted her and upset the apple cart?" Jeannie mind races again to the situation with her family, now way beyond the fact that Sue and Rosie, --yes, this Rosie being so smugly unreceptive-- colluded to keep an affair secret.

Jeannie sees Rosie's crossed arms, her unsmiling lips, and her jutting chin. "How could you be so mean? You *know* I didn't quit. You *are* mad at me about Sue."

Rosie doesn't say anything. She tilts back slightly on her heels and raises one eyebrow.

"Did you play my numbers?" Jeannie asks. "If you really thought I quit you weren't supposed to play my numbers."

Rosie's face colors. She looks almost as though the smugness has been slapped from her face. Now Rosie closes her eyes and her face changes as though Jeannie reminded her of something she'd rather forget, revealed an element of her even she doesn't like.

"It's not that." Rosie chews on the inside of her lip. "No, not that. It's crazy." She puts her hands on Jeannie's shoulders and then hugs her as Jeannie's emotions rocket from confusion and anger about Sue to a real fear that something terrible happened.

"We won," she whispers. "We won yesterday."

"What?"

"We won."

"What? We won?"

"The jackpot. The big one. The Mega Millions. One hundred twenty five, to be exact."

Jeannie stands in her entry, looking into Rosie's face, her hands still on Jeannie's shoulders. "Rosie?"

"I emailed everyone and I thought you were here to give me the money as a way to claim your part. But I see you're entirely innocent."

"I had no idea."

"What a crazy way for you to find out," she says this softly, as though she remembers that they used to be best friends.

"Oh, God." Jeannie's face is a crush of amazement and confusion. She says, "Oh, God," over and over. "This is so crazy. It's so crazy, everything that's going on now." *Dad unable to talk or walk. Mom feeding him like he's a child, his very weakness, paleness, absence. The craziness with the dealership, should I take it over? Sue saying, "He's the love of my life. And now I'm alone." Sara excited about her play. Yoga. Now this, this sudden stroke of good news, great news. Great luck mixed in with all the horrible.*

Jeannie starts crying, sobbing, her shoulders wracking, snot dribbling from her nose. In between the gulping tears, she apologizes, "I'm so sorry. I'm so sorry. It's too much. All too much."

"Jeannie?" Rosie says and then hugs her. She doesn't tell Jeannie it was her numbers that won. Instead, she says, "Let's forget you were late with the money. Keep it between us. And yes, I played your numbers."

Jeannie lifts her head. "I need to tell Mark. Oh God. 125 million. Million?"

"It'll probably be about 11 million apiece, but we'll have to each pay taxes on it. About 8 million after that."

"I dreamed, maybe we'd win $250,000 and could all go on a cruise, pay off debts. Not this."

"You're not going to give the rest back, are you?" Rosie laughs.

JEANNIE'S MIND REELS as she drives home. She stops to get some Roadhouse Joe coffee and sits in the parking lot drinking, trying to think. It's enough money to turn the dealership into a complete spa. Yoga classes. Massage rooms. Locker rooms with showers. A health food snack bar. Maybe meeting rooms for discussions, lectures, or book clubs. *That would mean firing Sue. But I can fire her anyway. Yes. If I'm running the dealership I can clean out her desk, put her things in a paper bag, change the password on her computer, hand her the sack at the door, and inform her that her final check will be mailed to her.*

Victory surges through her. Power hums.

*I can fire her.*

Clean, fresh revenge.

She shifts the car into gear and drives the rest of the way home.


MARK IS ON the phone, his eyes wide in surprise. Sara has left for school.

Jeannie mouths to him, "I need to talk to you," pointing at him so he'll get off the phone.

"Yes. She got home just now. Okay. We'll meet tomorrow night. Yes. I'll check the options." He turns to hang up the phone.

"Mark. We won the lottery." Now Jeannie bounces up and down with joy. She grabs his hands. It's beginning to feel real. "We won the jackpot. 125 million."

He picks her up, and swings her in a circle, swinging around until the room spins.

"We won. We won. We won the Mega Millions."

"I know. That was Kevin."

"125 million. Rosie just told me."

"We're all meeting tomorrow night at their house and figuring out what to do."

"What to do?"

"It's not so simple. First we have to create an agreement to memorialize the partnership for the lottery club. Then we have to set up an entity to receive the money. We could disperse the 125 million each year for twenty years. That entity, a corporation, a LLC, would protect our identities. It would be more money over the long run but it would be about, we figure roughly $900,000 a year for each of you. Of course, we'd have to give 35 % of it to Uncle Sam. So about half a million a year."

"That's a humungous amount of money. Remember when we were living on $3.35 an hour?"

76

"I do.  Or we could take the cash out. And have about 8 million, after taxes.  Even if we put that in an annuity, we should have 300,000 forever. And meanwhile the eight million would be there to protect Sara, our grandchildren. Generations."

Jeannie understands some things about money.  She heard her father talk about the economy, credit, and interest rates, manufacturing supplies, commodities all her life.  She worked in a car dealership and knows how it can be manipulated.  But she has trouble concentrating on what Mark is saying. It sounds like he's taking the win away, diminishing it in some way. His practicality, his logic is annoying. "You're not excited about this?"

"No. No. I am." He holds Jeannie to him.  "But Kevin and I want to help you, all of you. Dan's a C.P.A. so he can help figure it out, too.  So you, we, can make good decisions.  Many lottery winners have gone through their money and are in horrible debt in a few years, worse off than before they won. We want to protect you, us from that."

"That won't happen to us.  I'll get my dream.  A great yoga studio. We won't have to worry about the car industry anymore."

Mark has a wary expression on his face.

"You lawyers always look at what can go wrong. That's what you're taught to do.  This is going to be good for us. All of us. Taylor won't have to struggle. Marnie can pay off her debts. Chandra won't worry about being pink-slipped by the school board. This makes my father's stroke easier.  No one will have to worry about paying their bills."

Mark closes his eyes. When he talks again his voice is carefully modulated, "As long as no one goes on a crazy spending spree and massively escalates their standard of living. Bad money managers become disastrous money manages when they get a windfall."

"Some of us may want to do it on their own. I mean, hire their own people."

"They should. We'll start off the discussion and decisions."

"Well, I want to see it on the lottery page. Let's go check it." Jeannie opens up the bookmark and clicks *mega millions* and it pops up. She recognizes the numbers immediately. "They're my numbers, Mark. My numbers won!" She dances in the chair. "Our numbers." Jeannie understands the bargain she and Rosie made. Rosie will let the money float because Jeannie's numbers won.

"Your numbers?"

He leans over the computer as Jeannie strokes the various numbers. "I made up these numbers from our birthdates. Mine, yours," she touches each number as she says them, "Sara's, Mom's, Dad's and then the Powerball is 6 cause Sara and I are both born in June." Jeannie slowly shakes her head as she gazes at the numbers. "Our family. Our magic." Tears roll down her cheeks. Tears of joy, and something else, awe brushes her arms, back, neck with goose bumps, as though she has been specially blessed and honored. Her family. "Our family. Us."

Now she understands why Rosie was so weird. She knew they were Jeannie numbers. Only Rosie would even pay attention.

Jeannie turns to Mark and says, "You're wrong. Everything is going to be all right. Everything." She's been rewarded for the pain of the last few years.

"Too bad you didn't play the numbers by yourself. Then it would have been all ours."

"I would never have played if it hadn't been for my friends. I'm glad my numbers won for all of us."

Mark hugs me. "I'm a lucky man that you're my wife."

"But I'm glad it was our special numbers." The win, this spectacular win with her family's magical numbers proves something. But she's not sure what.

## *Eight*

*Inheritance takes on a special meaning when considering the wealth gap between blacks and whites in today's world because it links the disadvantaged economic position and prospects of today's African-Americans to the disadvantaged positions of their parents' and grandparents' generations. One in three white households will receive a substantial inheritance during their lifetime compared to only one in ten black households.*

SISSY STARTS TO call in her first patient when she hears her cell phone with Tara singing *I'll Miss You*, the tone Sissy downloaded for Tara's calls. She's the only one she knows who can download her kids' music to serve as their announcement. Sissy doesn't chide herself for the vanity of her pride, instead, Tara's soft voice pleading for a constant and consistent love imbues Sissy with Tara's affection.

"Hey, Sweetheart. What's the good news this morning?"

"Congratulations! We just wanted to congratulate you." There's silence on the other end and Tara continues, "Mom called late last night."

"She did?"

Tara whispers to Aaron, loud enough that Sissy hears, "I don't think she knows."

Sissy says, "What's going on?"

Tara hands the phone to Aaron. "You don't know? Woooh. I get to tell you? Well, Mom, sit down and take a deep breath. This is good news. Unbelievably great news. Marnie called Tara last night. You cookie babes won the Mega Millions."

"The jackpot? The big one?"

"Yep. About 125 million."

"Really?"

"Yep," Aaron laughs. "You're rich, Mom.  All of you are."

"Rich? I'm rich?"

"You should take us out to celebrate tonight!  Hell, you should take out all your kids, your grandkids, and the entire crew. The whole city."

"What?"  Sissy's heart pounds and she places a palm on her chest.

"Momma, it's for real.  Call Marnie!"

"Oh, Lord. Oh my. Let me get right back to you."

Sissy leans back in her chair and closes the patient's file.  The wooden top of her desk is scarred with doodles that some worker made years ago, the finish worn away in the spots where people rested their elbows.  The windowless office is a cubicle smashed between two exam rooms.  She flips on her phone and hits her email browser and sees a flurry of notes from Marnie, from Rosie announcing the win.  125 million.  The money, all that money, lots of yippee and hoorays and OMG along with an announcement of a meeting on Thursday at Rosie's house.

*My, my, my,* she thinks. *What my little dream book has wrought. Thank you, Momma, I know you're still looking after me. 125 million could make such a difference to so many people.*

She calls Marnie. "We're rich, super rich. Ohmigod isn't it a miracle? You. Me. Our kids. We shouldn't, any of us, have to worry about money again. Ever again. Can you imagine that, Sissy?"  Marnie's voice trills up and down, as though she is bouncing.

"Maybe we'll just have different worries," Sissy says. "Like what to do with it."

"Thank you, Sissy for inspiring us. And telling us about *Aunt Sally's Dream Book.*  Look at this. We'll have probably 7 or 8 million a piece by the time we pay taxes."

"It's not real."

82

"Not to me either. But I guess we're both, we're all, all seven of us, rich." Marnie stops for a minute and then adds, "It'll seem real when we have the money."

"When will that be?"

"I don't know. First, we have to decide together how we're going to take it. But we're rich."

"We're all doing okay as it is, we just don't appreciate it," Sissy says.

"Not me. I told you. It's a tiptoe, hope I don't fall off, each month. And you know, maybe Tara told you, but I had to borrow money from her. How humiliating."

"Shiiiit, Sweetheart. They're family. You supported her for decades. Turnabout is fair play."

Without stopping, without even taking a breath so that her frenzied joy is catchy, but unable to respond to anything else, Marnie asks, "You're going to make it to the meeting tomorrow? Aren't you?"

"Yes. I'll be there." Sissy thinks *125 million. Maybe it wouldn't be taxed if it all went to a charity. 125 million would be 6 million a year forever. That would fund a lot of farms. A greenhouse, too. A small agency helping people. Maybe even help build housing for homeless families.* Over 20 thousand people, a city in itself, right here, right in Detroit are homeless. Sleeping on the streets and in the parks homeless. Freezing to death in the cold homeless. Half at risk of dying on the streets homeless. Almost half of them are families.

Yes, that means children.

Little homeless children.

Then, Sissy calls Aaron, "You're on for that dinner tonight. Call your brothers and make the reservation, you pick a restaurant and get us a booth, or at least a quiet place where we can talk. But don't invite the crew. I have an idea I want to present." And then she calls Bob Catlin, a lawyer she knows who works for the Urban Coalition and the Homeless Action Network of Detroit. Sissy wants her own attorney. She's not going to necessarily go along with what her friends' husbands suggest. "You have time for me this afternoon? Looks like I'm part of a group that won the lottery. I need some advice."

"Hey. That's you?"

"What do you mean? How'd you hear?"

"It was on the news. Carmen Harlan announced that somebody in Southeast Michigan, probably Ann Arbor, is holding a Mega Millions ticket worth 125 million bucks. So that's you, uh? Couldn't have happened to a nicer person."

"It's not all mine. It's a group of seven. Can we meet? I want to know what will happen next." Now it seems real. It occurs to her that there could be a media frenzy fanning the public's embers of desire, jealousy and greed that could disrupt her life. Her kids' lives. Her job. And then the money wouldn't change them, the publicity from it would.

Money, what is it really? It has four uses: to purchase things, to assess a value on things, to prepare and fix future payments like a mortgage does, and to amass wealth through savings and investments. That's all it does. It doesn't love you, or provide happiness. It just provides unhappiness if you don't have it and you're hungry and homeless.

Lots of money creates false confidence and false invulnerability. It creates competition and envy.

"Absolutely. How about in an hour?"

"I'm on my way, Bob."

Sissy informs Carla, the clinic receptionist, she has a family emergency. Carla frowns until Sissy flashes one of her smiles and skips out of the office. "Hmmm. That must be some happy family emergency, Girlfriend." And winks as if Sissy is going to meet a man for a little afternoon delight.

SISSY SMELLS FLOWERS as soon as she enters Rosie's house. At first she thinks it's heavily rose scented potpourri or a diffuser, but then spots a bouquet of roses, lilies, irises, ginger flowers and birds of paradise two outstretched arms wide on Rosie's dining room table. Bottles of Champagne and catered trays of cheese, bread, and cold cuts from Zingerman's surround them. Rosie hasn't cooked. She and Kevin have bought dinner for everyone. *No more potlucks,* Sissy thinks when she sees the spread. *People are already changing their lives, increasing their consumption. The flowers are a hundred bucks, at least.*

Jeannie and Juliet laugh so loudly, their heads back, mouths wide open, and their clatter so giggly, that it catches Sissy in her throat. Marnie and Chandra hold each other's hands, bounce up and down, hooting. Taylor and Rosie and a man that Sissy doesn't know are huddled talking, their fingers clasping wine stems. Sissy is introduced to Kevin, and Mark. She already knows Jim from family parties at Marnie's and Dan from a dinner that Sissy and Juliet enjoyed after a conference, which he joined. Chandra's husband isn't there. He has to work. The men stand separate from each other, on the outskirts of the room, watching the manic happiness of their women.

Except for Kevin who is in earnest conversation with Taylor. It must be about the divorce. Dan has one hand plunged in his pocket, Mark's arms crossed over his chest observes Jeannie's happiness tinged with her perpetual anxious determination.

The men watch with no sexual interest, but with the attitude of examination and perusal she has seen in men attending a sporting event. With the win, their wives have conveyed the larger amount of money into the family and, in unforeseeable ways, their position in the family has changed. Although 1/3 of women in the US now make

85

more money than their husbands and Sissy has earned a higher salary than two out of the three men she's lived with, she realizes that's not true for any of these women. But what does she know, really, of these middle class white people? And their lives in a bourgeoisie middle and upper middle class city, largely white and sheltered. This money will test them, force them to examine and face the limits of well meaning and self-centeredness. Family and community.

*It'll test me, too,* she thinks.

Rosie works in her husband's firm. Juliet is a nurse and Dan is an accountant. He probably makes more. Jeannie's family has money, tied up in the dealership, now plummeting in worth. Mark is the big earner. Yoga instructors starting their careers eek out a living. She knows Marnie worries about money, and Jim? He's some kind of regional sales manager who travels a lot. He probably makes more, too. Chandra? She's a teacher. Her husband is a social worker. She may make a bit more, she certainly has better benefits. If you think about it, Sissy knows more than she thought. The threads of the sociology of our society are embroidered on our psyches. In spite of the fact we ignore it, class and money reach us as though they're pheromones. Unconscious and unbidden.

This influx of millions of dollars from their wives changes everything. Including the balance of power in some of these relationships. The women have the tilt of power unless they instantly refuse it. They congratulate each other as though they did something more amazing than pool their money and purchase lottery tickets. But then the number was one of theirs, she doesn't know whose, and perhaps its configuration tapped into magic, or blessing, or one of those mysterious forces of the universe, the strange balance of good and evil fighting for each of us, one at time, as we each fall one way or the other.

Sissy, whose life is in another city and with a different ethnicity, feels part of the group, and yet outside of it. Just then she meets Taylor's eyes. Younger. Poorer. A single mother. The stricken, shocked look on her pale face is not diminished even with lipstick. Sissy realizes they share separateness, this strange feeling of being welcomed but not belonging. Jeannie witnesses the similar expressions on Taylor's and Sissy's faces and recognizes them. Jeannie is a wild card.

A few minutes later, the men take over. It's amazing for Sissy to watch Mark and Kevin slide into their lawyer roles. The very tones of their voices change as they outline alternatives and the decisions that are before the group.

Then Kevin starts the meeting. "We have three months before we have to decide what we're going to do. We have to inform the state before we pick up the funds so they know how to prepare the first, or only, draw. So we should have our ducks in order before we make a move." Both his hands are jammed into his pockets and he withdraws one and sweeps the room. "Right now, no one knows you've, we've, won. It behooves us to keep it quiet so you're not hounded either by the press or by people pressuring you for money."

"But," Mark interrupts, "Our first and most important decision is how we're going to take the money. As an annuity, which will be about 900,000 for each of you for twenty years." Mark pulls down in his index finger. "Or we can split it up now and it'll be about 11 million in a lump sum each, but you'll probably have to pay taxes on it, 25% to the feds and 4.53% to the state so it'll be eight million. The experts recommend taking the pay off. Oh, you should probably keep 10% of that aside for more taxes, just in case." He pulls down his middle finger, swallows and continues, "There's an entire niche in the financial industry that purchases, at a great loss to the winner, what remains of an annuity because people overspend and borrow against their future."

"There's another way," Sissy says. "We could not divide it, but put most of it, either the annuity which would be about 6 and half million per year, or the entire 125 million in a foundation."

"Not take our own money?" Everyone looks at each other.

"We could draw money out of the charity at 5%. 5% is about 6 million a year."

"And divide that? Or donate it to a charity?"

"There're lots of options. We could pay salaries to some of us, like you Taylor, maybe you, too Jeannie. Salaries for our unique talents and passions in the service of helping others. Allie and Charlene could also be involved. This money could support us and our work and make significant change for the city of Detroit, helping and saving the lives of hundreds, maybe thousands of people." Sissy hears the pleading in her voice as she veers from preaching.

She's met with silence.

"There'd be security. You'd be using your talents. And you'd be helping others." Sissy removes the stridency from her voice. "Isn't that what we all really want from money? Security. And to be our own best selves?"

Each of the women glance down for a second and then search the expressions on their friends and partner's faces. Juliet pleats the crease in her trousers and then slides her fingers under the gold necklace that she always wears. Marnie frowns and chews on her lip.

"We can do that anyway. And make a difference in the way each of us wants," Jeannie says. "I can certainly start my yoga studio now, and maybe teach free classes at the community center. Or at the homeless shelter. We can give to our own charities."

"I'm just trying to raise my own kids. I'm not done with that yet," Taylor says. "This money is my *miracle*. Maybe I'm a selfish bitch, but I want to take care of me and mine. Now I get a chance to do that well."

"Do we all have to decide this together?" Marnie asks Mark and Kevin. "Can some of us take the annuity and others the pay out? Can we form a foundation with part of it?"

"We'll have to investigate. And we'll look into charities. If you donate some to a charity at the outset will it by-pass taxes? Maybe. We'll see. I suspect we could set up a legal entity that would accomplish that." Mark and Kevin frown at each other.

"It would be complicated," Kevin says, "And it would mean your lives were tied together, even in the next generation."

"Or two," Mark adds.

Sissy hadn't thought that far ahead, but it's true. They'd all be stuck together, for better or worse, into the future. More than a marriage. For better or worse.

"I know we can put half of our income into something called a private operating foundation. You won't have to pay taxes on it. Each of you could put five and a half million in the foundation. You'd still have five and a half million for yourselves. After taxes 3,850,000. Isn't that enough?"

"Sissy?" Marnie's head is tilted.

"I checked with an attorney I know who works with nonprofits and foundations." Her eyes meet each of the women's, sending a message that they need to check with their own private attorney.

"Meanwhile, an agreement must be drafted to memorialize our partnership and an entity must be set up to receive the money from the state. An account, a corporation," Kevin says. "It will help protect you, us from publicity."

Sissy nodded. "That's what Bob said."

"Meanwhile, none of us should make any big changes or decide what we're going to do with the money for six months. That's August. End of summer. Get the money. Keep it safe. And get used to it."

"Got it," Taylor rolls her eyes.

Marnie says, "Wait a minute. There's something else we have to consider. I know we're the ones that played, but I can't help thinking about the other cookie bitches. Vera. What are we going to do about Vera?" Marnie's voice rises. "But if we do something to help her, then what about the others? I'm sure Charlene could use money for her ministry. And maybe Alice could use the money so that she can stop this crazy bi coastal marriage," Rosie says.

"She's right. We have to do something to recognize them, to include them," Chandra says. "All our cookie club friends."

"They're going to be jealous," Juliet says. "And maybe angry."

"Why? They *chose* not to play." Rosie says. "It was their decision. We all deal with consequences. Every day. All the time. That's what being an adult is all about."

"They're our *friends,*" Marnie says. "This is our great news. We should figure out a way to share."

"How would we do it? Chose who is the neediest, like Vera? Or divide it equally. And then how much? It seems like a huge can of worms that only complicates things," Juliet says.

"How 'bout this." Rosie leans back and crosses her arms and then leans forward. "Why don't we celebrate together, all of us, and go on a cruise to the Caribbean and take them, too. All twelve. Have the biggest, best way-cool, girl's week out! Floating on a crystal sea where there's no cold, no snow, no ice, no sleet." Rosie's hands press into her knees as she leans toward the center of our circle. She glances at Kevin and he nods.

"Would Vera even be able to come?" Chandra asks.

"Her chemo ends next month and there's a two week break between that and radiation. We could schedule it then. It might be good for her," Marnie says.

"I'll arrange it." Rosie says, grinning. "We're going to party! We're so lucky. We're all going to have 8 million dollars. We're rich." She looks around the room and shakes her head, "Do you realize it, all you gorgeous women, we're rich?"

"Okay," Kevin says. "Let's have a show of hands. Do we want to shelter ourselves from publicity by forming a company to accept the money? All in favor of sheltering ourselves from publicity?"

Everyone's hands go up.

"Do we want to take the lump sum payment rather than the payout over twenty years?" Rosie asks.

"Yes."

"Absolutely."

"Everyone agrees to the lump sum?" Rosie question is met with nods.

"And each of us will decide whether we want to put some money into a charity of her choosing including Sissy's foundation."

Again a chorus of yeses and nods.

"Good. So when can we tell the other cookie ladies and arrange the cruise?"

"Tell them?" Mark frowns.

"I trust them to keep their mouths shut," Marnie says.

"We should share our joy with them," Juliet adds. They agree, but furrows remain on Mark's forehead.

91

"I'll arrange the cruise," Rosie says. "Oh we're going to have soooo so much fun!"

BUT TAYLOR CAN'T wait for the fun to begin. The next day, Taylor calls in sick at the library, drops the kids off at their schools, and drives to Somerset Collection, an upscale shopping destination mall about an hour away. Snow, dumped by trucks, is heaped in the median, along the edges of the highway but, between the piles, ground is visible. Winter slowly sheds its mantle. For over four years Taylor bought what she desperately needed at Value World and the Kiwanis on Saturday morning, buying used clothes for all three of them. The smell of dust and Lysol brought tears to her eyes. She hasn't stepped into a mall, or Target. She purchased underwear from the clearance bin at TJ Maxx. Somehow she couldn't imagine wearing panties that had been worn by a stranger no matter how many times they had been washed and bleached.

The mall glitters off the highway. A bridge, domed and encased in beige, complete with moving sidewalks, spans its two sides. Saks Fifth Avenue and Tiffany's on one side, Nordstrom and Macy's on the other. She parks in the lot next to a BMW. *I can buy anything I want.*

Taylor leaves her down coat, and picks up her old beige purse. The lining is torn so she pokes her hand through it to unearth her lipstick and smears it on.

*It's all in one's attitude.* She pulls her shoulders back as she strides through glass doors with brass handles as if she belongs, as if she's not wearing jeans she bought from Kiwanis for fifty cents and a sweater so worn it has pills all over it, especially under her arms. Strolling as though she's on stage, hipbones pointed, she picks up the

92

glossy brochure of the mall directory as she walks to the atrium. Three floors of shops, connected by humming escalators surround her. Rays of stores spread out like a star. Above her, a domed skylight emits natural light. Palm trees edge a raised shallow pool. Marble floors glisten. Elegantly dressed women glide up the escalators. A faint smell of vanilla wafts toward her.

Then she spots Tiffany's. When she enters, no one approaches her. She scans the jewelry cases. Locks, heart-shaped and square, gold and silver, some glittering with pave diamonds, dangle from bracelets, necklaces. The last thing she wants is a lock. She's free. Not married. Not poor. Not poor anymore. *Amazing.*

She turns, glances over rows of precious stone bracelets, pendants, and rings. Blazing with warmth and fire are orange stud earrings. She cranes over the glass, but still no one offers help. *I'm in my old disguise as a poor person,* she chuckles. She taps the glass with a forefinger, clears her throat, and says with a tone of annoyance, "Can I have some help, pleeeease."

She tries on the citrine earrings. Flashy. Lighter than they appear. $550 bucks. Ten times more than she spent the entire previous year on clothes. She fishes through the torn lining of her purse for her wallet, pulls out one of her charge cards, flicks a fingernail on it, and hands it to the saleswoman who takes it, and with tight lips, flashes it through the slot, examining the window.

*That tight ass clerk can take her supercilious attitude and shove it. And I'm doing this on my own, with my own money. Like all the shopping I did before Rick, when I was the headline singer and single. See. Women don't need men to provide status and wealth. We can do it ourselves, isn't that what the women's movement was about? I was doing it before I met him, and I certainly can do it now.*

When the card is Okayed, the clerk lifts her eyebrows, then hands Taylor the receipt to sign.

Taylor doesn't say a word, but signs the slip as though annoyed with the time it takes. The clerk meanwhile fastens the earrings in a robin's egg blue box, ties a white bow, folds tissue over it, places it in the characteristic Tiffany bag, and, with the box dangling from its the blue cords clasped between her forefinger and thumb, allows Taylor to retrieve it.

Next stop, BCBG. Clothes hang from racks without fanfare, but with an elegance that exemplifies class and confidence. Each item separate from the others, as though its very hanger is unique. At first no one approaches her, and she is free to browse uninterrupted, until the Tiffany bag is spotted. Taylor buys a top with a splashy arty design, a wrap snake print, an asymmetrical black tunic, perfect over skinny jeans, and a black purse with metal. Real leather, not plastic that will crack with a freeze. The lining is pliable chamois, the zipper slides easily and the iron studs add an edge without a hint of trash. The clothes have style and flash without garishness and are well made, no hanging threads, no untied seams. No smell of cleaning fluid or dust. Then Taylor spies a scarf that looks like an impressionist painting. By itself, it costs more than she's spent in the last five years on clothes.

*Winning the lottery has allowed me to be my own Prince Charming. Wow.*

She takes the new purse out of its bag, places the contents of her old beige one into it and slings the soft leather bag over her shoulder. At the next trash receptacle, she crams in the beige one. *Goodbye to old bad life. Hello, new one.*

At Nordstrom, she notices a black leather jacket, sniffs the rich musk. A zipper slants to a tunnel collar. Zippers hug the wrists. It has a tinge of hard edge. *That's the only bad boy I want anything to do with. No more assholes.* She zips the jacket, the sound flashing, and buys it. Matches well with the new purse.

She walks through the scent of tea oil into Saks, and notices that Chanel is offering makeovers. Yes. The young woman, Lisa, looks flawless. "Please try," she says just above a whisper as though they're sharing secrets. "I can show you some wonderful cosmetics, fulfilling your dreams for beauty."

So Taylor agrees. Sublimage cream, and express lifting firming mask, and correction line repairs, and make up. Lisa holds a wide brush and says, "Most importantly, after you apply your make up, brush down. Move all the little hairs on your face down. Very important, this tool." Lisa caresses Taylor's face with the gentle stroking.

*I love being pampered.*

"This collection is like a fantasy, flowers in spring time, but yet vibrant. A freshness, and dewy eyed look." With yellow nails, Lisa applies eyebrow pencil, shows Taylor how to do smoky eyes using a damp brush to apply liner, then light and dark shadows to highlight her bones, blush to bring out the apples in her cheeks, (build up slowly, here) concealer to camouflage the circles under her eyes, and diminish the lines between her nostrils and the corners of her lips. Lipstick liner, lipstick, and then gloss. Coats of mascara.

When Taylor looks in the mirror, she blinks in surprise. She looks totally unlike the woman who walked in a few hours before. Younger, yes. More vivid, yes. But different. Not quite exactly her anymore. Bright. Cheerful. More typically beautiful. The missing bow in her upper lip is gone, filled in with liner and coats of lipstick.

Lisa pulls out a drawing of a face and uses cotton swabs of make-up to show Taylor how she created her transformation. Taylor decides to buy it all. The mask, the foundation, the concealer, the eyeshadows, the three lipsticks, the shaders. When she sees the final sum, over a thousand dollars, a flash of fear engulfs her. *A thousand dollars on make up? Clothes and jewelry are one thing, they last, but make up? The Tiffany purchase was the cheapest of the day.*

Lisa slowly packs up the lotions, the tubes, the jars, the pencils, wrapping them in tissue and gently, like the treasures they are, and slides them in the Chanel bag.

*I can afford this. I can.* Taylor closes her eyes. *I'm rich. I'm single. I'm worth it. I deserve this, all this. And more. Much more. I'm entitled.* Taylor signs with a flourish.

She fishes the keys from her purse, puts the BCBG box and bag over one wrist. She stuffs the Tiffany bag in it, and carries the Chanel bag in her other hand, with the new leather jacket encased in a garment bag draped over her arm. She reaches her car and pops the trunk open, chuckling at the clutter of charger cords for when her battery dies, and motor oil she bought on sale at Murray's Auto. She nestles the shiny bags and boxes gently beside each other. *I have just spent more than this car is worth. Way more.*

It's only one in the afternoon. She calls her hairdresser, who has a cancellation. "Perfect," Taylor says. "I'll be there in half an hour."

Her hair is dyed its old auburn red color, with a few subtle streaks of brighter highlights, and cut into a sexy and sassy style. *No more just putting it back in a bun. No more tired old lady.*

While she's waiting for the dye to finish processing, Taylor makes a shopping list. *New iPhones for all three of us. New clothes for the kids. New iPad. New car, an SUV. New house, but not just yet. I'll wait 6 months for that. Yes. No more worries. No more Rick. I'll never have to*

96

*hear from him or deal with him again. When he dies I won't even know. I'll move away and be rid of him forever, start a new life in a new city with my new wealth.*

*I'm free!*

Her heart beats as she imagines the new her. Beautiful with red hair, up-tempo clothes, perfect face with smoky eyes. She'll be racy and exciting. In just a week everything has changed. *I think I'll start singing again. Why not? I can do this on my own. I'll be who I want to be. The lottery makes up for those wasted years.*

On the way home, Taylor gets a manicure and pedicure in coral polish to match her new lipstick, hair color and Tiffany jewels.

## Nine

*66% of people who received sudden wealth cited the ability to donate to charity, and 75% rated the ability to help family and friends as the positive results.*

EVEN TRACY COMES on the cruise. When she hears her friends won the lottery and all the cookie club members are sailing the Caribbean, she says, "Count me in!  Silver and I went to the South Pacific, Japan, China, and Egypt, but not there.   Besides,  how  could  I  miss  being  with  my girlfriends?" She  opens  her  arms.  "AND  I'm  already packed!"

Rosie arranges everything, like she arranged the trip to Cozumel when she, Jeannie and Sue were the three musketeers.  Jeannie worries about leaving Dad. Won't Mom need help?

"Quit fussing.   You think I'm incompetent?   I've taken care of Jack for decades.  You have your life, honey. Go."

Packing is a challenge, figuring out how light she can travel,  but  having  to  deal  with  security  and  the  3-1-1 regulations and disordering toothpaste and shampoo from the toiletry bag and the lotions and foundation from her make up bag is a pain. Then Jeannie decides, even though she doesn't really need to, she'll check the bag and pay the extra money.   What does she pack? A swimsuit. Lots of sunscreen. A pair of jeans, shorts, and tee shirts, some beach wraps, a few dresses. Pjs. That's it! Easy.

Rosie has opted to fly first class, "I just love getting in ahead of everybody else, not smashed in lines then stuffed in a tiny seat. No waiting." She strides through the first class security line.

Alice follows. "I was upgraded 'cause of all my miles,"  she  shrugs  away  her  grin  and  then  rocks  her shoulders back and forth, a movement which, if she were a child, says, "I'm better than you. Ha ha ha."

The very idea of crowds enclosed in one place makes Mark claustrophobic so this is Jeannie's first cruise and she opted to have her own stateroom. She had to pay extra for a single, but figured since they won all that money she could treat herself. She hasn't slept alone since she was in a college dorm. Oh, maybe a few times when Mark was away at a legal convention and once when she went to a yoga retreat. But now she has her own little room, all ship shape and tidy.

Through the porthole, the sea laps at the sky. Boats echo the waves moving toward the horizon, the edge of the earth.

Jeannie hangs her tee shirts, dresses in the closet and fills the dresser with underwear and PJs that Sara bought for her birthday. "They're purple. And soft," Sara said when she handed them to Jeannie. "You know me so well, my darling," she kissed her daughter. Now, Jeannie places toiletries in the bathroom medicine cabinet. Her make up bag on the toilet back. Stashes her suitcase in the floor of the closet. She brought a home fragrance oil diffuser scented with coconut and pineapple, and places the sticks in it. It has a wide bottom so it should manage any shifting. Beside, these ships are like floating motels.

This little cubicle, exactly like all the others filled with different people with different swimsuits and toothbrushes, makes Jeannie feel as if she's starting life over. She's as unknown and unseen as all the other voyagers in their cubicles. Anonymous. Her wealth invisible. Everything is new and fresh. Ahead of her are mysterious but limitless possibilities. The combination of exhilaration and anxiety tickles the back of her arms and neck with goose bumps.

Where's this coming from? *Must be the crazy combination of paralyzed Dad and the power of 125 million dollars. I'm still in jeans from five years ago, and a tee shirt patterned with the logo of a yoga retreat I attended. I'm a secret millionaire. No one would ever know. No one would ever guess anything about my life or me. In a way, it's like when I lost my virginity. Something profound changed, but it was indiscernible. I did not wear my sexual knowledge in my smile, just like this unaccustomed wealth.*

Her purple shawl drapes across the narrow bed, and she flips over the scent sticks to smell the coconut, evidence of her. *I have an impact as permanent as the smell of coconut and the flimsy shawl. So much for being a millionaire. I'm just another human animal after all.*

Attending the required safety meeting, Jeannie stands along the sides of the ship with a bunch of people she doesn't know, shifting from foot to foot as a crew member explains where the life jackets are stowed, insists everyone wear one. They look like they've donned pumpkin costumes for trick or treating. He points out lifeboats and how to board if there's an evacuation. The crewmember grins with shiny teeth and tells memorized jokes to deter the passengers from considering death and tragedy as they embark on a hoped- for joyous vacation. But that's what he's saying. They could go on a celebration and die.

It makes Jeannie think of her father.

Where are Rosie, Charlene, and Chandra? Jeannie doesn't see them among the smashed together people and they're on the same corridor.

She walks to Neptune's pool, her Kindle jammed into a tote, to meet the cookie bitches. It's somewhere on the fourth deck, adults only. (Does that mean nudity, or just no kids jumping up and down and smashing into you?) The ship is confusing, like a hospital, a maze of floors and long corridors that lead you-don't-know-where. She strides

101

around decks, up and down staircases, finds a casino, several bars, poolside grills, restaurants, an auditorium as she goes in circles, scanning the maps at the elevators, and then finds herself stuck on the right side, (starboard?) but it doesn't seem to have any access to the floor above which is where she needs to go. Abruptly, right in the middle of a corridor is a circular staircase that she climbs and then, Viola! A deck with a swimming pool and banks of chaises already strewn with blue towels and sunglasses and bottles of lotion. Adults, with bikinis and boxer suits, jump up and down playing volleyball in a pool. In the whirlpool, people lean their heads against the back, drinks in their hands. A sign says *Neptune Pool* over the bar.

Jeannie circles the deck, searching lounge chairs for her friends. No luck.

A mob of bathing suited people, gleaming with oil, surround a bar. They hold fancy drinks with spears of pineapple, umbrellas, some in a coconut, or in souvenir glasses.

Maybe the other eleven are slowly unpacking, or still wandering around hunting for Neptune.

Well, they can look for her.

She scouts several vacant chaises, retrieves a cobalt beach towel and spreads it over the wooden slats. Jeannie places the tote on the empty lounger next to hers saving a place for one of her friends, opens the kindle and resumes reading the novel, *Invention of Wings,* she started on the plane. She reads for a while, but keeps glancing to see if they've arrived, unable to lose herself in the book. At the bar, she orders a pina colada in a pineapple decorated with cherries and an umbrella. Then walks the long way back to her chaise, scanning the deck, but still no evidence of friends.

*See. I am anonymous. In a new life, or maybe Kafka novel where everything is tilted, amiss, transported to a twirked world with rules and requirements that can't be anticipated.*

Maybe she's on the wrong boat. No. Jeannie walked up the gangplank with Taylor, her hair dyed red and frosted, wearing a leather jacket, snappy with zippers and asymmetry. But she skipped off to another level, reminding Jeannie to meet everyone at the Neptune Pool.

A shadow falls over her and she raises her eyes to see the silhouette of a man. His head blocks the sun in such a way that spikes of bright rays scatter behind him. She only sees his outline, tall and lanky. "Is this available?" he asks pointing to the empty chair. He has a slight accent she can't place.

Jeannie shields her vision with her hand, squinting up at him and says, "Yes. I guess so."

He lies next to her, dark brown skin, and she notices his head of thick, curly hair, a robust peaked nose, and cheeks that cave in under his bones. His face says slight danger, aggressive and inquisitive. A spattering of hair, just enough to be interesting, freckles his body. He crosses one leg over the other, picks up the *New York Review of Books,* opens it. The paper shields Jeannie from the sun. She sips from her fancy drink.

"How is it?"

"Festive, sweet, and pretty," she answers.

"Yes it is. Very."

Jeannie head snaps toward him at his presumptuous chuckle after his armed innuendo.

He raises his brows.

She glances at her wedding ring, firmly surrounding her finger. She's barely taken it off, but a small mole has grown under it. Or maybe she never noticed it. Jeannie was so eager to get married, she never noticed the blemish on her ring finger. But it's there now. Something from within her. Has it grown on her wedding ring finger since she married?  Or had the ring covered up an unnoticed blemish?

"Thank you." Jeannie resumes reading.

"Do you like that Kindle?" He keeps her hooked in conversation. "I'm a writer and it's in my best interest to hate them." His eyes are very dark as they pin her for an answer to his question. She still can't place his slight accent.

"With it I carry lots of books.  I like going light."

"I'm fascinated by them, drawn to my own destruction. But yes, I can see you like light."  His eyes flit over Jeannie's body.  No one has looked at her like that in years. Since when?

She doesn't like how his eyes caress her, how his voice, so deep and rumbly, yet soft, tickles her.  She crosses her legs.

Then, dense shadows cover his swim trunks, his chest, with that spattering of hair.

"Hey, Jeannie. I've been looking everywhere for you. We've been fighting to keep a chaise for you in the Poseidon pool. What're you doing here?" It's Allie with a broad brimmed hat, a hooded white cover-all that goes to her ankles, and sunglasses.

"I've been waiting for you."

"Where's your cell phone? We've been calling and calling trying to locate you." Then she glimpses the man lying next to Jeannie.  "Oh. Well, we're all there." Allie stands glancing from Jeannie to the man. "At Poseidon."

"I'm Ricardo," he holds out his hand to Allie. "Sounds like she got the right god, just the wrong culture."

"Allie," she laughs.

Jeannie turns to him, "Nice to meet you. I'm Jeannie."

His teeth are even and very white when he smiles.

Jeannie stuffs her bag with her Kindle and towel, throws it over her shoulder, slides her feet into flip-flops, picks up the drink. She turns to Ricardo, licks her lips, to say something.

But he beats her to the punch. "See you around, Jeannie. We'll run into each again. We've got a week here." As though he releases her to join her friends. But only temporarily.

WELL, THERE THEY are, lying on the lounges, rubbing sunscreen on their legs, drinking fancy girly drinks. "Where were you? We started to get concerned," Marnie says.

"She was at Neptune. With some man."

"I get it. You went to the adults only pool and picked up a man and we haven't even left port yet," Taylor teases.

"I didn't pick him up." Jeannie defends herself. "I was trying to save those seats for you guys."

"Rrrrright." Vera teases.

"Vera, you're amazing. You look terrific." She wears a blond Marilyn Monroe wig, and a white suit. She looks a little tired, but nothing concealer and a little tan won't fix.

"Ah, the sun," she stretches her face to it. "Feel its heat."

"Yeah. A terrific relief from those grey, cold winters. Tell me once again, why do we live in Michigan?" Chandra says.

And just like that, Jeannie's sense of the anonymity with its aloneness and freedom vanishes.

"I love you guys," she says.

"We're so fucking lucky!" Taylor says.

"Hear! Hear!"

"Yes. We are," Charlene says. "Thank you for bringing us. Sharing your fortune."

They lift their silly decorated glasses, pineapples and coconuts. "L'Chaim," Allie says. "To us."


BUT THE TRUTH is, they still haven't figured out everything about the money. It's been three weeks, and they haven't even picked it up yet. Mark and Kevin are drawing up agreements for a corporation called *Christmas Cookie Club* to receive the money from the state, and additional agreements between the seven of the players. For now, each of them is charging her own expenses and sharing the expenses of the other five. Some decisions have been made, each one fraught with discussion and hurt feelings. Jeannie checks out Sissy who sits next to Charlene, drinking an ice tea, and scanning the crowd. For a second, Jeannie tries to look at the scene from Sissy's point of view and notices a young black couple holding hands between their chaises. The woman shifts on her side and whispers something in his ear and he laughs. A middle-aged man and woman both read. A black father teaches his daughter how to swim. Five men of diverse races surround three young black women wearing skimpy bathing suits and long extensions. The white people are doing similar things. Celebrating love, flirting, playing. Families. Couples. Friends.

When they decided not to pool all the money into Sissy's foundation, she was disappointed. Now, Mark and Kevin are creating a charity for her money, but she can only put in half of it. That will be almost six million dollars. Each of them can anonymously contribute to Sissy's foundation...it's being done in such a way that not even she will know who has donated. Sissy hopes to hire Allie to write additional grants. The first one will include a salary for Charlene to coalesce church groups, especially in suburbs, to aid with the inner city effort.

Jeannie imagines they'll become another three-musketeer friendship pulled together by their passion.

She envies Sissy's absolute convictions. Jeannie still hasn't decided whether she'll run the dealership, or close it. She could use the building for the ultimate yoga studio. That's the bigger financial risk. The taste for revenge on Sue is still in her mouth. It would be so glorious just to fire her and maintain the dealership, rubbing her nose in it. *Why is it so hard for me to make decisions? Why hasn't all my meditation made it easier and clearer? Instead they're less important. Whatever will be, will be.*

Jeannie meets the faces of Vera, Alice and Tracy, all three drinking margaritas. "Why not give them 5%? Or even one percent? One percent would be about 80,000 from each of us, times seven, divided by five would be about 100,000 a piece." Marnie suggested, working the calculator on her cell phone.

"Or we could each give each of them 13,000. Isn't that what you can give without getting tax penalty? That would be about 90,000," Rosie said.

"Count me out of that," Sissy said. They were at Jeannie's house for this discussion.

"Well then it would be about 70,000 for each of them. Do you know what a difference it would make, especially to Vera who started playing with us?"

No one responded to Marnie's pleading. Juliet ran her finger under the gold chain she always wears.

"Come on. We're rich," Marnie said. "We should share."

"Are you afraid they'll resent us?" Jeannie asked. "You think we'll lose our friends?"

"We're each giving to our own charities," Chandra reminded them. "I'm giving to schools in the village my parents came from in India. There're deserving and needy people all over this planet."

107

"I AM my own charity. Until my kids are secure, anyway," Taylor stated, leaned back and crossed her arms. "Not until I am absolutely financially safe. I never want to go dumpster diving again."

"Dumpster diving?" Chandra's voice screeched.

"What?"

"Really? You're kidding!"

"You don't know how bad it was. Dumpster diving and used clothes at the Goodwill and free turkeys and presents from Toys are Tots." Taylor closed her eyes and shudders. "I tried to get on welfare, but couldn't because I was still married. Never again. Never again. We were just this side of having to live in the car."

"I have obligations, responsibilities I don't know yet what I'm going to do about. I can't make this decision now," Juliet almost whispered. Jeannie realized then how little she knew about Juliet's life. Are her parents still alive? Does she have siblings?

"I think we should give more to our friends," Rosie repeated. "I think we should each divvy up 75 grand for the other cookie bitches." She was on her own mission.

As they so often do, they glanced at each other. Sissy announced by looking away that she was out of this discussion. Then she stood up and went to the bathroom.

Marnie said, "How about 100?"

"What is this a bidding war? One person says 50 G-s, another 70. Then another says 100. Are we proving who is the most generous?" Juliet prodded. She stood up then and shook her head slightly and her curls trembled on her shoulders. "Maybe we're really proving, who needs the win the least, not the most generous." She walked to Jeannie's counter and poured herself some wine.

Marnie frowned. "I think I'm one of those who needs it the most, and I'm suggesting the largest donations." Her voice was raised and her cheeks flushed.

"Why do we all have to do the same? Why can't we each contribute what we think is cool? Even if some of us contribute nothing."

Jeannie wondered if the one that grew up the poorest – Sissy? Juliet? --would be the stingiest. But then she grew up the richest and she's not the most generous.

Sissy is. She wins any competition for generosity. Maybe Sissy's munificence is partly the vanity of sainthood, her self-image devoted to a system of morality. It's who she is. Does her vanity stain the effect? No. It drives it. There's no arrogance to her lavish giving of herself or, now, her funds, and she seems without judgment regarding her friends' reluctance to match her devotion and generosity.

They didn't decide how to share their wealth with the other cookie friends. Except for the cruise. The cruise seemed safe.


NOW, THE DISCUSSION tugs at Jeannie's mind. *Where am I in all this? I don't know. I don't know what the right thing is anymore.* The sun blazes in a so blue sky, and the crowd laughs, flesh glistening, everyone with decorated drinks while she broils with emotions about her ill father, rages at Sue, and sorrows for her mother. None of it lessened by a new sense of privilege, and growing entitlement.

"To us. To life," Juliet says, smiling.

"Hey look! We're pulling away from the port. Going out to the ocean!" Rosie squeals.

They walk to the edge of the deck, lean over the railing, drinks in hand, and watch the dock and the city behind it recede.

A new horizon beckons.

## Ten

*On the average, lottery winners who are men give money to 3 friends, women to 1 friend.*

MARNIE STANDS IN the breakfast buffet line the next morning and sees Vera, Tracy and Alice leaning toward the center of their table. Vera whispers, Tracy shakes her head, and Alice lifts her face, chewing on her lower lip as she so often does.

*Will I interrupt them if I join them?* Marnie wonders. Then Charlene and Allie walk toward the table, holding piled plates, and slide next to them. *I guess it's okay,* Marnie grins and waves until Alice waves back.

Sissy stands in front of the omelets patiently waiting her turn.

The curving food line-- sticky sweet deserts, mounds of fruit, pancakes, potatoes, waffles, sausage, bacon, ham, oatmeal, scrambled eggs, bread, cheese, cold cuts, muffins of four different variety, bagels, smoked fish --- advances slowly as people scoop chosen items on top of others on their plates as though each new one is more delicious than the one before. *Why do we act as though this is the last food we're going to get and try to eat it all? The same choices will be there tomorrow, and the next morning, too.*

Sissy pulls up a chair to join the group.
Marnie glances at her own dish laden with fruit, cranberry nut muffins, and bacon and walks toward her friends.

"Anyone see Juliet?"

Just then Juliet comes with fruit, yogurt, and coffee. "Here I am. You guys missing me?" She laughs.

Jeannie is behind her. "I'm so excited about going kayaking today," she says as she sits. "Sea kayaking.

Gonna be way fun." Jeannie shakes her head and closes her eyes imagining thrills.

"Kayaking? No way. I'm hoping to find a Tanzanite. I understand this island has a store devoted to them." Taylor strides to the table just in time to hear Jeannie's comment.

"Hey, I'll hit the jewelry stores with you," Marnie says.

"Me too," Rosie adds as she steals a chair from another table and wedges it between Taylor and Marnie's.

"I'm snorkeling, floating over a colorful reef of gorgeous magical fishes." Allie's fingers twinkle the air as though each tip is a blue damsel nibbling branch coral.

"Yeah, I've signed up for that one, too," Juliet says.

"Where's Chandra?"

"Last seen she was piling up chips at the blackjack table."

"Looked like she won big," Jeannie adds.

"Chandra?" Marnie says, "Our cute Chandra is a card shark?"

They giggle.

"Yeah, she won almost 20 thousand!"

"Really?" Marnie asks.

Then Tracy interlaces her fingers, turns to Marnie and Rosie, sitting next to each other and says, "We were just talking about what you guys are going to do with all the money."

Dead silence.

Marnie and Rosie glance at each other.

Jeannie twists her wedding ring around her finger.

Juliet straightens her fork.

"I think you know what I'm going to do. I assume Allie and Charlene have told you. Most of my money is going into a special foundation. I hope everyone adds to it." Sissy checks the expressions on the winners' faces.

112

"Chandra told me you figure it'll be about 8 million each." Alice's lips are open, her lids slightly lowered. "I can't imagine what that must feel like," she sighs.

"Right now it feels like… *we* get to take you on a cruise!" Juliet says.

For some reason, not immediately discernible, her comment is met with strained looks, and silence. Tracy's fingers press into the backs of her hands, Alice chews on her lip. Vera wipes her forehead and inhales, exhausted. Allie and Charlene stab quick glances at each other, eyebrows raised as though they anticipated this very conversation.

Juliet jerks as though shoved. "Other than that I don't have a clue."

"I've, we've, been advised not to make any decision for six months. Not to buy anything. Not to give any away. To let the change settle in," Rosie says.

"Advised, by who?" Jeannie asks.

"We went to a financial planner, one who specializes in sudden inheritances and lottery winners. That was his advice. Meanwhile we're supposed to do research, imagine the future."

"I just want to be free," Taylor says. "Away from worry. Away from that bastard ex. Who is my ex!! Yippeee!! I can't tell you, begin to tell you, how thrilled and relieved I am that I'll never have to deal with him again. I don't even want to think about investments, retirement, any of that. I want to put it in the bank and *live* on it. Spend it." Taylor's eyes are closed. "Have fun. Start singing again. Start my life as though Rick never crashed into it. Except for the kids, of course."

"And you Jeannie? Are you going to do the yoga studio, women's center you dreamed about?" Alice's head tilts.

Jeannie shrugs, "I'm not sure. My dad's stroke has changed everything." She concentrates on her coffee. "Maybe that advice about not making decisions for six months is good. But the dealership can't wait for months. With Dad so ill, something has to be decided. I'm like a deer stuck in headlights." She lifts her head then and stares at Alice. "But I've been like that for several years." Jeannie's purple shirt bolsters the green in her hazel eyes.

The mood has changed. The excitement of the day: shopping for glinting gems that stole the sky, kayaking among fighting foam, laying on a beach with sand as white and fine as sugar, listening to the endless licking lullaby of surf, or floating over schools of fish flashing bright colors has dimmed.

They resume eating the scraps still on their plates.

Money.

How much will they give us? Or is this trip, this cruise, the total amount? Vera, Charlene, Tracy, Alice and Allie look at each other.

Money.

How can they each be multimillionaires with more than anyone needs for a lifetime, and not share with close friends? Especially Vera who is struggling for her very life?

Money.

They didn't do anything to deserve this. Not really. They took a chance on a dream.

Money.

What to do with it? How much to give families, friends who were once part of them, but now, not quite. Maybe never again, in the same way. The winners-- Marnie, Jeannie, Rosie, Juliet, Taylor --glance at each other.

Questions have seeped their way inside them like grits of sand in bathing suits, salt in hair.

## Eleven

*In 1826, Thomas Jefferson got permission for a private lottery to alleviate his debt. Held by his heirs after he died, it didn't raise enough money to pay his debts.*

JEANNIE WALKS TO the place on the dock where the Sea Kayakers are meeting and there's that guy. *What did he say his name was? Ricardo. That's it.* He stands beside a crewmember holding a sign saying *Sea Kayaking.* The badge on his chest announces his name: Glenn

Jeannie spots Allie and Juliet with twenty people surrounding a woman with the pony tail poking out the back of her baseball cap carrying a sign labeled *Snorkeling.* Another thirty wait to board a pirate boat for a ride around the island. The people on the shopping tour grab maps of the city and straggle through the town's streets. Ubiquitous steel drums throb.

"Where are the others?" Jeannie asks.

"So far just you two," Glenn says.

Ricardo smiles. "See how much we have in common?" he says as if resuming a discussion.

"Or how weird we both are," she quips.

"Exactly. None of your friends wanted to come?"

"Tanzanite and tropical fish took their fancy."

"Also good choices," which sounds like just small talk, just bullshit politeness, except for the way he examines her as though each word she utters is fascinating and scintillating. And except for the way he stares as though Jeannie has the most beautiful body in the world...not just her boobs, but the turn of her wrist, the funneling of her neck into collar bone, the lankiness of muscles pressing the bones of her arms.

"You guys familiar with kayaking?"

115

"Very," Ricardo says. "Led white water rafting tours in Cheat River through college."

"That's a five, isn't it?" The guide's eyebrows lift. "You'll take care of her, show her the ropes?" Glenn checks his watch.

"It would be a privilege."

"Come on then."

They get into Glenn's jeep and he drives the gentle curve at the island's edge to a dock with kayaks, life jackets, and paddles. Ricardo helps Jeannie find one that suits the length of her legs.

"I've kayaked before in our local river, well stream, but the sea will give me a challenge."

"Just coast with the surf. This is a breeze compared to a class 5 river," Ricardo reassures her.

Glen hands Ricardo a map of the shore, points out the mangrove swamps, some inlets where they might see an alligator. "But they're very rare, now," he warns. He draws a huge star on the shore and says, "Crystal Bay. A great beach for a picnic," and hands them each a sack lunch in a waterproof bag. Whistles. Life jackets they're supposed to wear at all times, waterproof bags for wallets and cell phones. Then a card with his cell number should they need it. Jeannie settles in a kayak and, before Glenn launches her, Ricardo does, calling over his shoulder as he hops into his kayak, "Don't worry I'll take very good care of her."

The sea is calm, not much different than the Huron River in winter, as it rocks Jeannie in the bright turquoise to the horizon. The sun warms her shoulders through her tee shirt. The cowries, braided into her hair, click setting a castanet rhythm as she strokes the water, flips her oar, and tugs the sea again. The paddle and the sea's pull synchronize, pulsing together.

She almost forgets about Ricardo behind her.

He easily gains speed and they stroke side by side. Then he surpasses Jeannie and leads them through an estuary to a mangrove forest, the bridge between the sea and the land. Roots twist to clasp trees to muddy, brackish water. Branches hanging with moss and air plants reach toward the moist air. Clouds of white butterflies flitter over the water. Bananaquits dance like sunbeams in the tangled forest. He pulls the paddle, turns it to its other side, and draws through the mucky water again, smooth as walking, it's that natural and customary.

Sun light sparks in golden patches on the water. A snowy egret balances on one leg in tree pose.

A startling splash. Sun spots collide.

Jeannie jerks.

Out of nowhere, an alligator snaps at the bird. Its teeth daggers.

Jeannie's kayak tilts. She clutches the sides. Releases her oar.

Slimy water as warm as flesh hits her thigh, fills her boat.

Lightening quick, Ricardo rights her, snatches her oar as it rushes by him.

The egret sits on a branch laughing at the alligator and the commotion.

Ricardo grabs Jeannie's boat, hands her the paddle. She plunges it into the mud, which sucks a hold on it. The alligator stares with devil eyes, its tail slithering underwater.

Ricardo shoves Jeannie down the stream, away from the alligator, from danger.

Her heart pounds. She's chilled from her sweat and stinks from the water. Then they're out of the swamp and into the sea again stretching no one can see where. But Jeannie knows. It goes all the way to Africa. The water is calm, clear and blue as the estuary is silt and obscure.

Pelicans fly over them, their wings bent in sinister corners, or straight as they coast on invisible currents.

The sand is white sugar, almost as fine as confectioners. There're no boats. No fishermen. No people. Just Jeannie and Ricardo and pelicans and palms.

They pull the kayaks to the shore.

Jeannie feels taken care of. *Isn't that weird? I don't like the feeling and I love it at the same time.* They perch on the sand, eat cheese sandwiches and chips and a lukewarm diet coke, isolated as if they're the only people in the world. Just the two of them.   Sand. Sun. Sea. Horizon. They watch the sea and pelicans. Elbows resting on knees. They wonder at the purple horizon, hunting the end of the ocean.

The beach is littered with smooth rocks polished by the sand and waves.  Jeannie picks one- green with black and white flecks. Another is black with a vivid pink stripe through it.   They're more beautiful than diamonds and have a compound, complicated history. While diamonds, so vacuous, empty really, only offer clarity.

"I could have been an alligator's next meal. Thank you." That eerie sense of her anonymity, of starting over, hits Jeannie.  Death. Life. A blink.  Like the stones, she is one of so many, so many. Unique only to her, precious only to her family.

He chuckles, all confidence and ease. "Not really, that was a small alligator and probably more scared of you in the kayak than you were of it. But I'll take that favor you now owe me."

"Uh oh," she says, "I guess I have to let you beat me at slots in the casino." She wins more laughter from him aware of the many different levels she plays.  Was she ever like this? Was she this carefree before Mark?  Or is this a new her fashioned by the entitlement of her wealth?

118

In the past, her money was her father's or her husband's.

They keep easy flirting, but underneath the patter, a current of Jeannie's thoughts stream. What would it be like if they were stranded here and only had each other? She glances at his muscular thighs under his brown skin, his slender fingers and wonder how he'd be as a lover. He's physically competent, comfortable in his body, and capable of managing the corporeal world while Mark is unable to repair the lawn mower, change the oil in their car. He hires people for everything that requires practical skills not associated with his work.

Ricardo's hair curls softly over his chest, as he leans back on his elbows, turns to her. His easy smile, his eyes sliding down her body reminds her of something long forgotten. Something she once felt, the suspense of the sexual unknown.

Mark and Jeannie are equal partners, best friends, and co-parents. It works so well in the life they have formed as they dole themselves to each other and their various roles. But somehow the man and woman part, the elemental part, has slumped through the cracks between jobs, caring for Sara and parents, dogs and bills and a house and a yard.

What would Ricardo's reaction be if she told him she's worth eleven million dollars before taxes? Would she seem more like a prize? Or more of a threat?

Jeannie fits Mark into this location. Could he casually sit here eating a cheese sandwich? What would he do if he saw an alligator close to her?

Could they have recaptured this male - female primal feeling? Would they just be loving friends commenting on the calm ignoring the potential of storm? Or would they turn to each other and, using years of practice with each other's bodies, their reactions foretold and predictable, make love. Their orgasms so taken for granted that they're the excuse for the day to end with the cuddling and quiet discussion that follow as they drift, at last, into the separate worlds of sleep. *If I were stranded on an island, would I choose Mark? Or Ricardo?*

Jeannie feels warmth emanating from Ricardo's thigh and smells lime from his shampoo. "Why are you all on the cruise together?"

"It's the ultimate girls night out," she says, suspicious, as if he's trying to find out about the lottery. How crazy that is, must be her sense of not deserving it. Even though it was her numbers. *Mark's and my numbers,* she reminds herself. An odd sense of things being particular and universal, extraordinary and ordinary simultaneously fills her as though her family and their birthdates are exceptional. Yet Jeannie knows they're not...not really...not ultimately...they're simply like grains in the sand.

She says that, "We're just grains in the sand, all of us."

"That's Buddhist. We may be grains of sand to the eyes in the sky, if there are any up there," he glances to the heavens, "but to us we are one-and-only-never-again grains. And you're very unique."

He thinks like she does. How terrifying. "How?"

"It's your grace. As though you live simultaneously in the minute, but realize that there's a history, questions that push or avoid the moment's solutions."

"How do you know that?"

"Writers arm themselves with careful observation of distinctive details. That's our stock in trade. Sight. Our voice rises from our vision."

"Like psychics?"

"They say that the only difference between writers and therapists is that therapists think they can make a difference."

Ricardo tells Jeannie he's on this cruise as research for a novel, part of a series of international thrillers having to do with counterfeiting and bank wire transfers. Some of the action takes place on a cruise and a Caribbean island.

Money. She tilts her head toward him aware that the lottery win would be fascinating to him. She also realizes he probably knows, at least theoretically, all the ways to hide it, loose it and wonders if he's proficient in conning people out of it or if those fantasies funnel into his characters.

"And do a man and woman sit on a beach as though they're Adam and Eve in just this way after he saves her life from a deadly beast?" She teases.

His eyes darken and soften and he says, "If I can chose the perfect words to describe the passage between us."

"Like aura." She holds her palm toward him and he places his, as if she willed it, a sparse span away. Tingling heat from him resounds with Jeannie's so their energy trembles. Amazement clouds their faces. She's had fantasies and wonderings about other men sexually, but always pushed away the thoughts, walked away from any opportunity, but this is compelling.

She doesn't know how it happens, because there're no words, no real reason that she comprehends the next thing that occurs. She doesn't know how they cross the bridge between sitting as primal male and female talking seductive nonsense, already adept at the game of being together, to crossing a line, but his lips tug at hers.

In return, she asks for more.

There's something about the smell of lime, the salt wafting from the sea, the sense of being the only man and woman in the world. There's something about the way his smile is slightly lopsided, and the small scar by his upper lip that persuades her. There's something about the long toes, tipped with short clean nails, buffed by the beach.

Before he pulls off her tee shirt and unties her bikini, Jeannie whispers, "I'm married." And twists her wedding ring, the mole underneath exposed to the sun.

"Not today. This week is ours. Only this one week." He retrieves a condom from him wallet.

"You knew?"

"I'm always responsible." He slides his hand under her head to kiss her.

*I can't do this*, Jeannie thinks.

He takes his time.

*I shouldn't do this.*

He throbs over her totally aware of her every reaction as he explores.

*Why not?* There's no answer. She arches herself to him.

She didn't know, not really, what a new lover is like. She's an adult. Not a kid anymore. There are no first times for anything. They've both done it all. He glides into her as though he's been there a hundred times before, (because he has) but never quite this way. Surprised at her wet feel, her slippery bridge. He just glides in and they rock, with the sea. They rock each other to a new home. He studies her nuances and moves accordingly. Surprisingly, he's as satisfying as he is thrilling.

Staring at the sun, Jeannie asks him if he wanted just a good lay or the closeness.

"Why do you need to diminish what we just gave each other?"

The second time they make love, she says, "I want to give you so much pleasure. I want to bind you to me with pleasure, as you have bound me to you."

"You already have."

"Good," she smiles. Jeannie doesn't want the tie to be hers alone. He's already shown her with his careful movements and complete control places in her body that she never knew.

AFTERWARD, AS THEY stroke the kayaks to the dock and she smells him between her legs, she realizes she hasn't thought of her father or Sue. Hasn't thought of them at all. Until now.

They're late.

Jeannie arrives at dinner after the first course is already served. Her friends worried about her, and she tells them they got lost in the estuary and about the alligator. She compliments Taylor's tanzanite as it sparkles like a sky diamond. But in truth, not as beautiful as the pebbles cast on the beach. She hears about the manatee that Juliet saw when she was snorkeling, his prickly whiskers almost scratching her, his eyes squinting. "I don't know how they were ever the archetype for mermaids. They're ugly." They chose between lobster or prime rib for dinner and go dancing in the Capone's Speakeasy, but Ricardo is not there. She didn't see him at dinner either.

When Jeannie turns on her cell phone, there's a text from Mark. *Hope you're having fun, darling. Sara and I are fine, just missing you. Love you.*

She imagines Mark and Sara eating dinner, Mark checking her homework, and tucking her in bed. Jeannie's family. Her other life. Jeannie texts him back, *I miss you, too. Went kayaking today and saw an alligator try to eat a white bird. Kiss each other for me.*

She pushes send, and thinks, *This is so easy.*

Later, she stretches in her bed --just like the other thousand beds in the other thousand cabins – she's shaken and surprised that she misses Ricardo.

Jeannie never thought she'd sleep with another man. Never thought she'd win 11 million dollars. She hasn't included either into who she is. *I'm news to me. It's as if somewhere inside me I knew I'd do this all along. I want him. A part of me thinks, why can't I just have sex with him—everyone else does this—why can't I just have him on the side? Would it diminish the wonderful things between Mark and I?*

*I have secrets.*

She answers her own question.

But she doesn't feel guilty. The sex with Ricardo feels right. They belong together. *I don't get that.* Jeannie astonishes herself.

## Twelve

*"How can we teach kids that hard work is the way to success if they hear radio commercials paid for by their government suggesting that the way to get rich is to bet money on a horse or a number?"* <u>Andy Rooney</u>

THE NEXT NIGHT, Ricardo holds Jeannie in his arms and says his life with its miseries and joys prepared him to appreciate her.  He actually says that.

"What miseries, tell me," but he doesn't answer.

They're in his cabin, it's after midnight. Jeannie spent the day playing bridge with Marnie, Juliet, and Sissy. Chandra and Taylor were in the casino.   She didn't see Vera, Alice, Tracy, Charlene, and Allie except at dinner and then they all attended a comedy show.  She didn't see him the entire day. *Maybe he's in his cabin writing*, she thought.

*I miss him when I'm not with him.*

All day, she imagines sneaking into Ricardo's room at midnight to do their elemental dance.

"I don't want any of them to find out."

"Secrecy makes it more thrilling," he says.

While she's on top of him, he whispers, "I'm so glad I met you before I died."

"A bit melodramatic, aren't you?" *Does he have an illness?* She wonders.

"I'm glad I met you while I still had some stamina," he says and they both laugh.

The next day, the third day, (Jeannie counts them like so many tanzanites on a bracelet) they again dock at an island.  The cookie club friends rented a boat for an off shore snorkeling dive. All twelve of them.

125

She's with her friends, without him, doing the remnants of her old life. She captures the old her, the Jeannie she used to be with them. The Jeannie before the money. Before Ricardo. She can do it...the old her...by rote. The line, lines, she's crossed are invisible.

Just like being an anonymous millionaire, she's an invisible adulteress. She coasts in the conversations. Hides her new self. They tease Chandra about her gambling. She lost half of what she won the second time she played. "But I'm refining my strategy," Chandra doesn't laugh. The next night she won 40,000. "So 52,000 altogether," she quickly nods her head as though she forms an exclamation point. "So far."

Vera clicks her tongue. "You should teach me."

"It's all math and focus," Chandra says. "You play a system and slowly win a bit with each hand and it mounts up. Like doing calendar spreads in options." She explains it vividly and they listen with blank faces. Finally, Charlene says, "I don't really understand what you're saying, but it sounds like what the banks did to create the mortgage mess."

"Well," Chandra tilts her head, "That was coalitions of questionable mortgages, this is betting on the future of a company and using statistics to predict its future." Chandra leans toward them. "Fibonacci predicted the sequence of everything starting with the reproduction of rabbits. There's a mathematical pattern to the organic world, the branching of trees, the uncurling of a fern, and the stock market. You just have to take advantage of the organic probability of what's next." A strand of Chandra's hair has loosened from her ponytail and hangs over the side of her face.

"The stock market was made by man. It's not organic," Sissy says.

"What about asset allocation and diversification?" Rosie says as she rubs lotion on her long arms. "That's what Kevin always pushes."

Jeannie wades into the sea to watch clouds of blue damsel floating among the coral, and swims after a parrotfish that almost allows her touch him. She floats over the endless sea, her breath echoing in the snorkel, wondering at her sense of power. *Is it being so peaceful at the sea? Is it winning money with my numbers? Is it Ricardo? Him, just him? Or that I've done what I've done? Is this how my father felt?*

She calls home from a phone on the island and Sara answers and tells Jeannie that she joined the track team and is going to a birthday party that weekend. She's trying out for another play! "This time with the Performance Network."

"But that's adult theater."

"Yep. But I play a kid. And, guess what? I've made the callbacks! Can you believe it?"

"Of course, darling. You were so good as Lucy."

"I thought you were just doing the Mom compliment thing."

"I would have thought you were terrific even if you weren't my daughter."

Sara considers this then says, "Really? Dad isn't home yet."

"Tell him I'm having fun. Tell him I said hello." There's a space of silence and then Jeannie adds, "I love you, Sara. And I mean that with all my heart."


RICARDO COMES TO her cabin that night, a coconut scented candle in a coconut shell lit for him.

When she's with him, she's happy and content and safe and secure.

But he'll go like the sun.

Like spring and summer.

She thinks of a hundred ways he can go. Lists them. Counts them on her fingers. His leaving, their separation protects her from being hurt, from hurting her family. *How much can we hurt each other in one week?*

On the third night, she tells him about Sue and Rosie and her father, detailing the entire story, tears rolling down her cheeks. Still. They're in his bed and he lies beside her clenching her hands and staring at the ceiling. When she tells him about her father's stroke, he turns on his side, examining the expressions fleeting across her face.

His hand is warm. He traces Jeannie's profile, forehead, nose, lips, chin, neck, between her breasts, to her navel. He watches bumps rise from the thrill of his fingertips. He watches a flush spread over her chest, and tests her wetness.

"Considering all that, I don't understand how I could do this," Jeannie shudders.

He clears his throat as though her story and her tears have moved him. "Maybe you had to explore it to understand it?"

"No, it's because of you. You get the credit." It's easy to blame him. As soon as he asks the question, she recognizes it's not about him, but about winning the lottery. Money is power. She doesn't have to be worried, or play it safe anymore. She has the freedom to be reckless, and self-centered. Entitled. She won 125 million for her friends and herself.

*I did.*

A surge of empowerment. The power of entitlement. Is that what her Dad had? Is that what so many men have? She turns to tell Ricardo, but remembers the strict prohibition about telling anyone. Once she tells him, whatever happens next would be predicated on his reaction to her atypical wealth.

*Ricardo, our affair, has taken me to the margins of suspicions where I don't know myself. But where I am the most me. And where I am absolutely in touch with the eternal now.*

"I'm not going to be able to say goodbye to you," he says.

"Could you promise me friendship, because if this continues, you'll be my only friend?" He already is, she shudders, pulling his blanket closer. The only one who has a clue about her now.

But he doesn't answer.

"You're scary."

"It's just this situation. Crossing a line that you haven't crossed before," he shrugs.

Jeannie doesn't understand what it is about him that turns her on so. Is it his spiritual, creative side? Is it her own shadow side, revealed at last? Or is it a shared secret, the theme of her last several years. Now, she, at last, has one, too. One that she has created. She repeats her own victimization, but it doesn't feel like treachery or revenge. It feels like fun and power.

THE FOURTH DAY is another one at sea and they sneak into his cabin after lunch while Chandra teaches Vera how to play black jack, while Sissy, Marnie, Rosie and Allie are at an afternoon Bingo game, while Taylor, Tracy, Alice, Juliet, Charlene are at the pool sunbathing, swimming, reading, drinking. Ricardo and Jeannie spend the entire afternoon inside each other coasting from the shore to the sky while time stops.

They're careful. They ignore each other in public, sense when they're in the same place and don't acknowledge each other. Once they lounge at the same pool, and Allie says, "Hey, there's that hot dude, Ricardo," and she nudges Taylor, "you should go scoop him up."

She glances up from her book, and then pushes her sunglasses up and returns to her novel.

Ricardo and Jeannie don't go on the same shore excursions anymore.

They make a point of disregarding each other, if anyone bothered to notice.

AT DINNER, ALICE, Allie, Vera, Tracy, and Charlene hang out at a grill but don't join Jeannie, Taylor, Marnie, Sissy, Chandra, Juliet, and Rosie at their table.

"Hey. Is this just coincidence? It's just the lottery players here." Rosie comments.

"I've been aware of a division for awhile," Sissy muses.

Chandra and Taylor meet each other's glances and shrug.

"We can't lose our friends because we won the lottery. Friends are too important," Marnie says.

"They're excluding themselves," Rosie says as she nibbles bread dipped in hummus. "We brought them on this cruise, but we can't make them *be* with us."

Sissy places her hands on her thighs. It's ironic that Sissy has figured out a way to include two, Allie and Charlene, in her plans and she only met them a few years ago while most of them have known each other for a decade.

"I overheard them talking at Neptune," Chandra says, "Alice made a comment that we're going to get almost 11 million each and all we're giving them is a cruise."

"More like 8," Taylor shrugs.

"That's what Charlene reminded them. And then Allie said, 'Besides, *we* decided not to play.' They saw me and stopped talking." Chandra's dark eyebrows arch.

"We need to decide soon how much money we're going to share with them and let them know," Marnie says. "We need to communicate with them more."

JEANNIE REPLAYS RICARDO'S lovemaking and scolds herself for lust shredding her integrity.

"Jeannie?" Marnie calls. "Jeannie? Earth to Jeannie?"

"Yeah?"

"Where were you?"

"Do you want the salmon teriyaki or the chicken Marsala?" A waitress asks at Jeannie's elbow.

"Oh. Salmon."

Jeannie spends the night dancing at the Capone's with Sissy, Taylor, and Rosie. When she shares one dance with Ricardo, she wonders if they notice how tenderly he places his fingertips on her shoulders, how she presses her torso into his chest and lets him carry her to an exaggerated dip.  He leaves before she does. Jeannie and Rosie walk to their corridor together. Jeannie enters her cabin, waits fifteen minutes, and then quietly leaves.

The next morning, Jeannie wakes early, before the sun and can't go back to sleep.  Her easy sleep is ruined.

Her phone beeps. There's a text from Mark. *Darling. I miss you so much.  Can't wait to see you tomorrow. I'll be at the airport to pick you up.  Kevin and I have been working on the contracts. Can't wait to show you how much I love you.  Until then, here's a cyber kiss.*

Her stomach turns.  She clamps her eyes shut.

*What have I done?*

*How will it feel to see Mark?  Can I just close the book on Ricardo? I think his name and my body responds.*

Jeannie texts back.  *Me, too!!!! See you tomorrow. Tell Sara I love her.*

THE LAST NIGHT, all twelve of them order champagne to celebrate the cruise, their friendship. They raise filled glasses. "To us," Juliet trills.

"To girlfriends!" they say.

Marnie places her hands on the table. "You know, " she turns to Alice, Tracy, Allie, Vera, and Charlene. "We haven't claimed the money yet but are setting up various companies to protect us from publicity." Marnie shakes her head, "We don't even know how much it'll be. But it's not 125 million because we've decided to get the payout. So it'll be more like 8 million by the time we pay what we have to on taxes. We've told you that before, right?" Marnie wants to give more to the ones that didn't play, and help out Vera, but she doesn't announce that. She doesn't realize how much 8 million sounds.

Allie shrugs and says, "I'm glad you guys won." Then glances at Taylor and Sissy.

"It's a big relief," Marnie reminds her. "It'll mean more fun and security for all of us." She sweeps her hand to include the entire table. It's her way of making a promise without being specific.

"Thank you so much for taking us on this cruise," Charlene says, raises her glass and toasts. "To you guys. Thank you."

Some people are grateful for what they have. Some people always want more.

Jeannie wonders, *Which am I? Both.*

Alice and Vera glance at each other. Taylor and Rosie and Chandra glance at each other.

Jeannie thinks about Ricardo.

They drink, ignoring the fizz, place the glasses on the tablecloth, and return to separate conversations. The cruise is over. The celebration is as finite and temporary as the bubbles in the glasses, the scent of coconut in Jeannie's cabin.

THE FINAL NIGHT, Ricardo says, right before he comes that he has an image in that space before orgasm that if there is a paradise, this is what angels feel.

They come together, tears flowing.

Jeannie wonders, *Is he writing dialogue? Will our words appear in his next novel? How much more delicious if he knew about the lottery. Such a great plot twist that could go so many different ways. So many scenarios. See how deceit grows, seeps into everything?*

"I'm not going to be able to let you go tomorrow."

*He doesn't know how tempting he is.*

"Isn't there a way we can meet, even if it's just for an afternoon in an airport hotel?"

"I might hate myself," Jeannie says, "I don't want to hurt you and I sure as shit don't want you to hurt me. Or Mark more than I have."

He shudders and squeezes Jeannie's hand.

"Let me consider if I can do this when I'm kissing my daughter goodnight and making love with Mark the day after I make love to you. "

"I didn't imagine this could happen," he says. "I thought we'd be a fun week. Surprisingly, I'm connected."

They make love again, this time, he says, his voice clogged, "Whatever comes next, thank you, Jeannie."

"Yes." She didn't expect to become tied to him separate from the thrill of cheating, and the rashness of empowerment. She didn't expect to win the lottery either. Hell, she wasn't even playing for the money, but the companionship. Jeannie keeps getting way more than she wants.

As Jeannie leaves his cabin that night, shuts his door as quietly as she can for the last time, her eyes red from crying, her crotch dripping from sex, she almost backs into

Rosie.  Rosie saunters toward the stairs that lead to their rooms, slightly tipsy from a night dancing at Capone's and drinking Piña Coladas. Her red dress outlines her hourglass body, her dark hair forms a shining helmet. She halts when she sees Jeannie. Rosie pins Jeannie with her eyes, then scans the rumpled hair, the smeared make up. And shakes her head slowly.

Jeannie flinches a smile, attempting to look casual, but grasps its transparent duplicity.

She's caught.

Rosie crosses her arms, "How does it feel to *be,*" Rosie spits out the word, raising one eyebrow as only she can, "your father's daughter after all?"

## Thirteen

*48% of lottery winners stay in the same job.*
*44% of winnings are spent after 5 years*
*19% of winners go abroad for the first time.*
*88% of Lottery winners still play weekly.*


AS SOON AS Jeannie arrives in baggage claim, she sees Sara and Mark holding a bouquet of yellow roses. Mark clasps Jeannie to him and whispers in her ear, "I missed you so much," pressing into her so she feels his prodding erection.

"Hmmmm. Absence makes the heart grow fonder, uh?" she whispers back. She thinks, but of course doesn't say, the quip that follows. *Fonder for someone else.*

"I love your hair, Mommy. So awesome," Sara's eyes are wide.

Jeannie touches her hair, she has almost forgotten the braids and is accustomed to the tinkling cowries.

"And guess what? I came in third in the 200 yard dash and my relay team came in first," Sara waves shinning ribbons, one gold and one blue. "But I didn't get the part with Performance Network." She turns her mouth down in a parody of the tragedy mask.

"Maybe you'll get the next one." Jeannie places her palms on her daughter's shoulders and brings her close again for a hug.

Mark bends over and says into her ear, "We have arranged for a bus to take us all home." His scent is almost as familiar as her own.

"All of us? And our luggage?"

"Yes. The publicity has hit the fan." He whispers, his head tilted so only she can hear. "Someone leaked and the media got hold of it. We've been hounded. Kevin and Dan. Silver has, too. It's not just the women who played. It's the entire club. We wanted to warn everybody before they got home. That's why the bus. We're just glad they didn't find out which plane you were on and besiege us here."

"How did it leak?"

"Let's get the luggage loaded."

Out of the corner of her eye, Jeannie spots Ricardo. His hands are plunged in the pockets of his leather jacket examining the bags rolling on the conveyor. What's he doing here? She realizes she never asked him where he lives, he never told her.

In one smooth motion, he spots a brown leather duffle, grabs the handle and jerks it from the turning belt. As he turns, he notices Jeannie. Mark's hand rests protectively on her shoulder. She embraces blazing yellow flowers, her other hand holds a girl's who already possesses her mother's grace. The three of them form an iconic image of the perfect family. All beautiful, well groomed, and healthy. All loved.

Is the image so different from the reality? Is he simply an aberration from an eccentric place in Jeannie's soul now to be erased as easily as bringing home someone else's grocery bag placed in the cart by the clerk and not bothering to return it? Is he that forgettable?

Their eyes meet. His are open with shock, almost as if he hadn't imagined a real family, a husband who loves her, a daughter. Jeannie is aware enough of his expressions (hadn't she watched his face tighten into a mixture of pleasure almost painful when he came? Hadn't she watched his eyes wet when she told him about Sue, his reaction to her story almost as important as telling the story itself) she notices the subtle change on his face. How had she been aware of all this and yet not known, not bothered to ask where he lived? Then he musters a wan smile. Gives her a slight wave, as if he's tipping an invisible hat, saying goodbye at last and forever.

Jeannie realizes she moves to him by the tinkling of her cowrie shells. Their eyes meet, the recognition of sorrow and surprise exchange. Then she turns to Mark and says, "I think I spy my luggage."

"Oh." Mark looks confused for just a minute, "How can you tell? They all look alike."

"I tied a blue bandana on my handle." It's so easy to lie when someone trusts you.

She walks past Ricardo, inhales his lime scent. His jacket brushes her arm. She merely wanted to be close to him again. Jeannie stands next to Chandra pulling out a red suitcase.

JIM, MARK, AND Dan cluster the group together, stack the luggage on three carts and push them toward the sign saying *Ground Transportation*. A bus waits and the men and the driver load the suitcases. A bottle of champagne is popped and glasses passed as the driver pulls from the curb. Only Alice's husband has not flown in from California for this event. Even Tony, Chandra's husband, who seldom joins the group, is in the bus. As soon as she sees him, Chandra chuckles, "Guess what? I won 83,000 in black jack! At the casino!" He nods at her and gives her a cursory kiss and she realizes something has happened. The women sit with their partners, Charlene sits with Sissy. Allie sits with Taylor. And Alice sits alone, plopping her purse on the seat next to her.

Allie notices how the women divide themselves. In the cruise it was winners and non-players, and now, it's coupled or single. *The hierarchies of the different roles our lives are parceled into,* she thinks.

Kevin grabs the mike and starts speaking. He's dressed in corporate casual clothes, when usually he just wears jeans. At first he simply welcomes the women. The forsythia is about to bloom and the crocuses are already telling us to get ready for celebration for we all have a lot of celebrating to do. He doesn't notice the glances between Tracy and Alice, or the concerned look that Marnie shoots Vera who sits across the aisle. Flynn holds her shoulder tightly. A tan has covered her with a healthier glow, but her gaunt face, and the way she worries her hands together, one hand massaging the knuckles of the other as though rubbing in lotion, betrays her anxiety. He doesn't acknowledge the rift between the players and non-players even though he senses it, predicted it.

"Mark and I have completed the documents developing a separate entity to receive the money. This will make distribution easier and each of you will be able to function separately in how you collect the money. All you have to do is sign it, and we can approach the state for the funds."

Alice rolls her eyes.

"But we don't need to talk about that now. We have a problem and that's why we've pirated you away from the airport like this. It's a problem for *all* of us." He stops and glances at Mark, lips forming a straight line. "We needed a chance to talk alone. Unfortunately," he pulls up his pants buckle as though preparing for battle, "the press has gotten a hold of the fact that a Christmas cookie club played the lottery and won. The human interest..."

But Rosie interrupts him. "How? Who told the press?" She sits near the front of the bus and turns in her seat and snares each of them with a glance, stops at Jeannie and frowns.

"Not me," Jeannie protests.

Rosie shuts her eyes and says "Who?" Her voice is loud enough to be heard over the wheels, the engine.

"It doesn't matter. No one did it to be malicious, it has just happened, so now we have a problem."

Dan reaches for a second cordless mike and says, "We've been barraged by telephone calls. Somehow they found out who attends the party, who decided to play the lottery and who didn't."

Silver stands and says, "This isn't just the winners. The media have been asking me how Tracy feels that her friends won and she didn't. They've been pushing to see if you're going to share."

"Me too." Tony says. "I've been besieged. Constant telephone calls at home and at work, reporters with cameras everywhere, even outside of my job."

"Hey. We have to speak one at a time and we have two mikes we can pass around so we can all hear," Kevin says.

Dan passes Tony the mike. His freckles stand out vividly in the winter pale. "They want to know how much you're going to split, what you're going to do with the money. It's as if they *want* you to fight."

"They do! It'll sell more papers, Internet hits. The media is fascinated by part of a group winning, and what's going to happen next," Dan adds.

"I told them you already are sharing. You're all on a cruise," Silver says.

"That's why we needed to do this." Kevin points a finger to the ceiling. "Warning. They're waiting for you. You may be surrounded by reporters, TV, who knows what, when you get to your houses."

"Do you want to go home? Or should we throw them off and go to a hotel?" Mark holds the mike, he waves it to see who wants to speak next.

"We could also take the bull by the horns, announce a press conference tomorrow. And spend today and tomorrow morning signing the papers and deciding what we're going to say," Dan suggests.

"It's simple," Allie says. "Some of us decided to play, some of us didn't."

"Meanwhile, we've had a wonderful cruise," Charlene says.

"Yes. And we're each going to figure out separately what we're doing with our money," Marnie says. "Won't that take care of it? Something else will come along. A serial rapist. A tornado. A flood. This can't be *that* important."

"It's hot news *now!*" Dan says.

"I want to go home," Sissy says. "And, please, my home is in a different direction." She stands in the bus, her hands on the back of the seat in front of her.

Kevin sucks in air between his teeth. "Well, as you can imagine, Tara and Aaron have been the most besieged. They're hiding at Weber's to avoid the press. It's gone viral that Aaron's and Tara's moms both won 125 million dollars."

Sissy rolls her eyes, there's a smattering of chuckles.

"Of course they got it mostly wrong," Rosie insists. "We all won."

"Is the press at Weber's?" Sissy asks.

"Nope. Tara and Aaron managed to escape without the press noticing. Amazing since the press is packed three deep around their house. It was on channel four news last night."

"I want to know how they found out." Rosie insists. "We all deserve to know."

Flynn and Kevin exchange a look, then Kevin glances at Mark. They know, all of them. They don't want to tell.

"Tell me," Rosie demands staring straight at her husband, eyebrows narrowed.

"We may need to know in order to handle this anyway," Allie says.

"She's right," Marnie says.

Surprisingly, Flynn stands up, holds the mike with one hand and places his other hand on Vera's shoulder. "Vera told the person who was making her wig. It was a rush job and Vera told her why she needed it so quickly. Unfortunately, her husband is a reporter for the news and also a blogger."

Marnie instantly imagines the media spin. A cancer patient struggles for her life and to pay her bills. Her friends win 125 million, take her on a cruise without helping her with her problems. The media will paint us as selfish villains and Vera into a sick and poor friend.

"So we need to present a united front," Kevin suggests. "A spotlight will be on each of us."

"I guess you were wrong, Marnie," Rosie says, her eyes narrowed, "wanting to share the joy and trusting them to keep their mouths shut."

"Hey, that's unnecessary," Allie cautions Rosie and shakes her head slowly.

"We can call that news conference and do it together tomorrow. That way we have more control. In a few months, there'll be other winners for them to be curious about."

"Do I have to be part of this?" Taylor asks. "I needed privacy."

"I didn't want my family to know until I figured out what I was going to do," Juliet whispers, but only Dan and Marnie, sitting directly in front of her, hear.

"Can this affect my divorce?" Taylor's voice screeches. "Can it? The settlement? I mean everything was done before I KNEW we won. Before the drawing even."

"I'm sorry. I'm sorry," Vera cries into her hands, her shoulders shaking. Flynn hands her a mike, which carries her whispered words. "My hairdresser just wanted to know why the big rush and I told her about the cruise and how it was scheduled in between my chemo and radiation." Vera wipes her eyes with the back of her hand. "She said how lucky to have such good friends, and I said, 'You think I'm lucky? They just won 125 mill!' I wasn't thinking. I was just happy and excited."

*Not just happy. Jealous and resentful, too* Rosie thinks, but for once bites her tongue in the face of Vera's sobs.

"I didn't mean for this to happen." Vera puts her face in her hands and gives Flynn back the mike.

"You were being impulsive, but you didn't have any malice. Nevertheless, we've got to figure out how to solve this problem," Marnie says.

"Why don't Mark and Kevin do the talking at the press conference," Taylor's lipstick is long worn off, making her appear pale. "That way we'll be protected and they won't know who we are."

"They already do. They know you're part of the group. There's already been a blog featuring stories about each of you."

"Shit," Taylor turns to glare at Vera. "You made a huge fucking problem for me."

Vera's cries escalate to sobs.

In the silence that follows the crumbs of Rosie's remorse at not sharing her money with the others are swept away, as though Vera's sin lost it for all of them.

Juliet stares out the window, rhythmically kicking her leg back and forth. She eases her hand under her tee shirt and feels the scar from her mastectomy.

Marnie's battle about giving Vera a greater amount of money has added confusion. But should she be punished for difficulty she inadvertently caused? When she didn't have any intent?

Tracy and Alice wonder if they'll seem like losers in the face of the millions that their friends and club members now possess. The public economic disparity may hurt their comradeship more than the reality would have.

Sissy wonders if she can use this situation to do her own spin and promote the foundation she dreams of starting.

Then the terrifying thought that has been pushed away to a deep recess of Taylor's mind explodes. "Can Rick go back to the court and get money from me if he finds out about this?"

Kevin and Mark both meet her eyes. "Yes. He can. In other cases, the divorced spouse has won," Kevin says, shaking his head from side to side.

"But my divorce was final *before* we won," Taylor's face reddens, her voice raises, her fist tightens in her lap.

Kevin's says softly, "But you bought the ticket while you were still married.  It can be considered marital property."

"I didn't buy it. Rosie did!" Taylor squeezes her eyes shut. "Oh, shit.  I'm going to have one month, one month with all my worries gone. Only one month without having to be plagued by Rick and poverty." She turns back to Vera, "I know you're sick and we're all supposed to feel sorry and protect you. But none of us were supposed to tell *anyone.* None of us." She wags her finger at Vera,  "Guilt doesn't do shit. You fucked up. Worst of all, I might have to deal with Rick," Taylor screeches. "He'll *torture* me again." Then, she crosses her legs and arms.

"Hey. Don't you talk to my wife like that," Flynn says.

Taylor glares out the window. Allie clasps Taylor's hand. Taylor wonders what will happen next to her. And Allie wonders what will happen with the hostile divisions between her friends.

## Fourteen

*On the national average, lottery gamblers with household incomes under $10,000 bet nearly 3 times as much on the lottery than those with incomes over $50,000.*

JULIET'S HOODIE PROVIDES a shield for her to check her lymph nodes, palpitate her breast. Dan, sitting next to her, participates in the conversation while the bus lurches down the highway and does not notice. She shifts to the window seeing twisted trees on I 94 scuttle by, a sign for line dancing at the Diamondback Saloon, and green signs announcing Belleville. In ten, maybe fifteen, minutes they'll be passing 23 and the exit for the trailer park.

Relieved that there are no more lumps, no more changes in her flesh, she slides her hand from her tee shirt, zips her jacket, pulls up the hood, and resumes witnessing black branches scratch the white sky.

The memory comes unbidden. Usually she shuts it down, but today she cannot prevent it. Her brothers and mother know about her lottery win and horrors pull. Time has passed. She no longer trusts what is memory and what is remembering the memory. For a long time she recalled only what she saw and sometimes the images had no meaning. The crushed leaves on the ground beside her, the wide open mouth and closed eyes of the boy on top of her were a bizarre kaleidoscope without narrative, when she was how old, was she 8? Or 9?

She must have been 9 because she saw the backpack with Josie and the Pussycats that her mom brought home from Goodwill. Juliet watched Josie on TV whenever she could so she was thrilled with the backpack, but the girls at school sneered, "Josie? That's retarded. No one cares about her anymore."

Juliet didn't cast the item aside to win peer acceptance. For once. Now, the backpack lay on the ground. A boy's boot stomped it. She thought he, like the girls, hated Josie and the Pussycats, but he wasn't paying attention to the backpack. He was waiting his turn. It just happened to be there. Like she happened to be there.

Sounds returned as random splotches. Bizarre connections. As the years went on, she learned the names.

Today, with the security of the millions, and the knowledge that she can no longer avoid her Mom, Larry, and Joey (most of all), the pictures, sounds, and smells coalesce. The terror, the pain, the shame along with them.

Outside the window, the scene plays on the budding but still bare trees, in the almost green grass.

She closes her eyes. *Think of something else,* she tells herself. *Don't think about the pain. Don't think about what they're doing.*

Like a movie with no off button it continues.

In the background, Joey screamed. "Stop. Stop it." But he was tied to a tree.

"Shut that asshole kid up," the boy with his boot on Josie ordered.

*Close your eyes. Don't look,* she thought. Or did she say it, did she tell him, did she protect Joey? Did she feel almost as badly for him as she did for herself?

No. Not really.

They walked through the woods on the way home, using a short cut as an excuse to play along the river. Well, not a river, a drainage ditch, but to them, (Juju 8 or is she 9 and Joey 7, just old enough to remember but way too young to do anything.) it was their river, their private forest with yellow trembling leafed trees in fall, white before they unfolded in spring. Miraculously, the precious surprise of ground dotted with tiny pink flowers, and vibrant violets came every year. In the fall, poking through the yellow leaves, plump red berries edged fat stems. The aroma of decaying leaves and the sticky sweetness of flowers thickened the air. It was quiet except for trucks on the highway they couldn't see, but the whooshing traffic sounded like she imagined waves in the sea.

Joey's muscles were still unformed on his arms, and his legs such skinny sticks it was amazing they were able to propel the rest of him anywhere and yet he had wiry energy, and prideful insistence. "I'm the man of the house, you have to listen to me. Doesn't matter you're older."

But Juju never did.

"Yep. He's the man," their mom said. Juju rolled her eyes, and Larry, playing on the floor, ignored everyone.

On the way home from school, they tarried in the quiet simple beauty. Climbed trees. Turned over stones for salamanders, saw a baby deer huddled under a thick shrub studying them with luminous eyes, watched the stream bubble as it tumbled, turning ordinary rocks into gleaming jewels.

Once, three teenage boys yelled, "Stay off our property, retards."

Juju ignored them, as though they weren't deserving of comment.

"It's not yours. It's the city's." Joey pretended he knew what he talked about, but no one knew whom it belonged to, if it belonged to anyone. It was an ignored parcel of do-nothing, know nothing useless land wedged between the trailer park and a cracker-box apartment house.

"You think you know so much, little smart ass. Think you're tough."

This time, the teens waited for them... Or maybe they just happened to be there and just happened to have the rope.

"You trespassing. You in our territory, asshole," one said. A red birthmark covered half his face. Red purple, almost as though his face had been cut in half and created from two separate fabrics, but not a color that she had ever seen on a person before. It was that vivid. More like the breast of a robin or a cardinal. Juju didn't understand what it was until much later: a port wine birthmark covering half his face. She thought his father smacked him that day and the redness would decrease in a few hours and be the light beige of the rest of his face. For a long time, she thought he took out his rage at his father on them.

"What happened to your face?" Joey asked with confused child's innocence, scared by uncertainty of erratic events.

There were three of them. Three. They seemed like men, but when you're 8 or is it 9, sixteen year olds seem like men. Stainface had a mustache, not a thick one, but one nonetheless. They were tall, lanky. Wore jeans, leather jackets. That was their uniform. All had long hair. One had blond hair down to his shoulders. One dark, long and straight. That was Stainface. The third wore tight jeans, a cobalt shirt with the sleeves torn off and bushy dark hair.

They had the rope with them. Why? Had they planned this all along? Or was it something for their clubhouse? A rope and a bungee cord. The one in the blue shirt and bushy hair grabbed Joey... "Gonna make you watch what we do to your sister, little shit."

Joey screamed, kicked his legs. The teen's hands, the one with the bushy hair, pinched tight around Joey's arms, he lifted him like he was a sack of potatoes. "You ain't shit, just a feather." Joey flailed little boy arms against

148

the bigger teen's torso. Joey was just a few inches taller than Bushyhair's belt, his arms pounded helplessly on his hips, ridiculously on his chest. Bushyhair laughed. "Think you a tough little shit, uh. Maybe we should do him, too."

"Nah, just tie him up and let him watch the fun," Stainface ordered.

Joey's heart pounded in his chest. *I'm the man in the house. I have to protect her.* He continued to punch, hit scrape, bite Bushyhair. He smelled the teen's dank musk.

"Damn little bastard. Thinks he's tough." Bushyhair brushed him away like an annoying insect.

The guy with the blonde hair punched Joey, he fell limply then Blondhair and Bushyhair quickly wrapped the rope around his torso and a tree. One of those trees with the white buds in spring and sun yellow in fall.

The world went black for Joey. Behind his lids were purple swirls and flashes. His rage fell to his feet like leaves. Useless against the almost men.

*Why are they doing this? Are they going to kill us?*

When he stopped screaming, when the sounds of slaps ceased, Juju thought, *They killed him.* Her eyes were clenched. She was too terrified to cry.

Stainface held her shoulders. She squirmed and he shoved her down. She kicked, but her feet landed nowhere except back on the ground. She heard them land with a slight crack of leaves, and a mute thud on the thick earth. Everything turned to a weird slow motion of noise and pulses behind her lids.

Still no sound from Joey. *They've killed him,* she thought again.

*What are they going to do? They're going to kill us?* Her head pounded, her arms were cold. She heard panting and screaming. *Is it mine? Must be mine.*

149

Joey squirmed against the rope holding him to the tree, he tried to kick, *I gotta keep fighting for my sister*, but the two bound his ankles against the trunk with the bungee cord. He struggled, the bark scraped his back as it tore through his shirt.

"Now. All the little bastard can do is watch."

"Have a thrill, asshole," Blondhair laughed. "You've probably been doing this for years."

"That little shit? No way."

She was already on the ground, Stainface thrusting her shoulders into earth that smelled sweet with decaying leaves. He tore off her jeans and jerked down her panties. Panties with cute little pastel bows that Mom bought in a pack of three at Meijer's Thrifty Acres.

"She don't even have no hair, just a little baldy," he said. "Gonna take it from you, whore. Gonna be your first." And then he plunged his wiggly, now not wiggly at all, into her.

Juju clamped her eyes tighter. Pain split her in two, pulsed behind her lids. He pushed her legs wide. He was going to tear her up her middle, split her in two pieces as he shoved himself inside her. Pain knifed from her thingamajig to her tummy, rang in her ears. Maybe she moaned. Maybe she screamed. She remembered saying, nonononononono, but maybe she only thought it, maybe she only screamed in her mind. She heard crying in the distance—a wail—she didn't know it was hers.

*Think of anything else. Think of Josie and her friends. Go somewhere else.* A bird cawed, a crow, she thought it was, crying a warning. She opened her eyes and it was there, in the sky, its black wings spread wide. *Let my mind go away. I'll be the crow. I'll be away from here.*

She stared at the crow, saw the purple red blotch across his eyes, cheek, his open mouth, and then her mind left.  It saw what the crow saw. The forest with its glorious yellow leaves and ripe red buds.

Off in the distance, Joey screamed. And then a slap. "You shut the fuck up or you'll get that again. Harder."

Then there was the next one.  Bushyhair pulled up her tee shirt and pinched her little nipples.  Little baby nipples. Not even breast buds yet. Grabbed and twisted. She wasn't going to give him the satisfaction of moaning. She stared straight up at the sky but he rotated her nipple until she screamed. He thrust himself inside. *Pretty soon this will be over.*  His bushy hair fell to her face, smelled rank of smoke and old sweat. She closed her eyes and there was the crow again, just behind her lids, in her mind.

*If I die, then oh well.* She thought about the crow as Bushyhair pushed pushed pushed pushed pushed, let out a funny sound, and stopped.

*He's finished whatever he needed to do.  Maybe it'll end. Will they kill me now?*

Then Blondhair was on top of her.  "Don't know about sloppy thirds, but it's here," he chortled. She clamped her eyes shut, heard the rip of his zipper and then his weight buried her as he forced himself into her.  This time she counted the agony from each thrust. One two three four five six seven eight nine ten eleven. He stopped. *It's over. I'm still alive.  Is Joey?*

Blondhair got up.

His zipper scraped the air.

Her eyes still shut. *If I didn't see it, it didn't happen. I saw Josie .  And the crow.*  But she didn't believe her own story. She already throbbed between her legs.  She felt them.  Each one.  Each  thrust.  She hurt up to her bellybutton, deep inside.

*What did I do?*
*What do I do?*

151

The three almost men stood around looking at her, scanning each other's faces, her body naked from the waist down, her shirt pulled up. Blood on her thigh. Juju didn't have any hair on her crotch, not yet, not even the straight ones that come in first.

*Are they going to kill me? Me and Joey?*

"Hope you learned your lesson." Stainface barked. "You come through our property again we do this again. But maybe you like it, uh? Want it again."

"We know where you little shits live…in that trailer park. You tell anyone, we kill your momma. Got it?" He growled.

"Or your baby brother," Bushyhair added.

Juju kept her eyes closed, listened to the crunch of leaves as they strolled away, until the sound muted.

*I can hear. I can hurt. I'm alive.*

Joey cried, "Ju-Ju, Juju"

*He's alive.* When she sat up, her legs hurt, those things that keep them attached to her body. The crease between her legs hurt. Blood smeared bright on her thighs. She wiped it with torn underpants. Carefully, dizzy, she stood up, thighs trembling, pulled on her jeans and crept to Joey, each movement hurt. Tears fell so fast she could barely see and stumbled. There were lots of leaves on the ground in the forest and they clattered an echo to broadcast where they were, what happened.

*Am I 8 or 9?*

Joey's eye was red and swollen. She unhooked the bungee cord, it snapped away and his legs were free. A piece of bark flew off the tree and hit her in her face. He kicked as though to make certain his legs obeyed his commands, to bring the blood and feeling back. "I'm sorry,"

"Shshsh," she told him.

152

The knot fastening him to the tree was another matter. Bushyhair and Blondhair tied it tightly and Juliet's fingers, which she had forcefully clenched, now quivered. She pulled at the bulge of the knot but it didn't budge. She tried another coil, tugged it with all her shaky might, but there was no movement.

"Hurry, Juju hurry."

"Shhshhh."

*Maybe I should go home and get a knife. Maybe mom is there already.* She tried to shove the loose end back through the loop, and saw a little progress, and then again pulled the bulge. It came loose. She untied him.

Juju hugged Joey close. They stood under the naked tree, and held each other. She felt nothing. Numb. *I am 8 or is 9 and he is 6, maybe 7. Kids. Poor white trash from the trailer park.*

"I'm sorry, Juju."

"You? Why?"

"I'm the man in the family." When his eyes met hers, they tilted down at the corners, darted away, were wet with fog rather than shiny. She saw defeat. She wondered, wonders even now, if her eyes changed that day too. Then he looked down as though he couldn't stare at her, couldn't see his sister anymore.

*My eyes changed too.*

*But maybe I am disgusting now. Unlook-at-able.*

"Did you see?"

Joey eyes remained on ruffled ground. He shrugged, shook his head. "I won't tell anyone. Not ever," he promised, as though telling someone meant it actually happened and never telling anyone meant it was only a nightmare.

"We're never going to talk about this again. Not ever," she said, her hands on his shoulders, her eyes piercing his. Even as a kid she knew once you put things in

153

words they were real. Otherwise they were just broken images and remembered sounds and smells that made no sense. "Not ever."

They both nodded. That's how they promised.

Juju took her notebook and pencil case from the Josie backpack.

She grabbed Joey's hand, and started to say *let's go home*, but said instead, "Let's go."

As she walked away, she thought, *We'll never come back here. To our freedom in the woods behind our trailer. Bye bye forest. Bye bye little pink flowers and baby deer.*

The crow flew overhead cawing goodbye.

Joey crept behind her on the path. His arms hurt, he pulled up his sleeve and there was a bruise purple as Redstain's face. Three slashes the shape of fingers. He wondered if the redpurple of Redstain's face had leaked from his fingers onto his arm. Joey saw only a little slit of ground, and Juju's heels as she staggered up the trail from his left eye. He guessed he could see. He hoped his eye wouldn't stay puffed.

His heart sank into his stomach and he puked up what was left of the free school cafeteria lunch. He considered lying on the ground, covering himself with leaves. *Maybe no one would find me. Maybe I'd be forgotten and unknown.*

Juju turned around, "Come on, Joey. Mom'll start worrying and we'll get more questions." She shook her head, "Your eye looks terrible." She chewed on the inside of her lip a bit and said, "What're you gonna tell Mom?"

*Maybe I'll just run away. Back into the woods. No, can't do that. This is my fault. My fault.*

"Tell her we were in the woods, climbing trees, and you fell and landed on something hard, a branch or a rock." She considered her words. *Always better to tell a bit of the truth when you're lying.* She walked close to him and

154

peered into his eye. "It'll be okay. Fine when the swelling goes down," she said.

*I have to protect Mom,* Joey thought as he shuffled his feet down the path.

JUJU BLED FOR several days after that, her thighs hurt and her labia were swollen and throbbing. A blue bruise flushed on her pubic bone and another on her chest, on what, in a few years, would be a breast. When she married, Juliet worried she was so damaged she couldn't bear children.

When she was diagnosed with breast cancer, in the breast Bushyhair had pinched, the thought occurred to her that his wrenching caused it. Of course, as a nurse, she knew that wasn't likely.

Joey's eye turned a vivid purple by night.

"I told you kids and told you to stay away from those damn woods. Now maybe you'll believe me. Why don't you ever listen? Don't go there no more," Mom scolded as she placed a bag of frozen peas on his eye. "Besides," she turned to Juliet, "I told you to come right home and clean this place up. Look at it!" She points to a sink full of dishes and tossed shoes and clothes on the floor. "You shoulda been doin' what you was suppose to instead of getting your brother hurt." She was already drinking and didn't want to be bothered with any more.

Juliet's bruises were easily covered.

Joey and Juliet kept their promises. They never told anyone. Juliet never told her husband, Dan, or her lover, Tom. She never told any physician. Joey and Juliet never mentioned the incident. She did not understand when she was exacting promises from Joey and herself what they would cost. It seemed simple and easy then when she was 8 or was she 9? It seemed the perfect solution. Just don't tell anyone and it would be like it never happened.

155

Juliet made another promise that day. This one to herself. When she was taking a bath and rubbing herself with soap even though it burned, examining the bruise on her lower abdomen and one spreading across her sternum. *I'm going to get out of this nightmare and never look back.* She studied how to cover herself with layers of perfect socially appropriate appearances and politeness. But the stain was too deep inside her to go away.

NOW AS SHE hears the clattering discussion in the bus, her friends arguing about what to do, she realizes she can no longer avoid looking back. She has to face the dirt she herself has brought into her life. How can she be super rich, so lucky when they are struggling so? Joey loved her. They were impotent to master their surroundings. She was the victim. But she survived. She took that horror and figured a way, a very flawed way, to protect herself. But from what?

From the minute she learned they had won the lottery, she knew she'd have to do something for her family. She has to face them, but she doesn't know how.

*I confused my rape with our poverty, as though it was one of the consequences. As though it was our fault. Something wrong with us that we were poor and raped.*

Tears spring to her eyes that she hides by wrapping her sweatshirt and its convenient hood even tighter.

## Fifteen

*By age 6, children are zealously devoted to the equitable partitioning of goods.*

JEANNIE STARTS TO unpack when Ricardo texts, *This isn't supposed to happen like this.* She deletes it along with his text from three days previously inviting her to meet him in Neptune at 11, and throws her dirty clothes into the laundry hamper.

*How can you be so near and yet so far? Where are you? I'm near Port Huron.*

She deletes that one, too, places the phone on the bedside table, and puts away her toiletries. She lights a candle in a coconut shell from one of the islands, throws her purple shawl on the bed and for a minute she's back in her cabin. Back with Ricardo. Mark comes behind her, wraps his arms around her, cupping her breasts. "So good to have you home. I missed you," he kisses her neck.

He's so familiar, so safe. Jeannie turns around, stands on her tiptoes, and kisses him. "You're such a good man. How did I get so lucky?"

"Good? That sounds like a brush off."

"No. It's a promise."

The phone beeps indicating another text. Mark turns to the sound, his eyebrows lift as though the innocuous alert is a warning siren.

It is.

"Hmmmm, one of the girls," Jeannie says, easy as pie. Then, she turns off the sound, and resumes the kiss.


OF COURSE IT'S not. It's Ricardo. *Send me your email address, Please.*

157

She wonders if he's heard about the lottery. No. He hasn't had enough time to drive to Port Huron, read the newspapers, or check for Jeannie on the Internet. His yearning is about her, or at least their great sex.

A few hours later Jeannie opens a new email account. The screen name is Yogacentera2 with a password from her cabin number and initials. She texts the address to Ricardo.

*I can't believe I'm doing this. Are all of us surprising to ourselves?*

People are only what they let you see.


THE NEXT DAY is the press conference. It has started when Vera arrives. Along one wall is a spread of pastries, cheese, crackers and fruit, coffee, tea, water, and a few soft drinks. Lined chairs hold a slapdash assortment of reporters who face a long table with mikes, glasses, and pitchers, their condensation slowly dripping on the cloth. Cameras, - green and red lights blinking, cords coiling on the carpet, - rise from tripods in the back corners of the room. Spotlights, also on tripods, beam hot lights to the table.

Kevin stands, a mike in hand. He's dressed in a sport jacket and slacks. Rosie sits next to him, staring with sharp, almost antagonistic eyes at the audience. Juliet, and Taylor are not there. Neither are Tracy or Alice.

Then Vera arrives.

"Oh, here's Vera Thompson, one of our cookie club members," Kevin says.

A reporter follows Vera and Flynn, strolls down the aisle, across the front and sits at the extreme left. Flynn takes a seat next to Tony. A chair is brought to the table for Vera. A glass of water is poured for her. She gulps the water, puts her hands in her lap and massages her fingers.

Kevin continues introducing the people at the table. Kevin likes to be in charge of things, to run them. "As I was saying, this is going to be an informal press conference, after all we're from the same community." Each woman has a sign in front of her with her first name. Marnie quickly writes *Vera* on tented construction paper and places in front of her. "That's why we're using first names. Let's keep it simple." He leans back and chuckles. "As you know, all these women are members of Marnie's Cookie Club. Some chose to play the lottery and some decided not to." He reminds the reporters that the women hadn't received the money, they don't know exactly how much they'll have, and they've been advised not to make any major decisions for six months. "This is Aaron and Tara, better known to you as Special Intent and Li'l Key, better known to us as Marnie and Sissy's kids. We know you want to talk to them and they agreed to come so you would back away from crushing their house. I know. I know…." He flutters his fingers and blinks his eyes. "…you're just doing your jobs."

His remark brings chuckles from the reporters.

"Now I turn this over to the women, starting with Marnie, the hostess of the cookie club."

"We're all thrilled to have won this money. As you'll hear in a moment, our good fortune will help other people, too." The blue silk blouse Marnie wears brings out the vibrancy in her eyes and the hues of her platinum hair. She's accustomed to public speaking through her training sessions and motivational speeches to other insurance agents. But as she tells a history of the formation of the lottery group from a cookie club, her voice trembles.

Vera's eyes open wide at the quiver in Marnie's voice. She's surprised that Marnie is nervous.

"Some of us did not wish to spend the time or the money playing. Some of us did not want to gamble. Some of us didn't have the time when we started, or were out of the country." She then mentions that Vera dropped out after the first month though the rest wanted her to continue.

Rosie grabs the mike next and stands. "So. I bought the ticket at Main Street Auto on my way to drop our son off at day care and go to work." She grins with pride. "Winning the lottery has been a big thrill, but I'm aware, we all are really, of the obligations. We have to shepherd the money for future generations and make positive, careful decisions. We, Kevin and I," she nods to him, "are following our advisor's suggestions and not making any major decisions for six months." Rosie looks up at the ceiling. "Oh, other than the cruise. Oh, and my car has over 200,000 miles on it and needs a transmission so I think we'll be buying a new car."

Jeannie doesn't say anything. Neither does Chandra.

Vera remains seated. Her fingers tremble as she reaches for the mike, and then she grips it so tightly her knuckles whiten. "It's my fault this is all happening, this press conference, that is." Her voice cracks. "I told Glenda, my wig maker, about the cruise. Guess I can't keep my big mouth shut, so I told her about the lottery win when we'd been sworn to secrecy. I was just so so happy for my friends, I couldn't keep the joy quiet." Her eyes roll around the audience. "Which one of you is Glenda's husband?"

A reporter raises his hand. "I'm Dalton O'Neil."

Vera nods at him and then talks as though he's the only one present. "I love Glenda. She's been so supportive and wonderful to me through my illness. But we didn't want this publicity. We wanted the space and quiet to figure out what we were going to do. I read the article that was in the paper when I got home and the blog you wrote. Yes, I'm Vera. The one whose cancer returned and decided to drop out of the lottery. But that was *my* decision. The group *begged* me not to quit," Vera's voice cracks in sorrow for herself. She's surprised by her relief and ease, grateful her cancer is public. At last, there's nothing to hide. "But I wanted my energy for healing and maintaining my life. The winners generously took us on a wonderful vacation timing it so I could continue my treatments. I'm so grateful. I have such wonderful girlfriends." She looks around the room again. Her eyes searching for anything else she should say.

Jeannie sitting next to her, notices the slight trembling of Vera's hand as she clenches the mike.

"Do I regret not continuing to play when they begged me to continue? I didn't have the strength then. We've all made decisions that we regret and we can never tell what is going to happen next. Unexpected luck or unexpected tragedy. I came today because I brought the publicity on the group and felt I needed to say what I feel. So please honor that we are private citizens who had some good luck. Or some not such good luck as the case may be." It's clear that's an oblique reference to her cancer. "And allow us the privacy of celebrating and healing in our own way. Thank you. Very much." She stares at Dalton.

Vera drops the mike on the table producing a teeth shuddering shriek. Then she swivels from the audience, gulps water, and remains in that position to hide her tears.

Sissy doesn't use a mike, her rich voice carries through the room. "Hello," she nods at the reporters. "Thank you for coming. I'm eager for this opportunity to speak to you. I have not followed the suggestions of our financial advisors because I know exactly what I'm going to do with my share of money and want to tell you about it." When she places her hand on her hip, a torrent of bracelets clatter to her wrist. She meets the eyes of each reporter. Her win right before Christmas of $10,000 inspired the women to form the lottery group. She fashioned the numbers from an old policy players dream book her mother used for years. Her comfort in front of an audience, fine tuned by preaching, is obvious as her cadence gathers rhythm and she rocks slightly on her heels.

"Ann Arbor is a glistening city with only the slight taint of a few empty stores compared to the devastation of Detroit, now bankrupt with a manager appointed by the governor, just this side of a ghost town. Now, snow drifts through the Fischer Body Plant, moss grows like putting green grass in Henry Ford's Office, ferns, weeds, and graffiti crowd Michigan Central's Railroad Platforms. Photographers come from all over the world to take pictures of Detroit becoming a ruin." She quotes statistics of homelessness; over five thousand sleep on chairs every night because there's not enough room for all of them to lie down. Almost half of the homeless are families. "That's right, with children. School kids are afraid to walk home past streets of vacant houses. Truth is," she stops, scans again the eyes of the reporters, "We're afraid of the homeless. Why? Because they could be us. Many of us are only one pay check, one bad decision, one illness from being on the streets." She draws pictures of the citizens, stories of bad luck, bad judgment, bad economic policies, bad mental health ending in deprivation and sadness. The herd of bracelets when she gestures punctuate her paragraphs. The spotlights make her skin shine.

Then she explains her dreams and hopes for a new Detroit rising from the ashes. A welcoming city where people grow their own food, are conscious of the environment, work to develop equalitarian communities, respectful of the environment, eager for the quality education. "Yes, that's idealistic. Yes, I know it's difficult. And right now we're struggling with bankruptcy and pension issues. And we're all aware of the forces that brought Detroit, the beautiful city on the lake, surrounded

162

by forest, to its knees: the collapse of America's auto industry, the corruption of the city, the rebellion and resulting flight from the city, and now this latest economic calamity. But instead of the prototype of a rust belt city, Detroit could be the model for the future. We live in the fresh water belt, too after all. Water is almost as precious as air. If we all work together we can do it. The American auto industry is reborn. And if we aim for the stars then maybe we'll get half way there.   That's why the name of my foundation is Phoenix."

Sissy sits down while reporters furiously text.   One has taken a video with his cell phone.

Then it's Allie's turn. The excitement in her voice increases, her gestures quicken as she details ideas about teaching skills to mothers of babies and toddlers at risk, meeting with teams of ex gang members to learn nonviolent strategies, and increasing realistic opportunities by developing internships with high technology companies. "It's a two pronged approach. We have to change the economic and social environment as well as help people believe in themselves and develop skills to take advantage of it. Detroit is ripe to become a creative Mecca for new entrepreneurs. That has already started." She finishes and hands the mike to Charlene.

The reporters shift in their seats. The press conference has become a promotion and they have lost their leverage. After all, tragedy and calamity and jealousy and envy and fear sell. Not hope and joy and good news.

Charlene's voice warms as she explains that she's an ecumenical minister who will be working with the sheriff's department, focusing on domestic violence. She's developing a plan to bridge the inner city with the churches and community organizations of the surrounding suburbs and in that way make metropolitan alliances. Maybe the churches can help build bridges between people and communities.

Then Special Intent stands.

The reporters sit up straighter, pull their laptops closer poised to write down every syllable.

He notices the shift in posture and chuckles, smiling at them. "You expect me to rap, but not today. Instead, I'm going to quote Jay-Z who said, 'You can say what you say, but you are what you are.'" Special stops to nod at the reporters. "What that means today, is that now we get a chance to DO what we've been sayin, to become who we been sayin we are. We," he glances at Tara, "are proud to be a part of what our mothers started. Our good fortune will spread and, just like our rap has gathered a following, so will Moms' foundation. This is a new chance for all of us in southeast Michigan. Me and the crew have always been rappin about our city and people, -- hell, it's OUR city and people, a reflection of us and we of it ---and now Moms presents us with another venue." He shifts his weight. "We'll perform at her fundraiser to launch Phoenix." Aaron stops two beats.

Tara standing next to him glances sidelong at him.

"And introduce our next songs. The profits from that album will enlarge Phoenix. That's in development now. So we ARE what we SAY." He tilts his head toward Tara and smiles, giving the wink that fans recognize as part of a secret language.

Tara's hair is a soft red, she wears only a bit of make up. Sweetly smiling at the reporters, she's the Madonna about to give birth, her belly shouting out her fertility. "We feel soooo lucky, soooo thrilled at the opportunity to help our family make a difference. My Mom's cookie club has, like, always been about charity, and giving to others." She places a palm on her belly. "They've donated cookies to safe house or the hospice since the beginning. Now we're, the family we've created," and her arms sweeps Marnie, Sissy, Allie, Charlene and then touches Aaron's arm, "Will work as a team to create some change. My sister, Sky who's a lawyer, will help too. We hope you will join our dream for Phoenix. Pleeeaaaaze publicize *this*! You always want to publicize us. Publicize this because this IS us. Help us make winning the lottery important in the good that money can do." Tara grabs Aaron's hand and holds it high, bows her head slightly, as though they've just finished a concert.

There's applause when she sits.

Sissy has used the press conference to launch her foundation.

KEVIN SEEMS CONFUSED what to do next. It's almost anticlimactic, but he grabs the mike and says, "Time for questions."

"This is for Special Intent. What's the focus of the album you're working on?" A woman reporter in a low cut maroon top asks.

"My lyrics have often been about the Big D. If Motown can flourish again, the country can," Aaron says.

"Hey, can you give us any preview?"

Aaron raises his eyebrows, "You'll have to wait for the big launch. Please come. Email the foundation and we'll make sure you have tickets. And then, do me a favor," he leans toward the reporters, "*write* about it. Spread the word. We *need* you."

"Li'l Key. When's your baby due? And do you know its gender?" A man in a suit and tie asks.

"Thank you for asking. She's due in two months."

"How're you feeling?"

She laughs, "Pregnant." Her voice has the husky edge that's developed by constant singing and is surprising for her diminutive size.

Vera glances at Marnie. *Good. The attention is all on Aaron and Tara. Sissy managed to take it away from us. And spin the negative connotations in the articles to a positive. I hope it rubs off on all of us and I'm forgiven. Especially Taylor. Nothing bad should happen to her because of my lack of discretion.*

"Why aren't all the women here? Where's Taylor? And Juliet? And Tracy? And Alice?" Dalton asks.

"I'll answer that," Kevin says. "Different reasons for each of them. Right now, Alice is on a plane flying to her husband. Juliet planned to come, but came down with the flu, or food poisoning. The others were either uncomfortable with the idea of speaking in public or had plans they couldn't cancel."

"Are they available for private interviews?" He's not going to let it go.

"We're here to answer your questions," Marnie interrupts.

"Allie, why did you decide not to play?" Dalton asks.

Allie reaches for the mike, but doesn't stand. She clears her throat. "My father died when he was only 44. I realized that the most important commodity is time. Not money."

"What kind of car are you going to buy?" A reporter in a pink blouse asks Rosie.

"Oh," she glances at Jeannie. "I don't know yet. Maybe a Volt. Probably something from Jeannie's Dad's dealership."

"Hey. Jeannie. I understand your numbers won. Do you think you should get more?"

Jeannie had not anticipated the question and sips on her water stalling for time. She inhales, hearing her own wind brush through her nostrils. "No. I'm glad it was my numbers. It makes me feel specially blessed because I

166

figured out the numbers from our birthdates." She smiles at Mark. "I'm glad we all won."

"Are there other members in the foundation?" a man in jeans and a *Michigan* tee shirt asks Sissy.

"We're going to have a board of directors," Sissy says, "but it's too early for me to have that figured out. But hey, I'm open for suggestions. And someone from the media could be valuable."

"Sissy. You're a Christian woman, isn't playing the lottery gambling? And doesn't the Bible caution against that?"

Sissy laughs. "I play because you can do good things with money. It's not the root of all evil. Selfishness and greed are. That's what my momma told me. Besides, playing is fun. You think I'm doing good things with the money I just won?" She pins him with her eyes, he bows his head texting.

The woman in the maroon blouse raises her hand, "Chandra. I understand that you won some money at blackjack."

Chandra soothes a strand of hair behind her ear. "Yes. I read books and stuck with the suggested system. It's a question of playing the probabilities with each hand. Sometimes systems work." She glances to the ceiling. "I'm a mathematics teacher and understand statistics and calculus." She starts to explain more, but the reporter shuffles a cell into her purse and so Chandra stops.

No one raises a hand to ask a question.

"Okay, I guess we're done," Kevin says. "Thank you for coming, and I hope we'll see some of you when the state gives us the check. And, more importantly, at the foundation's launch."

A flutter of blinding camera shots, and then the sound of equipment being shut down, snapped shut, and stashed in bags. Spotlights are shut off. Special Intent, Li'l

Key and Sissy are outside the room, laughing and joking with the reporters.

Allie dispenses coffee and places pineapple, melon, and strawberries on a plate. The pastries sweat in the glare of lights. Kevin pours a glass of water, and hugs Rosie with one arm. Flynn hugs Vera, and says, "You were so brave." No one says anything aloud until the reporters depart, the TV cameras are totted away and the friends are left with shuffled chairs, sweating pitchers, and the discarded scraps of food.

"Thanks Vera, You cut off the nasty stories by being here and by your comments." Marnie touches her arm gently.

"When I read that stuff they said about me, like I'm a pathetic sick cancer victim and you guys ignored my plight, I knew I had to come."

"You were wonderful," Charlene hugs her.

"Sissy helped. Between the two of you, they don't think we're greedy bitches," Rosie says, crosses her arms and tilts back. "We did good."

They high five each other and toast with glasses of water and Diet Coke.

"I'm so glad that's over. I'm sorry Taylor wasn't here," Vera says. " I came partly to assuage her rage and she wasn't even here." Vera purses her lips together as though kissing the air.

"I'll tell Taylor," Rosie promises.

## Sixteen

*Julius Caesar used daily lotteries to raise money for construction and Rome's wars.*

AFTER THE PRESS conference, Jeannie picks up her mother and they visit her father. He sits in a chair at the rehab center, feeding himself.

"Look what you can do!" Mom's voice trills with excitement.

He looks confused, as though he doesn't recognize them. He places a wobbling spoon laden with pudding down before he can decipher who they are and remember how to smile. He stutters, "Eannie."

"He still has trouble with consonants," Mom reports.

He smiles at Jeannie with one side of his mouth.

She pastes a grin on her face as though he's the same father he was a few months ago, and she is the same daughter. His cheek is dry dust. When she kisses him, he smells of antiseptic and, faintly, urine. Jeannie cringes at his helplessness, his frailty. *Even our everyday lives are full of the kindness of duplicity.*

On her way home she drives to the dealership, lets the car idle in the parking lot, and surveys salesmen and customers through the glass display windows. Jay and a young couple stroll around a floor model and then disappear into his cubicle. Sue's helmet of shinning hair drapes over a stack of papers as she scans information from her monitor and checks it with a printout. When Sue lifts her face, Jeannie notices etched lines between her brows, her lips pull down at the corners. *Not so easy, kid, is it?*

As soon as Jeannie enters the main door, salesmen's heads snap up. They're hoping for an additional customer, but instead they get Jeannie with the uncomfortable association of her sick father, their boss.

*Do they know about the lottery win?*

Sue flexes a metallic grin, crosses her arms, and pulls her shoulders back in her turquoise blouse. Jeannie watches this routine, not sure if it is a defensive or offensive. *I wonder if Rosie has told her about Ricardo.* The thought chills her. *Sue probably knows about the lottery win.*

"I was just going over last month's figures, getting ready to send your dad a report."

"Don't send it to him. Send it to me."

"Oh." She slumps. "How's he doing?"

Jeannie considers her response when Kurt, another salesman, joins them. "Hey. Congratulations about the lottery win."

"How'd you hear?"

"Are you kidding? It's everywhere. The newspaper, the Internet, TV. You and the cookie ladies are hot."

"Good for you and the cookie club," Sue says.

Jeannie shoots Sue a vicious look.

A bright flush spreads from her neck to her cheeks. "So when's your dad returning?" Her voice now even.

"Yeah, I was just going to ask that," Kurt adds.

The young couple leave, brochures and papers in their hands, and Jay strides toward Jeannie. He shakes his head slightly, "And. How's Jack?"

"Slowly improving," Jeannie says. She doesn't tell him he's concentrating on feeding himself and learning to speak. She doesn't tell him he's not Jack Jeffries anymore.

"I assume until your father's back, you'll be in running things, and reporting to him?" Kurt asks.

Jeannie turns her body to Jay and Kurt avoiding Sue. "My father is not returning. About six months ago, he, along with headquarters, arranged that, if something like this would happen, I'd be the general manager. Corporate looked over my years working here and decided I had credible experience."

Sue drains of color, brows raised.

*She was taking classes and training to run a profitable dealership. My father promised her much he had no intentions of honoring.* For the first time, Jeannie realizes that Dad knew full well he was playing with fire by not taking his medication and prepared accordingly, angry at his own decision to please Sue.

Now, Sue realizes her future is at Jeannie's whim.

Jeannie meets Kurt's eyes. "We're not sure what we're going to do and need more information." Amazing how she can hide in the editorial *we*. "So, there'll be a meeting next week with all staff, including service. We need accounting reports from each separate department, sales figures from you," Jeannie nods at each of them, "We want your visions of the dealership one year from now and five years from now. That's the most important part." She pauses. "Actually we need those recommendations from each of you Wednesday and then let's have a meeting on Friday night after the dealership closes."

"Great idea," Jay says, "I've been thinking about how to optimize the changes in the industry and have ideas for reorganization."

Sue's stricken look is Jeannie's small victory. *I can so easily fire her. Zap. She's gone. Or I could be her boss and lord it over her for years.* Jeannie understands Sue's desperation for her father, but could let her twist in the wind like she let Jeannie do for so many months. Years, really.

*Some people put selfish desire over righteous love and consideration.*

*Bad people? Her?*

WHEN JEANNIE RETURNS home, reporters are stacked in the driveway. "How does it feel to win 125 million dollars," one asks.

"What are you going to do with the money?" She frowns at him and sure enough there's a flash of camera. *I need to remember to always smile. Next time I come home, I will not park on the street, but pull right in the garage*, Jeannie thinks as she walks in her house and shuts the blinds on the front windows to shield herself from the prying.

When she checks her email in her secret account, there's a letter in her inbox.

*This wasn't supposed to happen like this. We were supposed to be recreational, fun sex. We were supposed to be a compartmentalized week. But I've fallen in love with you. Don't let us float away. Please.*

Jeannie reads the message several times. Then closes down the email and opens her usual one flooded with mail. There's a letter from her supervisor when Mark was in law school. The restaurant chain he worked in closed, he lost his house; his pension and his savings only produce $10,000 a year. Luckily he is 56 so he can withdraw it. He lives with his children. Can she lend him money until things get better?

Yoga friends congratulate her. A few are simply excited that she can build her yoga center. Others ask for jobs when she opens the studio. "I'll do anything! Answer the phone, handle your website, email. Be your personal assistant. Even clean up," one suggests.

The woman who lives two doors down the street sends Jeannie an itemized list of bills with a suggestion that Jeannie pays them. She doesn't even say please. If Jeannie could pay her mortgage, $2500 a month which ballooned along with her equity line when they put in the swimming pool and hot tub, (remember you, Sara, and

Mark came to several parties) and another $600 a month for heating, that would make things so much better. That's only $3,100 a month and will be nothing to Jeannie now. What did Jeannie do to get so lucky? She's been playing for years. She adds a thank you and a smiley face after presuming that Jeannie will agree.

Jeannie deletes her email, and shuts down the computer, but her fingertips remain on the space bar. Money, and its power have complicated her life.  She inhales.  *It's my life.  I can do what I want. It's my numbers that won.  I exhale.  I'm okay. Yes.*

## Seventeen

95% of lottery winners remain married.
56% of people who win a million quit their jobs.

AS SOON AS Juliet arrives home, she unpacks her suitcase in the laundry room, drags it, including travel cases of toiletries, to the basement. Within ten minutes, except for a slight tan and lightening of her hair, it's as if she were never away. Juliet has no intention of attending the press conference. She peers from her upstairs window. The reporter who was staked outside her house is now gone. After changing into jeans, a tee shirt and old shoes, she drives toward the trailer park.

She pulls into the Red Robin lot at the edge of the forest. The drainage ditch is part of a protected wetland and no one has bothered to go through the necessary paperwork and engineering to build houses or another commercial building. Instead, its edges have been nibbled away: some to Red Robin's parking lot, and some to an addition to the apartment complex using existing roadways and sewer system.

She enters the forest. Like a homing pigeon, she has no trouble finding the deer path that she and Joey travelled in spite of overgrown grapevines, Virginia creeper, poison ivy, Solomon seal, and Jack in the pulpit. The trail is still as snaky, as littered with decaying leaves. There's an extra curve here and there where trees died, fell, and forced the deer to redesign their route. When she inhales the dank richness of earth creating more life, smelling the same as her childhood, tears spring to her eyes. She tiptoes across a log over the stream bubbling foamy water, flooding its edges.

She has returned to Eden.

Spring Beauties, those delicate pink flowers whose name she didn't know as a child, are in bloom. Wild woodruff carpets the floor. *Hepatica, gallium.* She knows the names of the ephemeral spring flowers that will vanish when the trees leaf out. Vanish and be reborn, not like the mastodon that vanished forever. *Not like my childhood that vanished forever. Here. Right here.*

The trees are thicker, oaks and spindly maples crowd out the aspen. From her peripheral vision, she sees movement, turns, and a deer faces her. Five feet away, it watches, ears pointed toward her. They stare, the deer frozen, glowing eyes unblinking. Juliet is aware movement will cause it to bolt. The deer's immobility is its primary defense as though motion betrays its existence. When Juliet takes a step, it leaps away, white tail the only evidence of its velocity. *Is it the progeny of the baby decades ago continuing regardless of jeopardy or time? I guess I am, too. Still alive, now my progeny producing progeny. I wonder if other children play here, if other teenage rapists and abusers stalk here, as incessant as the seasons. Evil as persistent, as inevitable, as social misery. Along with spring,* she reminds herself. *And joy.*

She has no trouble recognizing the exact place. There's the oak tree that became Joey's stake. She runs her palms, her fingers up and down the trunk over the rough bark. Near its base, she notices a fissure, crusty with twisted bark, a hole she pokes her fingers in and digs out mealy wood. *Did the snapping of the bungee cord make this scar, as though the tree wept at its misuse?*

Leaning against the tree, she stares at the spot where she lay. Now an aspen grows, its base surrounded by trillium as though her little girl virginal blood transpired into the flower. She coaxed the same species to spread in the shaded areas of her garden. Clumps of blue bells, the flowers still tight buds, cluster at the edges. Up above, the sky is that wan blue so common in spring when the earth isn't convinced that summer will arrive once again with all its glory.

There're no crows.

JULIET SAW STAINFACE again. It was a spring day like this one. She and Marnie had just become friends at Pioneer High School and roamed South University examining the cosmetics at the pharmacy, giggling over the dirty cards at Middle Earth, and trying on dangly earrings that neither one could afford. Instead, they bought macramé bracelets made from embroidery thread. Two for a dollar the sign said. They divvied up fifty cents each and tied them on each other's wrists.

"We'll never take them off. Friends forever." Marnie squealed and they twisted their pinky fingers around each other's.

"Forever," Juliet repeated. *I belong somewhere. Somewhere beside the trailer.*

The *friends forever* turned out to be true. At least so far.

They climbed up stairs to play games at Pinball Pete's, then walked into the dimly lit Brown Jug and sat down at a booth. Juliet perused the menu as if she often sat in a college restaurant with a friend, drank water with lemon in it, talked, and ordered food. *I'm able to do anything I want, really want. I just have to work hard and do it,* she thought, as she ordered a Famous Brown Jug Burger and coke, crossing her leg and swinging it while smiling at the cute waiter who, amazingly, flirted back.

"He must not know we're just in tenth grade," Marnie whispered behind her hands.

*Or he doesn't care. Or he likes it,* Juliet thought. She glanced sidelong and ran her fingers through ironed hair. They giggled at her display as though it were only silly and not a manipulation to be practiced. She thought, as they wandered through the fraternity and sorority mansions, Victorian and Tudor style homes of the faculty and physicians at the hospital, *This is what I want. This.* She pointed to an arts and crafts style home with a spreading front porch, paned windows, festooned with baskets of pansies and said to Marnie, "This is my house. This one."

Marnie pointed to a Victorian with a tower, narrow windows, ornate molding. "That one is mine. We'll be neighbors."

Alone, on the bus home, she daydreamed a future. She wanted only what many had. It wasn't like she wanted to marry the king of England, or be a movie star. Her rules: Study in school. Get a good job. Save money. Marry a professional man. A man who goes to the University so she can be safe.

That day, roaming around the University area and the middle class neighborhood with Marnie, flutters of the possibility of living in a place like this were cemented. High school initiated a chance for a new life.

Her optimism and power continued as she walked home from her bus stop passed Kroger, TJ Maxx, and Bob Evans. *I'll live on a street with trees, and lawns, and flowers, and garages.* She watched her feet on the crumbling cement so she wouldn't trip, looked up, and saw Stainface.

The same red birthmark covered half his face. He wore a baseball cap, but it merely shadowed the purple half of his face, it didn't hide it. His shoulders were broader. She closed her eyes hoping he was an apparition, a haunting of the futility of her dreams, and when she opened them again he'd be gone.

But there he was sauntering toward her, now only a few feet away.

He glanced at her, looked her up and down. Her hip hugging jeans, the purple tee shirt that said *Pioneer.*

Their eyes met.

Juliet's mouth opened. Her stomach twisted.

He showed no sign of recognition. Had she changed that much? Would she always be an 8 or 9 year old to him? Or had he attacked so many little girls that he couldn't remember all of them?

He continued north on Carpenter.

When she got home a few minutes later, she wanted to crawl in bed and hide. But her Mom sat on the couch drinking a beer and watching *Dynasty*. "Did you and your new friend have a good time?" she asked hopefully.

"Yeah, but I got sick from lunch." Juliet entered the bathroom, puked up the burger and fries souring her since she walked by Stainface. Washed her face. Then took a shower.

When she came out, Mom put the back of her hand on Juliet's forehead. "You don't have a fever," Mom remarked and poured some Pepto Bismol.

Juliet choked down the chalky pink liquid trembling in the cup, crawled in bed, covered her head with her quilt and waited for her heart to resume normal beating.

*NOW, ALL MY teenage goals have come to fruition. I studied, saved, married a professional man, live in a house with a garage on a block with trees,* she thinks as she strides up the path, her hands plunged in her jacket pockets, to the trailer.

Beside the trailer is her mom's car, a 1995 Honda Civic. A 1983 Ford Ranger sits on ramps, waiting for an oil change, a tire change, a new transmission, something. It was like that the last time she was here. And maybe the time before that. Another job never completed. An idea as rusted as the car. Motion and goals gone to waste. A basketball hoop leans on its pole.

She knocks on the aluminum door, the metal curlicue shield on the window twisted out of shape. Joey pushes himself from the sofa, reluctantly pulls himself from watching TV. His guitar lies on a chair. His expression doesn't change when he sees her. He simply opens the door, shuffles back, plops back down, and plunks his socked feet on a coffee table littered with ashtrays, car magazines, advertisements, and beer bottles.

"Where's Mom?"

Joey shrugs, "Not here."

Juliet gets herself a glass of water from the kitchen sink. On the windowsill, a miniature violet that she bought Mom for Mother's Day several years ago, flowers wildly, the plump blooms providing spots of clean color. She sits on the chair next to the sofa.

*Jerseylicious* plays on the TV. "These people crazy," Joey says.

"I'm glad you're here. I'm glad it's just us."

For the first time, Joey looks at her. His brows come together in that same expression of bewildered curiosity he had as a child.

"I went to Eden."

"Oh, the raggedy woods," he says.

"There're flowers growing where it happened."

He stands, strides to the refrigerator and pulls out a coke. "I know. Trillium blooming now. Soon it'll be the blue bells." He shoves the bottle at her. "You want one?"

"I'm fine."

"I planted them."

"You?" *Joey made a grave for our childhoods?*

"You're breaking our promise?"

"Yes."

180

"Couldn't let the place contain only awful memories. Something as important needed to be marked." His soft whisper contains a tenderness she never heard from him.

"I spend half my mind pushing the memory away. Today it came back in full."

He gulps the soda standing over her, and then sits down. "Just today? Every single day and every night it's there.  Used to go over it, changing the outcome. If we had just gone home that day, or went down by the stream instead of by the tree, if I had kicked Stainface in his balls, if I had picked up a stick I could have beat up the Bushyhair and rescued you." He plants his elbows on his knees, and leans forward, the coke can dangling between his fingertips, his chin on his chest.

He mumbles, "I thought about you, and what they did. How you left the family that day."

"I didn't know you paid attention."

"And me, I knew I could never leave Mom. We made opposite decisions. I was stuck here shoring up the edge of the forest from its evil. Trying to maintain civilization."

"The forest? It wasn't the forest.  It was just those kids."

"No. No it's everywhere, in the forest, too. See how the oaks and maples crowd out the aspen? See how the hawks kill the bunnies and squirrels, see how the deer destroy the plants?  See how the rich exploit us?  Well, Larry and me anyway. You rich now. We, human beings, destroy to live. So do the other predators. So evil is in all of us.  Some more. Some less. What they did to two children, we were just little kids, was evil. Just for sicko fun. Now, I monitor the forests."

"What?"

"First I planted those flowers.  Now, I walk through the forests, make sure it isn't happening to any other little kids. Never got to rescue nobody though. But I've faced my own shadows." He turns to her. "How 'bout you?"

*Tom. Dan. The years of glib lies. Broken promises. Ungiven hearts.* Her fingers slide under her chain.

"Why you always do that?"

Her hand falls to her lap and she shrugs.

"That some kind of talisman, some magic, or just a nervous tick?"

"A nervous tick," she says and runs her fingers through her curly hair.

"You lying." He swills more coke. "Sure you don't want something? Seems like we gonna talk about this, we need some brew, some weed, somethin. Shit. We probably need some heroin, but I ain't got none of that."

"I'm fine," she interlaces her fingers.

"Funny how you can just be playin around, shit happens, and presto! Everything is different. Good is bad. And bad is good. Life forever changed."

"Uh?"

"I'm just sayin."

"Joey."

"I knew I couldn't be the man no more."

"Joey." Her voice is clogged with tears.

"And you, Juju? You came here to talk, but seems like I've been doin the talkin."

She clears her throat. "You're right. I left the family that day." She starts to wind her index around her necklace and jerks her hand away. "You're right. That one decision, made that terrible day, led to a bunch of others like dominos. But yes. My hunt for safety started that day. "

"Did you find it? Seems like you too scared to even face us."

Juliet looks down. "I feel safe." She glances around the living room, duct tape holding up some ceiling tile, the afghan her mom crocheted with yarn from Meijer's, matted and grey with years of use and washing. Smeared windows prevent the sun from streaming in and spotlighting the grim. "But in making my life about leaving here, about not being trailer-park trash, I forgot to make it mine. I forgot who I was, who I am."

"So you help others to avoid yourself."

"Nope. Can't take credit for being altruistic. Nursing was simply a job."

"You made the wrong decision, but hell you was just a kid. It's not about the trailer park, it's about people. After all Iggy Pop grew up here. Right here. Each and every one of us is capable of anything. And I made the wrong decision too."

"Yes."

"Don't say yes so quickly. You don't know all the decisions I made. But the first wrong decision was to stay here forever to protect Mom. I could have used my guitar playing to help get us out, worked a little harder at it. Or school. But," he shrugs, "I guess, the fuckin truth is, after that day, nothing seemed worth shit. And you know, this don't bother me none." He nods at the easy chair with the split in the Naugahyde and the stuffing spilling out, the rugs on top of rugs to hide burn holes, spills, and provide extra layers of warmth, the drawings done when they were kids, yellow and faded with age, still stuck to the walls with masking tape. "It's home. All our years and memories. And I don't buy the whole system. Look at this," He kicks at the piles of magazines, advertisements, coupons urging how to live, coaxing them to buy more, fill the house with more. "As if then we'd be happy. Think all that material shit prevents evil or guarantees happiness? Rich people have their own brand of evil. Them bankers and Wall Street dudes too. Just as evil. Maybe more so 'cause they have more power. Selfish to their own desires just like those mutherfuckas that abused us."

Juliet starts to argue with him, but instead stares at the TV screen, the women snarling at each other, snatching each other's hair. Joey shakes his head, "See. Foul nastiness everywhere." He grabs the remote and turns it off.

The silence is loud. Then a car horn blares from the street.

Joey blurts a bitter chortle with a harsh tone. "Sometimes you can zap it away." He shakes his head fast. "Got a question I've been wonderin about since I been grown enough to understand what happened." He faces her again. "You ever enjoy being with a man or they scar you too bad."

*I didn't expect this.* "Well," she sips some water, "at first, the pictures always came back. But after awhile they dimmed. No one knows, but you. But. Well. I'm always alone."

"Yeah. I don't catch no feelings either. I make sure of that. Lovin you and Mom is heartbreakin enough. Can't help feeling bad about what I'm doing and so sorry for the girl I want to cry. So I just avoid the whole thing. But what you just say? You like sex or not?"

"I find comfort in sex. No one knows me. Not Dan. He doesn't know any of this and no one can know me without knowing this. And I pretend with everything. Including sex. It's easier." Her fingers slide up and down the chain.

He wags his finger at her gesture. "You have a secret. When you think of it, you do that necklace thing. What's your secret? You a lesbian?"

Juliet frowns and chortles, "No." Then looks at him, her eyes a washy blue, like his, she realizes.

"I wouldn't blame you none." He leans back on the couch, and drapes his arm on its back. "You know what,

184

Juju? Sex is the closest most of us get to God. But all I've gotten is the Devil."

She squints at him, confused.

"You know why you here today?"

"To talk to you."

"No, I mean why you remember, why you want to talk *today*. Because you won the lottery and you feeling guilty."

"You know?"

"It's everywhere. News. YouTube. Ann Arbor cookie club won 125 mill. You shoulda played with us, and helped us out when we wanted you to join our little family bets. The lottery, hell," Joey tightens his fists and pulls his shoulders back, "it allows the system to continue. We know we ain't climbing up no ladder to riches, that Horatio Alger myth is just a fairy tale now, but maybe we win the lottery and become rich. It's the fantasy that keeps us poor bastards in control. It's how capitalism keeps on working. All those bullshit lies about how we're going to get rich. So we actually identify with our own oppressors."

Juliet pinches the crease she irons in her jeans, runs her hands down her thighs.

"Well. I got my revenge. Our revenge. You might as well know since we're talking."

"What?"

"That asshole with the big red birthmark, remember?" Joey lights a cigarette and blows a plume of smoke.

"Stainface."

"I saw him working at Home Depot, recognized the fucka with that half red face right away." Joey squints. "For years that face was my nightmare. And I wasn't shit to him. Ten years passed, I was a man. Almost. Seventeen."

185

Hair rises on the back of her neck and she grips her fingers together. *I opened Pandora's box. Now I witness the furies."*

"I followed him, knew his work schedule. And one night, beat him. Pounded him with my fists. I was bigger than him then, not no six year old pipsqueak. Funny how he seemed so gigantic back then, when I was a kid. But, by that time I was almost grown, he was shorter than me. Heavier though. I had the element of surprise. A storehouse of rage. Beat him. Kicked him with steel-toed work boots I bought at Home Depot. Got him with his own goods like he got you with his shit." Joey stares at the blank TV while he sucks on the cigarette, his voice measured as though he narrates a scene. "After the first punch, I said, 'Remember me? You tied me to a tree and raped my sister. Remember me? You and your fucking buddies pulled a train on my sister and she was just a little kid.' I hit him again.

"He squinted givin me that mad dog look, and goes, 'You just as stupid as you was then. You think I'm going to let you beat the shit out of me and live?'

"He pulled a knife. Not a big one. One of those switch blades people carry. Flashed it. Sliced my arm open." Joey taps his arm and she notices a six-inch gash, now bubbly with scar tissue, across his forearm. "I punched him and he slashed my shirt, only nicking my chest instead of stabbing me 'cause I spun away and kicked him in the chest.

"He fell. I kicked him again, and grabbed the knife. 'You took our souls away. This the get back of a soulless man. You piece of evil shit,' I said.

"He laughed, just laughed, as though he enjoyed the pain. Laughed through the blood in his mouth."

Joey holds his head back and pushes his fingers into his forehead, tossing his head from side to side, the cigarette dripping ashes on his pants.

He almost whispers to the ceiling, "Then he said, 'You fuckin' little perv. Got off on watching us fuck your sister, didn't you? Too bad we missed her ass. Maybe I'll come get that next time. She should be grown now and like it. I still know where you live.' " Now, Joey faces Juliet and growls Stainface's words. " 'Or maybe I'll get your Mom.... You assholes haven't moved from that shitty ass trailer.' "

Juliet inhales as though slapped, air hissing through her teeth.

Joey closes his eyes and whispers. "This time I protected you, and Mom."

"What?"

"You don't understand?"

"I wouldn't have imagined," Juliet whispers and shakes her head, then turns to him.

Joey's eyes shut, his lips pulled tightly together. "If he hadn't threatened you and Mom I woulda just walked on. Knocked his teeth out and be done with it. Didn't think it evened the score, but figured I got some payback. Later I would have realized that he'd have to kill me. I, we could have charged him with child abuse and rape. He'd be labeled for the rest of his life. He couldn't let that happen."

"Did it solve anything?"

"Think about *that* all the time, too. I hadn't thought it through when I started hitting him. He escalated it and I defended myself, you, and Mom."

"How did you get away with it?"

"I started having nightmares again, not about the murder, but about your rape, me struggling against those bungee cords. Always his face. I'd wake up wet and trembling and see again the spreading pool of blood by his head. Two days later, the News had an article about a man

187

killed in the Home Depot parking lot.  He had served time for rape, and drug possession. They figured it was a drug murder, and, I guess, they didn't look too hard. They never arrested anyone."

"Is this justice?"

"Think about *that* all the time.  Can't figure out if I'm a survivor, an avenger, or a protector. Or all of them."

*Horror builds on horror. Violence begets violence. How do you judge the gang rape and abuse of kids with self-defense murder, on any scale of justice? There're answers all across the spectrum on that.  A lot of people would applaud. A lot would think Joey should be in prison forever.*

Joey looks at his sister, her perfectly groomed curly hair, the slight aroma of some fresh lemon scent, the perfectly toned body and narrow waist gripped with a belt. "What's fair? Fact I can't get a full time job with benefits though I've put in 186 applications ain't fair. None of this is fair."

Juliet leans back on the sofa.  Sadness for Joey engulfs her. *He's a victim as much as me.  How did I not realize that?*

"But it does change something. Might save some other little girl.  Some other little boy.  Maybe his own damn kids. One less raping asshole in the world. And, you know what? It was after that I started taking care of our spot.  It was after that I started patrolling the forests." He stops. Juliet hears her own breathing, her own heart. "Figured I had to turn it all into something good. Some redemption for me. For you.

Tears stream down Juliet's face. It's the first time she's cried about her rape.  Is she crying for herself, for Joey? Is she crying for Stainface, too? For all of them? The forgotten kids.

"Don'tcha just love how life takes unexpected turns? Knowing we got a tiny bit of revenge make you feel better?"

She hugs him. It's tentative, her fingertips rest on the tops of his shoulders.

Then Joey grabs her close and gives her a bear hug, pulls back and looks at her. "So whatcha gonna do with all that money? You think it's a prize for suffering? Will all that money make things better?"

## *Eighteen*

*Income refers to a flow of money over time in the form of a rate (per hour, per week, or per year); wealth is a collection of assets owned. In essence, income is specifically what people receive through work, retirement, or social welfare whereas wealth is what people own.*

PEOPLE ARE WHAT they let us see. And I don't even let myself see myself, Jeannie thinks as she opens her email. It's late night, early morning, Mark and Sara both sleeping. She slips away from their warm bed and comes here to this computer, to a virtual secret love nest to write to Ricardo. She wouldn't have predicted any of this. *I'm a mystery to myself. A continual astonishment*, she thinks with a sense of wonderment and pride. Yes, pride. She's not the simple middle class, almost middle-aged (when do you become that?) mother living out routines. *I'm not. I have secret rooms inside me. I'm exciting. No longer mundane and ordinary.* She lets her fingers transport her to Ricardo.

They haven't seen each other yet. She keeps backing away as though to see him here, to have sex with him in Michigan makes her an adulteress. But the thrill of having something all to herself that she knows is wrong is unpredictably delicious.

*I wonder if Rosie has told Sue.*

*Probably.*

He answers immediately. He's awake, has been awake, waiting for her. They do this every night. Every night they make virtual love replaying everything they did to each other, detailing everything that there is left undone. This time he writes: *Meet me at the Westin Hotel, at the airport terminal at 11 am tomorrow. Pppppllllleeeeaaaazzzz.*

191

Yes. Yes yes. Index finger, middle finger, ring finger. That's how she types it over and over, eyes closed so she can feel him close to her. yesyesyesyes.

She returns to bed.

"Jeannie?" Mark reaches for her.

"I had to pee."

He spoons her. He can't smell Ricardo on her. Cyber sex has no aroma. He doesn't notice Jeannie's heart beating. She synchronizes her breathing with his until she drifts back to sleep.

Mark and Jeannie have a good relationship. At least she thought so. Mark satisfies her. Loves her. Knows her. Accepts her. All that. Everything that's supposed to be important. A good marriage. But sex with Ricardo is thrilling. It's new. It's wrong. It's hers. Just hers.


SARA IS IN school. Mark is at the office. Ricardo has texted the room. It's the same number as his cabin. Of course. He thinks romantically. Consistent symbols of them, the few they have, are important.

The sun blares through the sunroof in Jeannie's car. She wears new underwear. Carefully washed hair. Coconut perfume to remind him. How will it feel to see him here? A part of her hopes he has lost his luster. She laughs when she thinks of the word and its core. Lust. This is a new Jeannie, an adventurous selfish person unleashed by the lottery.

He opens the door. His dark eyes are bottomless, no way to see into his soul, he simply mirrors her. Aaah. They stare at each other and then so slowly, so gently as though his lips are petals, he kisses her eyelashes, brows, the tip of her nose as he makes his way down her body.

They make love with a thick ache to reclaim the territory of each other. Snatching off clothes, grabbing

192

flesh, smelling still exotic scents, rubbing, plunging, slowly watching each other, shaken by new implications.

"I didn't want you to mean this much."

"How much?"

He doesn't answer. Even he doesn't have the words to measure the extent of love or lust. Which is it? Love or lust. Lust. Crossing boundaries to be bad.

"I won eight million dollars in the lottery." Jeannie says when we're finished.

"I know."

"You do?"

"This morning I Googled you and it popped up in some crazy blog. And the Michigan lottery page."

"Oh. Does that make me more ..." She searches for the word, "Valuable? Desirable?"

"You already are that."

He lays beside her, holding her hand, both of them staring at the ceiling talking as though to look into each other's faces would cause them to lie.

"You knew though, before we met. Right?"

"Yes, that's what we were celebrating on the cruise."

He nods, taking in the information. "So how has being rich changed you? Rich and in the perfect family. It tore my heart out seeing you with your husband and child. You looked, the three of you, so like you belonged together."

"And you wanted in."

He inhales sharply, a gasp more than an inhale. "I wanted that with you."

*Now I guess I have everything. A perfect family. You. Eight million bucks. Everything.* But she doesn't say that. Instead she says, "You think it's in the genes somehow?"

He squeezes her hand hard. He knows exactly what she's asking. "No. It's human. A human pull. But why now? The lottery win?"

"No, it's you. It's us."     She might be lying. "Somehow to get closer to my father than I've ever been? To understand him?"

He relinquishes the blankness of the ceiling and turns toward her. "Did it work?"

"When you stop being the victim, then you're free to victimize," she says.

His brows shoot up with alarm. "But I hope that neither victimizing or being the victim is even the issue." His voice trembles through the sheets to her.

"I don't want to hurt Mark. Am I hurting myself? You?"

Ricardo moves over her, tastes her forehead, arms, nipples leaving wet trails of him as though she is a continent and he is the road. Once again Jeannie opens herself. And once again they stir the skies.

*Sin ceases to exist if you're exposed to it enough. So does the value of money.* Jeannie doesn't know if she just thinks it or says it. But she knows it's true. And it gets easier each time. As the lies mount, so do the small deceptions. As you overbuy, goods mean less. Spending money, even ridiculous amounts, is easier. Having new lovers can become the same collecting. Then you are alone. Jeannie sees all this. She feels anger at her father for so easily casting away her mother.

Now Sue is alone. Maybe without a job. That's my decision.

*I hope they had fun while it lasted,* she thinks without bitterness or rancor, but with both wishes and sorrow. *He never cast away my mother. Mother was too important to him. That's why he never told her about Sue. Never left her.* Chills of epiphany crawl up her arms. *I'm not telling Mark.*

She must say it, or Ricardo has read her mind, or senses her distance because he says, "I think we've learned everything we had to teach each other."

She's quiet for a minute then says, "I hear what you're saying to me."

He goes to the bathroom and he says, "No. There's one more thing you have to teach me."

Jeannie doesn't respond.

"I don't want to learn it."

She knows what that is. And she knows that she will teach him.

"I'm grown up. I learned a long time ago I don't always get what I want." He walks toward her. "Or what I so rightly deserve. And this, you, are …."

Jeannie kisses Ricardo goodbye, softly. And says, "It's been……" and then stops. Unsure the word to say.

"I know. There's no word."

"No. There isn't."

She closes the door quietly behind her.

SHE WAS TRYING her father on for size. He didn't fit.

He taught me though. *Things I could have done without ever learning.*

*Now what?*

## Nineteen

*400 families make more money than 50% of the bottom half of Americans. In other words, 400 people have as much wealth as a hundred million.*

THE NEXT NIGHT, a Tuesday, Juliet waits for Tom, like she has many other Tuesday nights. How many? Over five hundred, she figures. She is dressed in street clothes, her legs crossed as she slides her fingers up and down her chain while examining the apartment she and Tom decorated over a decade ago and remembering their thrill when they discovered the Monet water lilies bedspread at Macy's. The small counter in the kitchen is bare except for a coffee maker. Plain white plates are precisely stacked inside the white cabinets. The burgundy sofa faces a table with a TV and DVD player. It could be a room in a residence hotel. And then she realizes her house, where she has lived for over twenty years and raised her children, is similarly anonymous. Perfect, but soulless. Set up as though to advertise furniture or be photographed for a House Decorating magazine. *I live a carefully presented life, but I forgot the most important thing. Me. Expressing me. I became the opposite of that trailer. It was messy and chaotic, so I was obsessively neat. It was crammed with various clashing colors and clutter so I had only white, or beige. Mom is chubby, so I'm trim. I became simply* not *them. My persona so carefully presented I almost believed it.*

A tear trickles out of the corner of her eye when she thinks of Joey. *I'm disgusted by my own dismay at poverty. It's as though not making it in America is a crime, and the poor and struggling are modern lepers.* There are more Joeys, so many more, than there are middle class.

*Who was I before the rape?* She struggles to remember. Other than Josie and her girl gang of pussycats, she can't.

Then she hears noise outside the door as Tom shuffles his weight. A paper bag crinkles as it's switched from one arm to the other. A clang of keys and the slide of the bolt, and Tom steps in. His eyes widen and he grins when he sees her. "Here already? Thought I'd beat you." He kisses her cheek. "Brought us Chicken Vindaloo and Naan." He raises the bag.

Her resolve ebbs as she warms to his familiar smile, his dark hair with grey clustered distinguishingly at his sideburns. When she blinks, she sees him, as he was fifteen years ago when he was the charming, out of reach doctor, hair still black. Her own stomach turning, heart beating, dry mouth excitement. Her panties wet with wanting. Her longing for an internal solution, a telling and being known and accepted greater, so much greater, than her desire.

There must be something in her posture now, sitting in one of their chairs, finger wound around her chain, shoulders pulled back, the furrow between her brows that catches him. He narrows his eyes, "What's up, Sweetpea?"

The endearment is meant to disarm her.

"Let's eat," She stands and retrieves their placemats and silverware, but notes her false gaiety.

"OK," he shrugs.

She pours wine while he dishes the Indian food, the aroma of curry, ginger and cardamom imbuing the apartment with a counterfeit warmth and home.

At dinner, they talk about changes in software that modifies record keeping, and politics between nursing and administration. They discuss a new Thai restaurant. "Maybe I'll get take out from there next week," Tom says as he stirs sugar into his decaf.

198

*Should I tell him now?* Instead she comes to him and kisses the curve of his ear.

After they make love, she says, "That felt close. Comfortable." Her throat tinged with gratitude and sorrow.

"Comfortable?" He chortles.

Then she turns to him. "This is the last time I'm coming here. I don't want to do this anymore."

"Just like that? After all this time?"

His shock alarms her.

"What's going on?"

"I've been living a dishonest life. I've been dishonest with everyone, but most of all myself. I have to get on a track that I'm proud of while I still have the time." Her voice cracks. The cluster of tears she fights pools in her eyes and she blinks.

"Let's face it, Tom. We never planned to spend a decade sharing a secret apartment. In the beginning it was fun, but we thought we were building a life together. We were planning to be *whole* with each other, to make *us* right. But that never happened. Instead this hideaway..." She sits up, leans against the bed backboard, and pulls the bedspread with her. "Has become an avoidance." She stops. "Well, I'll speak for me. It's allowed me to hide from everyone. Including myself."

Tom rubs his brows with one hand, shaking his head. "For me, it's an oasis. A refueling. It makes it possible to get through the massive bullshit of the rest of my life."

Juliet grabs his hand and squeezes it. Turns to face him. "Don't you see, that's the problem. We could have been, should have been the cure for our loneliness and what was missing in the rest of our lives. Instead, we, this, allows the inadequacies in our lives to continue unchanged. Like a band aid that staunches the bleeding while an internal hemorrhage continues unchecked." She swallows and wets her lips. "The rest of our lives become a lie while

199

we playact in a thousand small ways. It's just that we, only we know, even know. We could be together in our total lives. We could make it different, couldn't we?" She pleads.

"I guess we had to end sometime. One of us had to the have the strength."

She hoped that he would claim her. She only wanted to stop their cheating, secrets.

"Is this about the lottery?"

"No. Well, maybe. But in a surprising way."

He narrows his eyes, his face darkens as he leans closer to her. "So what was I? Was I an ace in a hole in case Dan's business faltered? So that you would never be poor again?" He growls. "A doctor makes good extra bank, uh, Sweetpea?" He spits the love name at her. "Now, I'm unneeded and discarded."

"Do you realize what you're calling me?"

"If the shoe fits...." Outside, a horn beeps, once, and again, impatient. Then the car alarm goes off, the screaming ricocheting inside Juliet.

"It's come to this?" Her fingers slide up and down her chain, a familiar gesture that is her faithful symbol of him, of his claim on her. She jerks her hand away. "Is it easier to be angry than sad?"

He doesn't answer.

She turns away, smelling their sex clinging to the sheets.

"I resent how you did this. First as a fiat accompli. Not discussing it with me so we could deal with this problem together like we have so many others. You made a dictatorial decision to end us."

*But I didn't. I just wanted to end our secret life. But clearly all he wants is this, simply this. If he wanted me, he'd would have said, 'Well let's make us whole now. Let's get divorces and be together.' But he didn't.*

"And second with the implications of you being rich and now not needing me, " he continues.

Juliet hugs her knees to her chest and stares at the wall across the room. "Didn't you hear what I said? Didn't you listen to me? I didn't end us, just the lies and secrets. The lottery made me realize how dishonest I've been with everyone, myself most of all. Like I said, I'm trying to set myself right." She turns to him. "I love you. I had so much hope for us, but we ended up…." Her pupils shift as she hunts for the word. She doesn't cry. The tears tighten in her chest because he doesn't love her. But of course, he doesn't even completely know her. *But how can he love me when I don't?*

"What's next? We're never going to see each other again? How do you get a divorce from an affair? And we've lasted longer than many marriages. I am, was, committed to you."

"Tom," she places her hand on his arm and softens her voice, "you were committed to this. One evening a week. We were a compartment you opened and then shut." She inhales. "How do we end this? I don't know. One of us has to have all this donated to a charity." She sweeps her arm around the apartment. It's easy to think about logistics, much easier than fatal disillusions and crushing bereavement. How to say goodbye to a lover? Think about the material goods. Maybe that's why couples fight so hard over whom gets the table, the dishes, and CDs.

"So like *you* to consider the to do list rather than the emotions." He nods at her. "What do we do about the leftover love and companionship?"

She turns away. "That's the problem. My problem."

"Well, you can do that. The sofa, etc. I'll take care of ending the lease, etc." Now, his voice is the same as when he orders lab tests for a patient. All traces of anger and sorrow erased. He's once again the professional man, the physician in orderly control.

"You know, Tom. We both cherish the same illusion. Images of smooth, competent perfection. I have to figure out how to be free of them."

A silence follows as though something else needs to be said. They're tearing themselves asunder when there's been no fight, but a decision born from the realization, they both reluctantly agree, of the wrongness, failure at the core that one, only one, insists be set straight.

"Will we see each other again?"

"Of course," she chuckles. "How can we avoid each other?" She refers to the hospital, the web of professional and social obligations they share. "I care about you, Tom. We've been helpful to each other." Her eyes fill with tears as she remembers his nurturing when she was fighting her cancer. Automatically, one hand touches her breast.

He stares at her, eyes wet, while he shakes his head sadly. "I'm still here."

He could, even now, even at this brink, promise love and marriage to her and she'd tell him her secret. She would. But he doesn't respond to her opening.

"Maybe someday, after several months, we can be friends."

"I love you, Juliet. Remember that. Maybe not enough. Maybe in a small compartment instead of my entire life. Maybe not how you wanted, but what I knew of you, what you gave me I loved. You. Have. Been. Loved," he says each word distinct. Then his voice catches. "And this," he nods at the bed, the neat kitchen counter, the TV and finally her, still huddled with the bedspread, "was the highlight of my week. When I was most me." He stands up. "I'm always here for you, if you need me."

In the past, that would have felt like sufficient security and kindness. But now Juliet sees Tom returning to

202

his doctor role. Sure enough, he slides on his trousers, and shirt, rushing his arms into his lab coat.

He leans down and kisses her forehead with the same automatic kiss he would plant when saying goodnight to a child.

She doesn't cry after he leaves. Instead, she dresses and stuffs a drawstring garbage bag with the take-out boxes, a carton of cream, a dried apple, and outdated yogurt from the fridge. She unhooks the lobster clasp of her gold chain and releases it into the white plastic watching it slink into the remnants of their last dinner. Then she ties the drawstrings tightly, locks the door, and heaves the white bag into the container in the alley as she strides to her car.

SHE TAKES A detour on the way home and stops at the trailer park. She parks the car while her iPod plays Gershwin's *Porgy and Bess*. Shadows of Mom and Joey move on the window shades. They sit at opposite ends of the sofa watching TV. The sides of Joey's face jiggle and then Mom turns toward him and laughs. Juliet can't hear the laughter. She only sees her mom's black silhouette. Mom opens her mouth wide, her throat trembles. Then, she pushes herself from the couch and wobbles, knees hurting, into the kitchen. She disappears, the light goes on above the sink and, a few minutes later, the shadow of Mom returns to the living room with two cans. The dark silhouette that is her mother, not flesh and blood but one-dimensional, shifts on the window shade.

Mom stops in front of the specter of Joey, hands him the can and then toddles the few additional feet to her side of the sofa. She faces the parking lot, but in the darkness, with the car's lights turned off, there's no way she can know that her daughter sits there. The blobby amorphous form that is Mom, settles back down on the sofa. Juliet considers knocking on the door and joining them. Maybe she, too, could drink from one of the cans. Beer? Pop? Maybe she wouldn't feel left out.

Mom nestles into the cushions, her shoulders form a soft cave for her body. They sit there side by side. Not talking. Watching a program together, their shadow selves content.

Juliet arrives home before Dan and stands under the shower draining away the sweat, the scent, and sense of Tom's touches. Tears merge with water running down her face when she reviews, not only the years of making love, of kindness, of laughter and caring, but also the hopes that she held when they fell in love. She would risk opening up and telling him about the rape, maybe when they moved into the apartment, maybe when he left his wife, maybe when she left Dan, maybe when they were married. The hoped for maybes were merely ramparts for her shame and a soothing narrative so she could live with lies. Maybe someday, she'd be known. Maybe someday she'd no longer be alone. That illusion preserved the myth of her ultimate integrity. All the maybes are now played out and she's left with this shower, this hot water beating her curly hair, shoulders, breasts slightly damaged, Pilates trimmed stomach, and thighs while the shadows of Mom and Joey continue to watch TV.

By the time she gets out of the shower and puts on pajamas, Dan is home. She kisses him, the same perfunctory, almost absent-minded kiss that Tom gave her, and she smells the musk of another woman. His voice is as mechanical as her kiss when he asks her how her staff meeting was.

"I'm not going anymore. That's my last one."

"What? How come?" His eyes are wide.

She's at the moment that she's feared. The easiest thing to do is tell another glib lie. Her heart pounds. Light seems to tunnel so the edges of her vision narrow. When she inhales, her chest rises. It's now. "There're a lot of things going on we need to discuss," Juliet clears her throat.

Her distant, forced calm sends trickles up his spine.

He places his thumb in his pocket, his fingers splayed on the outside of his leg, a gesture that he does when he's feeling insecure.

"I don't know where to start."

He sits down, places his elbows on his knees and turns toward her. Her hair is still damp, a ribbed white towel draped over her shoulders. He shrugs waiting for her to begin this forced discussion.

She licks her lips and then gets herself a glass of water. "You want some?" she calls.

"No."

She stalls, she wanted to do this, but hadn't considered how to start. Juliet stands at the edge of a cliff without a strategy.

"We need, I need to figure out where *we're* going to know where *I'm* going."

He squints at her. "What are you talking about? The lottery money?"

She sits next to him, her glass already frosty under her fingertips. "There're things about me that I've never told you, never told anyone and I'm tired of living unknown. And we, we've built our lives together, we have a family together, all this," she nods at the walls of the room expanding her motions in such a way to encompass the universe of their house. "So I thought I'd try to tell you..." Juliet reaches her hand to hold his. Her hand is so chilled, the warmth of his palm, and enfolding chunky fingers reassure her. She starts by telling him that she went to the trailer, well, not the trailer but the woods near it. And she tells him about the rape, --pressing, gripping his

205

fingers, her eyes seeing Joey tied to a tree, -- the three men, and how they hurt her. She sits beside Dan staring at the carpet, clutching his hand. He doesn't move. She uses clinical terms. Penis. Vagina. Breast. Forced penetration. First Degree Child abuse. Her voice is so soft he leans toward her.

She tells him of the pact she and Joey made.

Color slowly drains from his face. Touchier lamps spread ovals on the ceiling that drip to the tops of the walls.

She describes years of shame and disgust and thinking that it was her fault, her shame. She tries to describe the nightmarish feeling that it would never end, that they would never go away, that the boys poking her, pulling her, forcing themselves inside her would continue forever. There must have been a reason that that she was targeted. Something about her. Something wrong with her. She settled on her poverty.

After she tells Dan, still staring at the carpet, her only recognition of him the sweat building in his palm, she turns to him and says, "I've never told anyone. I've never said any of this ever. I never even tried." That's when she notices how sickly he looks as they sit in their white living room, the cushions providing splotches of color.

By then his head is back on the couch and a tear trickles down his face. *He loves me. I should have done this years ago.*

"My poor Juliet." He blinks, shuts his eyes trying to sort out the conflicting thoughts. "Why are you telling me now?" The mucus in his throat blurs his words.

This might have been a gift after they got engaged or after they were married. But now it's a confession of years of betrayal because he was blind to a crucial fact affecting them all, hanging like a powerful, but invisible

206

magnet pulling each day, each love making session, each moment of happiness or sorrow.

"I couldn't tell you because that would make it seem more real. Someone else would know and I couldn't hide it from myself. I pretended it never happened."

"Each time we made love, specters were with you, with us, and I didn't even know so I couldn't even fight them." He whispers, then shakes his head slowly from side to side as the reality becomes clear.

"Yes." Juliet pulls the cream colored afghan around her.

They're quiet, not sure where to go next. Then he says, "It explains so much."

"You're right. We've both made accommodations to my omission. You, too."

He looks down. She considers confronting him about the woman she smells on him, but thinks that would be her using offense as a defense. And she can't defend herself.

He nods at her. His face flushed with fury. "So where does Tom fit in?"

Her heart pounds so loudly he must hear it. The rug she studies is a Persian carpet she bought because the soft beiges and subtle browns meld into the maple floor, indistinguishable, unnoticeable.

"You think I haven't known? Of course I have. I'm not that obtuse."

She sums it up. "He doesn't know. I never told Tom. I saw him for the last time tonight. What about the woman I smell on you, who I don't even know and can't fathom."

He doesn't answer.

"Revenge fucking? Friend with benefits? Commercial sex partner? Love affair? What?"

"You list it so casually and easily."

"I want, we need to figure out where we're going to go from here. Can we go together? WE can build a new life together, or new lives apart.  WE can do what we want. If we can figure out what we want."

"That's the hard part."

"So who is she, what is she to you?"

"Through the years it's been all of the above," he releases her hand.  She'd been holding his fingers so tight they're slightly stiff now.

"And this one?"

"I can't believe we're talking about this. Like this," he whispers, disappointment in his voice.

"What do you mean?"

"So controlled, so dispassionate.  I don't know if it's a testament to our friendship and understanding or proof of how done we are."

"I don't know either."  Juliet picks up her water from the Noguchi table.  "But I wish you well. Separate from me. I don't blame you.  I blame me. A lack of courage or immaturity. Or denial," she shrugs.  "I don't know."

"You never know anybody, do you?" Weariness fills his voice.

"Not unless they want you to. I want you to know me." *It's my only chance. It's so terrifying.*

He nods. "Did you end it with Tom? Or did he?"

"I did."

"Why?"

"Because we weren't going anywhere and the continuance of our secret was part of why I don't like myself, continuing the self loathing since that incident, since my childhood." She leans back and puts her palms on her thighs.  "And why now?  I don't know. I think I feel safe enough to deal with what happened to me.  I think I feel safe enough to finally tell you, tell someone."

He squints at her.  "The lottery money?"

"Maybe.  I'll be okay financially no matter what happens, I guess." She sips from the water, and says with a sense of surprise and awe, "You know, I thought I was raped because I was poor. Stupid, I know. And blamed my Mom. Blamed our poverty. That's why, really, I've been so distant from my family. But now, I know it was bad luck, and bad people. I'm safe enough, secure enough to do something about it." Her head tilts, she tells him simultaneously to realizing herself. It's the first time that she says words that weren't rehearsed. "It never was really about money. I just thought it was. I just realized this second."

"Why me?"

"Who better than you? I want someone to know me, love me," her voice catches with tears, "I hope it's you. My husband, the father of my children? I love you. You, us, is the best I've got. Best in my life. It's late, I know, but I'm trying to set things right." She clears her throat. "Is it too late?"

He clamps his eyes shut. His head tilts on the sofa back, his neck has thickened through the years, dewlaps adding the girth.

"You weren't, aren't culpable, except, I don't know," she shakes her head. "I guess the distance between us was okay because you never forced the issue. You never said, hey there seems to be a veil between us, an absence."

"No. I made accommodations. I thought that's who you were…. obsessive about getting things right. The complete nurse."

She laughs. "Being a nurse was an easy and perfect disguise. So easy to hide in procedures."

"Remember, I kept asking, in the beginning, was there something else you wanted me to do? Anything. I'd do anything." He turns to her, his eyes opaquely blue, not like the sky, but a vague blue not grey enough to be

209

startling. "I tried everything. And it got better, but it wasn't, I don't know, ever free and easy.  It was always work."

"Yes."

"Was it different with Tom?"

She shuts her eyes. "Different, but the vague visions were always present."

"It was you. Always you. I don't know if this is good news or bad."  He sits back and then says to the ceiling, almost as if she isn't there, isn't even necessary, "Strange, isn't it, that new information sheds light so history is changed." Then, tentatively, he reaches for her hand.

## Twenty

*The rich are always going to say that, you know, just give us more money and we'll go out and spend more and then it will all trickle down to the rest of you. But that has not worked the last 10 years, and I hope the American public is catching                                                                on.*
Warren Buffet

*THE LOTTERY HAS changed everything,* Juliet thinks. *I'm starting over as though I'm a nine-year-old girl in a middle-aged woman's body. A little girl grown old. A grown-up little girl. I'm no longer a poor little girl, but a rich one with the wisdom and the folly of all the years.* Juliet stops her thoughts. *That's all the money changed, really. I have money now. I'm still that same nine year-old.*

Juliet watches Dan standing in the line for beer at the Top of the Park. Her hair is damp from dancing and she gathers it to the top of her head, winds a band around it, and tightens the ponytail.

*Why me and not Joey?*

*I was lucky. Well, no. I had ambition born of fear, successful because of dutifulness rather than a passion. I dutifully did my homework. Biology was the forest encased in a safe place, nature with its orderly progression and wild serendipity to study and dissect. My counselor suggested I get a nursing degree at Washtenaw Community College. I could walk there from the trailer park if I had to. I didn't know what else to do. It was a way out.*

*"At the end of the two year degree, you'll have a job. We need nurses. And the pay is good," she said. A wage to support an apartment, maybe a condo. I could. So I did.*

*It wasn't luck. It was hard work. Determination. But isn't luck in that too? The luck to have the genes to be able to learn the material. Memorizing was easy for me. Joey, too. Larry, too. But they didn't use their own skills. Joey didn't even take his musical talent seriously.*

Dan leans over to place his order, while Juliet saves a small table. Lady Sunshine and the X Band have just finished their first set. *Honky Tonk Woman* plays through the loud speaker. "Here you go," Dan brings over two beers. "Look who I found." Marnie and Jim, Jeannie and Mark are with him.

JULIET DOESN'T BLAME herself for the rape. In the last five months, that blame slipped away on quiet toes. Nothing about her, not her curly hair, or tall size, or exploring the woods, made the rape happen. Three vicious teens took their rage, their power, their need to control out on her and Joey who were easy to victimize. They were children. Poor. She was a girl. It was simple.

But she can't figure out, begin to sort out, how she feels about Joey killing Stainface even in self-defense, even to protect her and Mom, and planting flowers on the spot in the forest as though she, no they, were buried there. No getting around that my little brother wouldn't eat anything but grilled cheese sandwiches for three years, and wanted to be called Joey-Boy after that kid on the Walton's, and slept with me every night for a year after our attack.

Slept with me and wet my bed. Our bed, really, I guess.

Each night, warm urine hit my thighs and woke me up. Each morning, I hissed at him to wear a diaper or those pull ups that Larry still wore. I was tired of being peed on.

I was afraid the kids at school would smell it.

I rose early to take a shower.

212

"Why does this room smell so bad," Mom screeched. She felt my bed. "You start back wetting the bed?" she narrowed her eyes at me in disbelief. "You waaaayyy too old for that. Maybe we better take you to the doctor."

I shot Joey a look.

"It was me. I had a nightmare and crawled into her bed. I wet it."

"Well, pull off those sheets and go wash them." Her fists were on her hips, legs spread wide as she shook her head of curls and growled, "What's wrong with you kids?"

Little Joey's skinny arms gathered the pee sheets into a crumbled ball.

"Luckily we have a washer and dryer right here," Mom forces open the bi-fold door, "Or I'd be pissed as hell at having to lug this mess to the Laundromat." The washer and dryer were recent purchases that had been on lay away for a year before they were delivered and installed.

Mom woke Joey for a few nights. Then she forgot. And he resumed peeing on me.

All night he clung to me.

But he kept our promise. We never talked about the forest.

So, while her friends talk about the next party at Marnie's, Rosie buying a condo in Naples, Sissy's foundation getting a major grant, Juliet watches Dan, in a conversation about U of M season tickets with Kevin.

The tune switches to *Hold on, I'm Coming*, and the smell of a cigarette drifts to her. Beer and cigarettes, the smell of her childhood home. Her house now has the aroma of various diffusers, Ylang Ylang and ginger in the bedroom, vanilla and lime in the kitchen, green tea in the living room, and almond in the linen closet.

I had the toughness not to remain that victimized little girl. Was it strength and determination? Or fear and anxiety? Doesn't matter. I did it.

Now, it's time to do this.

THE NEXT DAY, driving home from work, she calls Joey. The phone ringing, amplified by the Bluetooth speaker is louder than holding a receiver to her ear. She steers the car through the edge of town. Rush hour hasn't started so she glides through the synchronized green lights at 35 miles an hour.

"Heeeeyyy." His voice a husky whisper like she just woke him.

"Hi, Joey. You alone?"

"I don't know. Why?"

"I've been thinking, Joey, I want to tell Mom what happened."

He fumbles around, she hears the flick of a lighter, then a long hissing inhale. "Why you want that?"

"I've told Dan. It's done wonders for our marriage."

Joey snickers. "I bet. Now he's trying to make up to you for all your sexual pain. And you giving him all the chances he needs to figure out just how to do it, uh?"

She hears envy of her apparent success. "I'm trying to be closer with the important people in my life." She makes a right turn and arrows around the campus area, a cluster of restaurants, head shops, video and book stores. Now mostly empty of people. The students are gone for the summer.

"You didn't tell him…."

"That's your secret. Not mine."

"Why Mom need to feel bad about something else in her life, something she didn't even know happened? She'll be upset and guilty she didn't protect us."

White impatiens and fuchsia petunias blaze at the base of Bradford pear trees planted in cement creating a barrier between the stores bordered by sidewalk and cars.

"Don't you think sometimes people know without *knowing*? Sense things? Maybe parts of her life will be clarified."

"Clarified, uh? Sheeeet. Your life *clarified*? Knowing about Stainface *clarify* anything for you?"

"We all paid for decades." *PAID,* she thinks, *as though it has to do with money. Why do I see everything that way? SUFFER that's the word.*

He shucks air in between his teeth, a scraping sound of sorrow and exasperation.

"It explains things about you," she says softly to Joey.

"Reveals, maybe. But what the fuck does it *explain*?"

She's in front of her house now and pushes the button for the garage door on the roof of her car, absent-mindedly watching it slide open. Her car glides in. "Maybe why you're always high or stoned avoiding reality."

There's silence. "You're so wrong.  I'm that way because of what *he* did to us. US. He set me on a path and I'm too far along to jump to another."

"It's never to late to be who you want to be."

"I'm the world's most forgotten boy."

She hears him swallow.

"What you don't know is, I'd been smoking rock and after I beat him up, I stopped. Joined AA. Just ended it. Quit beer and pot too for about five years.  For a while Mom went with me.  I figured I was worth something since I'm an avenging angel."

Juliet closes the garage door while her car continues to run.

"Can I help, Joey?"

"Help me? Well, I could really use a new car."  He laughs. "Don't tell Mom."

"We haven't been loving since…"

"Mom didn't rape you. You ain't really good at compartmentalizing shit, are you?"

"I just stay away from everybody."

"Well then, you're telling her for you. Not for her. But you're an adult. You're not nine no more. Live with your decisions."

On the wall of the garage is a rack of hanging shovels, spades, leaf rakes, a coiled yellow extension cord, a scarecrow with a jaunty patched hat and silly smile that she put out each fall. The mix of oil and gas from the lawnmower, and the car's fumes shift around her. Maybe he's right.

"In AA they have a making amends step. It's more than an apology."

He inhales on his cigarette.

"The guideline is, you don't make amends to someone if making amends will hurt them. Then it's for you and that's selfish. Will telling her make the two of you close? Help her in any way?"

Juliet turns off the car, switches the phone to mobile, opens the car door, and says, "I'll think about it."

It's worked with Dan. Yes, there're resentments, memories that return and, as they replay them, they see each other's lies and are plagued. It's not always pretty, and certainly not the Hallmark card life Juliet wanted, but they remake the narrative of their lives, and learn from each other. She looks forward to making dinner, and Dan comes home. On time. They tell each other their day. It's not a big deal, really, so simple, really. The minutia, the ordinariness of their work, the people they interact with, their children, sometimes calling or Skyping them for a family conversation. They lie in bed, talk, make love, as he explores her body with his new knowledge, learning ways to enjoy each other.

*I'm not alone. The last time I felt close like this was with Joey and Mom and Larry. Before. In spite of the pee, Joey sleeping with me. Even though neither one of us were even conscious. Maybe that's what was happening in another way with Tom and even Dan. I just wanted the cuddling, certainly not the sex with all the accompanying images, or an intimate relationship with the pitfalls of secrets, compromises and loss.*

"Whatever, Juju. You've always been on your own agenda. Regardless of us. This time around, develop some loyalty."

"I'm working on being that person I want to be."

"Yeah. Riiiight. Don't make that at our expense."

She realizes how far apart they are.

Click.

He's hung up.

She stands in the garage, the cell phone in her hand, slides her purse on her shoulder, and then walks inside to start cooking.


DINNER IS OVER, and Dan stretches out on the chaise, still sipping iced herbal tea. Fireflies wink sporadically in the garden.

"Come and sit with me." He pats the arm of the chaise.

Juliet lies against his chest. The stubble of his chin grazes her temple. "You smell good," he tells her as she grabs both of his hands. "The lemony smell of you. Always fresh."

"I feel your heart beating against me."

"Good. That means I'm alive," he laughs.

"Thank God we are," Juliet says. At first it's a nonchalant quip, matching his, but then she hears her own words from a different vantage point. "I'm so glad that we're alive to get here, to arrive where we are right now."

217

"Yes," he whispers into her ear and brushes the tip of it with his lips. "To understand the story we've been living and get to know each other."

They listen to each other's hearts and breath. Outside a Morning Dove coos its last goodnight. Or is it the first good morning?

"And rich. We're so lucky." He hugs her close so she knows he's not simply talking about the lottery win.

After she tells him about her conversation with Joey, she asks, "What do you think I should do about Mom, my family?"

"You want to get closer, and you want to help them. And you want to continue healing yourself. Three things. But really, darling, Joey may be right. How would telling your Mom help? You think it'll help your relationship like it's helped ours. She can't do anything about it now." He sips from his tea, offering her some. "Why don't you try other ways to help her...? Every time I see her, she seems in pain."

"Pain?"

"Always with her hand on her low back, limping. You don't notice?"

"I notice that beer in her hand."

"Maybe she's self-medicating. Why don't you hang out with her? Do things. Go for lunch and a movie, a massage, get your hair done, buy her some clothes. You know. Girly things. Fun things. The fun things that money buys. Bet she'd love that. "

Why hadn't she thought of that? It's so simple. She has to get over her slight embarrassment of being with a mom who wears baggy clothes that are twenty years old, some of which are stained.

"You think she'd feel criticized?"

He chuckles. "That's you criticizing her."

"Mom doesn't like change."

"Don't know until you try. They sure could use a car that works and isn't half the time in the shop or waiting for one of them to get around to fix it. And with the way prices are, a gas credit card."

THAT NIGHT, AFTER they're in bed, Dan puts his hand on her hip. It's his customary way to initiate sex. At his request, she has told him everything she can remember about the rape. She talked turned away from him with his arms tightly clasped around her as though preventing a fall from grace. He listened. Asked questions. His heart raced against her back, his tears dripped on her shoulder blades. Then, Dan went over her body, kissing her gently, asking her body to forgive men. Tears struggled down her cheeks. Slowly, as the weeks passed, the smashed pictures faded away.

She thought of other things when they made love. She needed eggbeaters and Lactaid milk, to schedule training for her nurses in the new software, to try the recipe for asparagus and shiitakes for the next party. Ridiculous minutia. Anything but his lips surrounding her nipple, his fingers nestled in the groove between her legs. He misread her moistness for readiness, but it was, she knew, beyond her control. Now she wants him, but for years it was simply her body's way to predict and prepare for the intrusion that would soon follow.

"So do you come, or do you fake it?"

She held her breath, pressing her lips together. How do you forgive a spouse for lying every time you make love? And isn't a feigned orgasm, a lie?

"We're already at an edge here. There's nowhere to go but better," he said.

"I fake it. I've come, though, but with myself."

As if he were trying to figure out what to say next, his hand, almost absentmindedly, almost mechanically, stroked her hip, her thigh, and then back to her waist, as she lay on her side facing him. "Don't fake anymore. I'll never know what works. And sex isn't just about the climax."

She wet her lower lip, nodded, and inched toward him for a kiss. How did he know all this?

Sometimes, now, if she went through a series of fantasies, the same fantasies she used when she masturbated, she could come with him. That was recent. But she wasn't with him, she was with a scenario of her own control.

SO THIS NIGHT, his hand is on her hip, which he uses to pull her toward him. She wants to get through the sex so they can cuddle. Should she tell him? Or would that destroy his earnestness to please her?

"Don't close your eyes," he says. The aroma of Ylang ylang coasts from the bedside table.

She notices the fringe of lashes on his lids, a few of them white. Freckles beside his eyes. Beyond him, the sage walls of the bedroom, the color of a grayed spring. He kisses her, licks her, travels down her collarbone, sternum, breast, nipples. His silky hair tickles the flesh surrounding her navel.

When he is inside her, she closes her eyes. He kisses her lids and whispers, "Open your eyes."

Their eyes link.

"It's me, Dan. Hello, Juliet."

They move together leisurely, eyes fastened. "I never noticed the slight yellow flecks in your eyes before, the way they're rimmed with grey." He shakes his head, stops rocking and examines her face, his palms on either side of her cheeks. "Aah, Juliet, you're so dear to me. My person, my companion."

They continue their slow waltz.

"You're so sweet. Really very sweet." He notices her moist eyes, his voice fatherly.

It's as if she sees him for the first time. Dan. Her Dan. The person who has been with her these years. All these years. Her son has Dan's mouth, the hesitant smile that shuffles its way to a grin. Her daughter has his quickly tapered fingers, thick where they meet the palm. As they rock together, eyes joined, a new emotion saturates her, amorphous and soft, like a sheet of silk, or the settling of a warm breeze that changes everything, but is barely perceptible.

Does he feel this sense of oneness, their connection, at last united?

She stares into his eyes.

Locked together, they continue their dawdling rhythm.

"Do you feel it too?" she whispers, afraid if she speaks it will infringe on the enchantment.

His brows lift slightly, as he whispers, "Yes. We're together."

AFTERWARD, AFTER THEIR speed became insistent and they break the spell for the joy of orgasm, and then stir it up again until they're spent, she asks, "So that's the sex that is even better than cuddling?"

Dan laughs and pulls her on top of him, his hands on the cheeks of her ass, drawing her closer as if to obliterate the separation of their skins.

"I didn't know that could happen. We were... some place else," Juliet's hair brushes his chest.

"In the world we made together. A separate oasis."

Out of the blue, she guesses it's out of the blue, "I'm so lucky. Ahhh. Sex and money." She counts the ways.

"Two ways to get happiness," he says.

"I'll take that sex over money anytime," she says.

221

He laughs.

Immediately before she drifts to sleep, she wonders if another woman showed him that spiritual side to sex and taught him how to get there, or if he stumbled on it that night. The answer, she realizes, is in what wasn't said. He would have told her that he, too, never experienced it. They promised each other no lies, not even little white ones. In her mind, Juliet thanks her, this anonymous other woman who taught Dan how to make sex so beautiful. She whispers, but he's already asleep, "Thank you, Dan. Thank you for showing me pleasure with you."

LATER THAT WEEK, Juliet takes Mom to Red Lobster. Mom wears bell-bottom jeans that were once fashionable, but now emphasize her spreading hips and bulging stomach. She quit hiding the gray in her hair and thin curls fluff around her head sporadically.

When did she get so pallid? Weren't her eyes a deep brown? Age spots dot her hands and her forearms, the knots of veins and stripes of tendons visible under powdery skin. Yet Juliet is touched by her attempts to make this festive. She penciled in dark eyebrows, but the freshly applied too dark lipstick makes her lips appear shocking slits in a pale face.

Mom sits down, places the napkin on her lap, and giggles. "Oh, this is my favorite restaurant. And yours too."

"Mine?"

Mom lifts her stiff eyebrows, "Yeaaah. Useta be, anyway. Don't you remember your little song? *I love popcorn. And I love shrimp. But most of all I love... popcorn shrimp!*" Mom wags her head with each word as she chants the melody. "I thought you were so cute and the song so clever you should be doing a TV advertisement," she giggles. "'Course that was a long time ago." Mom looks

222

at the daughter sitting across from her. The imperceptible make-up applied so subtly that no one would notice the brushed brows, the matte eye shadow. Even her lipstick appears to be naturally glistening lips. Mom tilts her head. Her daughter is so beautiful.  So perfect. Of course she's rich now, it's easier to provide a smooth veneer of comfort and happiness.  But even before the lottery, Juliet was always faultless.

Juliet doesn't completely understand why, her eyes fill. "I had forgotten."

"You were such a sweet girl, so happy.  I remember how you loved that backpack, what was the picture on it? Ah yeah, Josie and the Pussycats. Remember?" Mom's brows lift with the memory of Juliet's happiness when she brought it home. Then Mom's overly red lips turn down. "You were so sad when you lost it, you didn't seem the same... as though you didn't recognize yourself anymore."

*I was right.  She knows without knowing,* Juliet thinks.

The waitress arrives.  "Here're some of our famous rolls. Ya'll want something to drink, or are you ready to order?" The aromas of yeast and cheese greet them.

Mom says, "I'll have that crunchy popcorn shrimp."

"Me, too," Juliet giggles, and picks up her glass. "To a celebration of old times.  Before I lost Josie." *Before I lost Josie.* Her words ring in her ears.

Mom clicks her clear glass against her daughter's. "You kinda found her again. With those Christmas cookie gals.  And winning that lottery is better than that raggedy backpack. By a long shot," she laughs.

"I never thought of the Christmas cookie club as a girl gang, but you're right.  Like the Pussycats with adult craziness, disagreements, and fun, but like the Pussycats relying on each other." Juliet's mind races, she'd give up the millions to redo that fateful afternoon when she lost

Josie. *But now, right now, I'm happy. How can I have regrets? I wouldn't redo anything because then I wouldn't be where I am, who I am.*

"Josie and the pussycats are better than the lottery, Mom."

Juliet watches Mom's thoughts, unspoken and maybe even unrecognized, dance across her mom's eyes. Then Mom says, "People are always more important than anything." She flicks her fingers together as though feeling the air like a material, the weight of dust and time passing.

The waitress brings their popcorn shrimp. Juliet picks one up and pops it in her mouth. "Tastes just like I remembered!" and then she swishes it in the cocktail sauce, "Even better with a little spice."

Mom laughs.

"I love you, Mom," Juliet says, another shrimp between her fingers.

"I've been waiting a long time to hear you say that again." Their eyes meet. They stop in mid gesture, Juliet holds the shrimp, and her mom holds a bottle of ketchup. And then, almost as though to turn the sentiment into something commonplace between them, her mom squeezes ketchup on her curly fries and salts it. "But you were off doing your own thing, your life. Way I figure is, children are more important to their parents than the parents are to their kids."

They're quiet as they concentrate on the shrimp and coleslaw, Juliet considering Mom's statement. Then Mom says, "We haven't done this....ever. The lottery has changed you."

"Well, it gave me a safety net to risk making changes in my life. I've been thinking about my family, you. What would you want? This money is a blessing. Would you like a new house?"

224

Mom places her palms on the edge of the table and pushes against the seat back. "Leave where I've been living for over thirty years?"

"There're condos right around the corner. You wouldn't have to leave this neighborhood. Still be able to walk here."

Mom concentrates on her fries, shaking her head back and forth.

"What about a new trailer? Would you like a new one, on the same lot?"

She squinches up her eyes, chewing her fries. "I don't know." She picks up a shrimp. "Sounds like a lot of work. How would all our stuff look in a new trailer? It wouldn't feel like home anymore. I like living with all those memories of you kids when you were in your playpens, and coloring on our table, and playing Barbie. All those faded drawings you kids did are on the wall. Besides, I lived there with your father."

"Well, we could frame our paintings and reupholster the furniture. I mean, if you would like to spruce it up, we can do it. We can hire people to do all the work."

"I can't say that trailer was ever my dream, but..." Mom shrugs. "It suits me now, I belong there. It's who I am. It's home."

"Think about it. Check out those new condos."

"You know, we all wish you had played the lottery with us. I guess when your friends started doing it, it was okay. When it was just ole us, well...." She examines her plate hunting for the next morsel, but puts her fork down, and picks up a roll. "Ah well," she sighs. "It is what it is. But no. I don't want to move. That's what you wanted. And you did it. Don't think I'd be any happier someplace else. I always bring me and all my little joys and sorrows wherever I go."

"It's whatever you want, Mom. You. But hey, how 'bout we have a little fun with my lucky money today. Maybe we could go on a shopping spree... we haven't done that since you took me school shopping at Meijer's. Remember?" Juliet was six, too young, then, to understand the difference between buying clothes at Meijer's and at the Mall. Was the pleasure any less? "It was so exciting. Remember that little granny dress, with the long skirt."

"I had to sneak it out of your room to wash it!" Mom laughs.

"Except this time it'll be on me for you! And we won't have to worry about prices! And we can go anywhere you want... the Mall? Downtown? Target?"

Juliet watches as her Mom's eyes light up. "I haven't bought new clothes, since I got on social security."

"Then how 'bout a movie?"

"What is this, some kind of late Mother's Day? What am I, Queen for a Day?"

"You deserve it. Maybe you'll be Queen for a Day once a month, how's that? Mom." Juliet places her hand on her mom's. "I realized I want to spend more time with you and use some of this money to help my family. And we need to do something about that hip pain that keeps bothering you. After all...." She lets the sentence trickle away. She thinks of saying, *you helped me out when you could, as much as you could*. And she thinks about saying *you're my family after all*. And she thinks about saying *and I love you*.

At last she settles on, "Sometimes spending money is fun." Juliet grins. "And I guess, I'm finally growing up."

## Twenty-one

*After winning the lottery:*
- *1% have plastic surgery*
- *3% move kids to private schools*
- *12% join health clubs*
- *32% gain weight*
- *44% have spent it all after 5 years*

"SO. TAYLOR. HOW'RE you doing?" Rosie's whisper indicates she's asking about the most recent divorce settlement that they sent. But, in truth, she needs to talk with someone. She and Kevin have just had a fight. She left his office, like the dismissed help she once was. Since, she's gone out of her way for Taylor, she hoped Taylor might help her. She calls Taylor, "Hey, whatcha doing? Are you busy?"

Taylor is shopping before going to get a facial, would Rosie want to come?

Rosie makes a mistake and opens the conversation as they're walking into Sixteen Hands to examine the jewelry. She asks how Taylor likes the settlement. It's so much easier to be Rosie the paralegal, than Rosie the pregnant woman whose husband is furious.

"Okay," Taylor rocks back on her heels, crosses her arms. Her dangling earrings jingle as she moves. She stands in front of a case of ceramic salt and peppershakers decorated in cheery colors. "I guess that's the best we can do." Taylor exhales with exasperation. "That and the civil suit we'll file against him. Fucking bastard."

"Soon this will be over. You can get on with your life."

Taylor runs her fingers through her red hair, her earrings tinkling like tiny sharp bells. "That's what I thought when I signed that stupid settlement back in March. I had a month, one fucking month, of freedom from him and poverty." She crosses her arms, shakes her head, her fury only slightly dimmed to vexation. Then she realizes how enraged she's being. "I don't mean for you to get the brunt of this. I know you've done what you can. No one can beat Rick. His narcissistic evil wins in the end."

"You've won. You just don't see that yet." Rosie imagines for a moment Kevin leaving her, Kevin taking half of her lottery money and leaving her with two kids. But in this case, it would be her fault. And the lottery money is a marital asset.

"You sound like Allie." They rally a laugh, but both are rueful rather than joyful. They move to a rack of scarves. Taylor examines an orange one with tangerine and sky colors worked in felted concentric circles.

"That would go soooo great with your hair and that tanzanite," Rosie says while fingering a scarf that is hand-painted deer prancing among silk dragonflies in red and deep purple.

"Gorgeous with your long neck, Rosie," Taylor encourages.

"Sooooo. Girlfriend scarves," Rosie trills. She doesn't want to damage the moment by talking about her problems. She'll bask in the comradeship of buying things, something she and Taylor do oh soooo well.

When they finish purchasing the dual scarves and stride once again down Main Street toward their respective cars, Rosie asks, "Hey. Did you decide about Naples? We're leaving in three weeks. Got plenty of room." Rosie shifts her packages. "Maybe if you get away from here, you'll feel better. After all, you're a millionaire. You've got two great kids. You're beautiful and sexy. You've been given a new

228

life, and scads of money while you're still young enough to enjoy it. Forget Rick. Count your blessings and be happy." She tells herself this, too.

How can Taylor just forget all the horrible things Rick did? Never. Never. "No. The kids are going to camp in a few weeks. Think I'll enjoy being alone."

"Well, if you change your mind, last minute is okay, too," Rosie smiles. "We'd love to have you and there's a lively social scene. We know the owner of a jazz bar, maybe you could start singing."

"Maybe..." Taylor placates Rosie who tries hard to make it right when it can't be. Not ever.

Rosie realizes she can't tell Taylor about the pregnancy, not then anyway. Shopping was just what she needed.

In her car, she dumps her purse on the passenger seat next to her and she hears Jeannie calling. "Rosie? Rosie? Is that you? Hellooooo. Hellooooo. Are you okay?"

Rosie picks up the phone, "Jeannie. Ohmigod, how are you?"

"You called me?" Jeannie's voice is confused.

Rosie had pocket-dialed Jeannie, or rather, purse-dialed her. *But maybe that's a sign that Jeannie is the person I need to talk to. After all, she used to be my closest friend.* Rosie inhales, "Jeannie, are you free? I mean can we get together?" Too early for lunch, and she's already gone shopping. She remembers Jeannie's excited grin taking the kayak out in the Caribbean and how she and Jeannie and Sue used to float down the Huron, "Maybe we can go for a canoe ride or something and talk? Please."

There's a beat of silence on Jeannie's end and then a cautious and drawn out, "A canoe ride? Okay." She stretches the word, confusion still in her voice. "It's a beautiful day. I'll meet you at the livery at Gallup in half an hour, is that good?"

"Fabulous. Thanks."

Rosie picks up sandwiches and Cokes, stuffs them in the Igloo that's always in the trunk of her car, and has paid for a canoe by the time Jeannie arrives. They put on the orange life jackets and push into the black water.

There is not much wind, the forest calm on either side of the river. Ducklings chase their mothers. Shadows of fish glide in the water. As soon as the current carries them, Jeannie asks, "What's up, Rosie? What's going on?"

"You know me well." Rosie is not sure how to broach the subject and enjoys donating her control to the river's current. "I'm pregnant."

"Oh." Jeannie strokes the water, drops flick in the sun, "But I can't read you. Is this good news? Are congratulations in order?"

"For me, but not for Kevin." As she pulls the water she relays the conversation with Kevin. Rosie hadn't consciously recalled, but this conversation, this year with a second pregnancy between these two friends who have been so tenuous, and estranged, is a repeat of many conversations they had years ago, before Ben, when Rosie wanted to get pregnant and Kevin didn't want more children. Some things don't change. Some issues return over again in different guises. "Kevin has been dreaming boats. Retirement. Cruising around the world. You remember. He never wanted another set of kids. One was more than enough."

They're comfortable talking, sliding into familiar places, as their oars hit the water simultaneously. They pull to a small island and climb up the short bank to eat.

"You're sort of headstrong, Rosie. You do what you want and then mop up the consequences in such a charming way you're always forgiven." Jeannie hesitates, and adds, "Or almost forgiven."

"But the relationship pays the price." Rosie meets Jeannie's eyes and they both know they're talking about Rosie's betrayal of Jeannie. "Do I do that, Jeannie? Betray the ones I love the most? You? Kevin?"

"You do what *you* want to do. You don't confront if your wishes clash with the people you love. That's the dishonesty. The betrayal. You lie about yourself by omission."

Rosie nods, wraps her arms around her knees. "That's true. I'm too afraid of being rejected and inadvertently make it more likely."

"You'll turn yourself into a pretzel and an exemplar of efficiency trying to make everyone happy," Jeannie comments, starring at the diamonds glittering on the water. "So now what? You and Kevin are in different places in your lives. I guess that's the real problem with your age difference. He's ready to retire and you're still nest building."

Rosie laughs. "I've always wanted lots of children. I felt so alone being an only child," she sighs. "Like you. With all that unrelenting attention on me. Didn't you hate it?"

"I wanted lots of kids too. It didn't happen." Jeannie chuckles, "Thank God for my sweet Sara. My one flower." She stuffs the rest of the sandwich in a bag then interlaces her fingers and wraps them around her knees.

"I guess Kevin and I both have to imagine what we want and figure out how to get it."

"Maybe you could spend the next five years floating around the world on that yacht he wants so badly. Home school Ben, like he suggested. Then settle someplace during the school year. There're ways. You'll figure it out if you pull together."

"Thanks," Rosie says.

"For what?"

Rosie doesn't answer, but drinks her soda. "Soooo what have you decided about the dealership?" Rosie asks.

Jeannie knows she's asking partly because of Sue, and partly because she wants to turn the attention away from her. "Still trying to figure that out." Jeannie wants to coast over the bombs ticking in their knowledge of each other that can easily destroy this renewed closeness.

"Perfect opportunity for you to get revenge on Sue." Rosie stares at the opposite shore. Above the thick forest a cedar house with windows that span the first floor and peak on the second stretches across the top of the hill. Below is a boathouse, several canoes, kayaks, and rowboats rock gently by the dock.

Jeannie reviews how to respond.

Rosie brings her thick auburn brows together, narrowing her eyes. "Soooo, since Ricardo, maybe you see things differently. Have you told Mark about him yet?"

Jeannie shivers. A breeze picks up, and she pushes her straw hat tighter on her head. "Nothing really happened with Ricardo. Nothing," she lies. "And my decision about the dealership will be what's best for me and my family. But you're right, the flirtation with Ricardo opened a window into understanding Sue and my dad." She thinks, but doesn't say, *However, Sue was one of a long line of dalliances. Ricardo was a one-time event. But ethical issues of adultery don't disappear because of this distinction. Ricardo didn't have the permanent effects of Sue. Am I lying to myself? Rosie is the only one who knows about my affair with Ricardo—and I doubt she believes it was only a flirtation.*

"Good. So you've forgiven her? Them?"

"I've forgiven you, Rosie. I understand the terrible position you were in." Jeannie faces her friend, shakes her head as sorrow fills her eyes. A red wing blackbird flies so close to them that they see the glitter of his eye, the bright ribbons on his wing a blur.

As though thinking the same thought, they stand and stretch, ready to launch the canoe. Before they get in, Jeannie asks Rosie, "What would you have done if you were me?"

Rosie's voice is soft and tender. "I don't know. I'm soooo glad I wasn't in your position. All that pain and betrayal."

"Thank you, Rosie. Thank you." She turns to hug her friend. She knows she has nothing to fear from Rosie.

"No easy answers sometime, uh?" Rosie says. "And winning the lottery doesn't solve them."

"It makes it easier though, uh?"

Jeannie's arms raise and descend gently on Rosie's shoulders. They draw each other close, knocking off Jeannie's hat, which she presses back on. They push the canoe into the river. The splashing water, humming crickets, in the lazy current accompany their thoughts.

## Twenty-two

*In the year 2000, 300,000 deaths were attributed to obesity, 291,000 deaths were due to poverty and income inequality.*

AFTER THE CANOE ride with Rosie, Jeannie knows she has to make a decision. She can't go back and forth.

*Who am I, I don't even know anymore?*

She learned how easy it is to let immediate desires carry you to a place where you don't like yourself. And get stuck with sin. The magic from her numbers winning the lottery has washed away her moorings.

*Who was I before? Before Sue and my father. Before that betrayal.* She lies in *Savasana* concentrating on inhaling slowly. Expanding her ribs. Counting to 6. Then holding her air in. Then letting it out as she counts to 8. Simply count. Simply breathe.

Truth is, she feels peaceful lying here, in the now. But there're limits to the now. It avoids how the present determines the future. Because she knows, (all she has to do is look at her father) everyone pays in the present for the mistakes, the foibles, and the pathology of the past.

*We make a new future with each now. Like it or not. So we can't just ride in the now without thinking about the future we form.*

*I have to do something, but I don't know what is the something I have to do.*

She tells herself: *It's my decision. Not what I'm supposed to do, but my desire.*

But she doesn't know any more. She distrusts her own desires.

As though all of them are evil and sinful.

No.

235

Breathe in two three four five six seven. Stay full. Exhale two three four five six seven eight nine. Stay empty. Empty. Start again and again. Until sometime there is the last breath. Jeannie wonders, *Will I know it when it's here? Or is it just the final one and important because none follow?*

Having an affair was so much easier than this choice. Maybe it even occurred as distraction. Easier to stay up writing on the Internet than making a decision. Jeannie can't predict or trust anything because anything can happen. It's all crazy luck.

If she doesn't make up her mind the dealership drifts. Even now they ask what her plans are. Their lives hang on her verdict. They treat her as though she's the boss, but she doesn't do the boss things: Provide a consistent marketing plan. Go over the sales charts. Network. Hang out after work. She doesn't even go there every day. Sue's sales continue to be stellar, she notices, scanning the report. But she doesn't get excited. With confusion and hope in his eyes, Kurt asks about her father. He figures her distraction is a result of concerns about her Dad. Jay shoves sales reports with a wide smile at the positive news.

"Whaddya think?" he asks with a gleam on his forehead.

Preoccupied, Jeannie answers, "Looks good." Then, she musters earnest praise, "The internet promotion seems to be working. The industry is turning around and we're helping that happen." She shuffles through disinterest to maintain contact so a resolution isn't an inadvertent result of inattention. And returns to the bliss of the now.

Maybe the answer is in her lacks. Like the final breathe. Yes.

*Do I want to run the dealership? Do I want to run a yoga studio? Do I want to run anything? Has winning the lottery robbed me of my passion, but quickened my entitlement and a belief in my own magic and lust?*

She doesn't want to hurt people. She already hurt Ricardo. She doesn't want to damage her father's legacy or his business by indecision.

*Do I just want to exist in this eternal now?*

She breathes in, try to get to it. Try to get to the peace, but it doesn't provide an answer. It is its own answer. Another escape, like drugs or sex, but without obvious negative consequences. Another way to avoid the complicated and disorderly world complete with pain and unpredictability. How to live a life? Enjoy the pleasure and calm and when that changes, escape into the eternal now.

Then tinkling soft bells ring and Molly says, "Wiggle your fingers and toes," as she brings the class back from relaxation.

Jeannie wanted the yoga studio for more than five years. She wanted to run the dealership since she was in high school. But she's not a kid anymore, she doesn't have to do it because she wanted it once, she doesn't have to follow in her father's footsteps.

Unexpectedly, her heart beats in her throat. She's laying on her right side, heart to the sky, legs and knees bent. *That's it. I don't need to step one foot in front of another following what I thought I wanted once upon a time.*

Chills walk up and down her arms.

The affair with Ricardo was another way to be like her father, replacing her need to run the dealership with a more twisted way to follow in his footsteps. "It's my dream that someday we'll run this together, and someday, it'll be all yours," Dad said when he drove her home from her first day of work, and then winked. "It'll be our special family link and our father-daughter connection will be our special work link." His warmth sifted over her. He charmed his daughter like he captivated everyone.

*The dealership started as a way to be with Dad. I can't win anything from him anymore. It isn't a way to share something extraordinary. I can simply love him in spite of it all.*

Telling Mark about her affair would unburden her, but unnecessarily hurt him. *I have to carry this guilt alone. I don't want to change my marriage. I love Mark. He's the most important man to me. My partner.* Chills run up her spine once again. Of course, Mom is the most important woman to Dad. He didn't want anything to change their relationship. *Why didn't I ever see how much he loved her, I focused on his inadequacy, his imperfect commitment, his entitlement.*

Her heart pounds in her ears.

Her body is drenched with sweat. But she's clear. Jeannie is in the now.

*I don't want to run the auto dealership. I don't. It has nothing to do with revenge against Sue, or wanting the approval and love of my father. None of that matters.*

And then Molly says, "We'll close with the endless Om."

Jeannie inhales, and then exhales her Om until all breath is gone. Surrounding her, other Oms start and finish according to all the other breath patterns until an Om that has no beginning or ending fills the room.

FIRST, SHE SITS in her car, calls Mark, and tells him.

"Well, of course. You don't need to hold onto it for your father or mother. You can do what you want to do. You can do the yoga studio. The dealership would make a world class yoga studio."

"Nope." She doesn't realize this until she says it. "I want a cozy, warm house. Or a loft downtown. I don't want

238

to be in my father's old space. I want to find my own. I realized there are three different things: managing the dealership, owning the franchise, and owning the building. My father did all three, but they aren't stuck together. I can untie them. And I don't have to decide what to do with all of them right now. I might not even want to run a yoga studio. I know though, absolutely, I don't want to be general manager of that dealership. I'm not winding my life around winning my father anymore."

"Jeannie, that's great." His voice is soft and caressing. "I bet Sue or Jay could be general manager. Maybe your parents could keep the franchise and the building. Your father might get well enough that he'd like to keep a hand in."

"Exactly. Let's wait and see."

"A new studio will be all yours, if you want it…"

"All ours," she corrects him.

Jeannie calls Sue and tells her she'd like for them to get together. "What's your schedule like this afternoon?"

"This afternoon?" There's hesitation, a hint of fear in her voice. After all, the last time Jeannie saw Sue, Jeannie accused her of causing her father's stroke and confronted her with how little she knew him.

"I think we should talk." Jeannie makes sure her voice is soft, almost sweet and friendly, to help her feel at ease.

"What's this about?" Sue doesn't trust Jeannie.

"Your future," she tells her. "Want to have lunch, or would you rather take a walk? We could go to Gallup Park." Jeannie gives her the choice, and feels her soften.

"Okay, the park." She wants to keep moving.

"I'll meet you by the livery. Noon okay?"

"Yep. See you then." She clicks off.

IT'S THE LAST of August and fall is coming. But now, right now, the trees are still green. The lawn is lime green. Fluffy clouds creep across the blue. As though set by a designer to complete the picture, a single swan swims down the river. A couple floats by in a canoe and Jeannie thinks of her and Ricardo's trip down the alligator filled estuary. Seems so long ago.

Sue walks toward Jeannie. Sue's turquoise cardigan sways with each step. When she sees Jeannie, she doesn't smile, but nods. They're not going to pretend. They haven't been together, arranged to see each other for several years. How many? Four maybe... since Jeannie saw her and Dad together downtown and realized they were having an affair.

"It seems like a lifetime ago since we've been together," Jeannie says. No point in beating around the bush and she's not going to play at being nice. They're too tangled. But, Jeannie is no longer mad at her. *When did the rage and hurt have ebbed away? What finally made it die?*

They fall into walking together. Each right feet lands at the same time as they automatically take the same walk in the same direction that they had so often when they were best friends. They curve away from the livery and concession stand, walk to the river, and over the bridge. For a while they don't talk. They watch their feet land simultaneously. Sue wears wedge sandals of squares of vibrant colors. A turquoise and silver anklet and a stack of toe rings on her middle toe. She's turquoise and blue and her shield of dark hair glinting burgundy. She's lost weight, Jeannie notices. She wonders if Sue is dating anyone, or sleeping with another married man, or just hanging out with friends.

"Well." Jeannie starts but doesn't know where to go from there. Just go. "I wanted to tell you first, before I tell the others, what I've decided. It's been hard sorting

240

through what's my desire from when I was a kid, what my father would want me to do, what I wanted to do to get revenge on you for your affair and betrayal of me." There she said it. Just like that, just like one of my motivations.

Sue inhales sharply.

Jeannie turns to her, her head is down and she examines her feet with their turquoise nails landing on the path.

"To finally understand what I wanted to do for me, for my life, given the situation now." Jeannie stops because she'd said the most important thing.

"I'm sorry," Sue says almost in a whisper. "So sorry how this all turned out. I, we, didn't mean for this to happen. It's almost destroyed me."

Jeannie puts her hand on Sue's arm. "I know."

"I just fell so in love with Jack...

She doesn't say *your father* but turns him into a man, simply a man, by using his name. Turns him into another male and, for a moment, Sue and Jeannie into girlfriends again.

"I couldn't help myself. You understand now, don't you?" She shoots Jeannie a look so she'll know Sue's referring to Ricardo.

*Should I lie and say nothing happened, like I told Rosie? Is there a subtle threat or blackmail in her comment so that I need to guard myself?* Jeannie thinks. "Not really. Neither one of you protected yourself, and he endangered himself."

"Me, too. Look, I lost you." Her voice catches and she clears it. "That's been a source of pain for both of us."

"A pain that bound you closer." A vile vision of them placating each other for hurting her, putting her into an untenable position flits across Jeannie's mind.

"He loves you so much. You don't know how important you are to him."

Jeannie glances at the river, a mother followed by five almost grown ducklings swim for the far shore. *I don't need my father's fuck to reassure me of his love.* "Well," Jeannie chortles. "Now my mother and I take care of him. He can't even be left alone."

"It's so tragic. The fact he didn't take his medication.... It makes me hate myself."

For a moment, Jeannie wants to take that away from her. Wants to reassure her, and tell her he was the one responsible for his own health. But Jeannie doesn't know the pressure Sue put on him, Jeannie doesn't know the pressure her being thirty years younger put on him. Or his own need to preserve his self-image. Jeannie says simply, "We never really predict anyone."

They walk over the river and stand on the bridge. The water is murky. It appears clear and blue from a distance, but when it can't reflect the sun, stirred up mud lurks in the slight current.

"So, you haven't told me yet. What have you decided?"

"At first, I thought I'd be the general manager. It was okayed by headquarters, but I would do that for the teenager I used to be and for my father. Then I thought, I'd sell the franchise and keep the building, my parents own it, you know. Well, it's in my mother's name. But she doesn't want to be bothered. I realized I didn't want to put a yoga studio there. For me the aura would always be my father's charisma and self-destructive charm. We may simply keep the franchise and the building to support them. I don't, we don't, need to make all those decisions right now. We can wait to see how much Dad recovers."

Sue nods and resumes watching her feet land on the black cement.

Jeannie chuckles. "In a way, you and Dad did me a favor. It forced me to examine who he was, and my

242

relationship with him. No woman, not even a daughter, could get more than his need for a reflection that fed his narcissism. And thus I understand more who I am, and find peace."

They walk a while further. There're no flowers. Just the winding water, the kept paths, and wooden bridges, the fields for picnic tables. It's mostly empty except for a few people fishing along the edges. A mother and a toddler play on the swings at the playground. The couple in the canoe is long gone. The swan drifts around an island in the middle of a river, hunting for his mate.

"Business is really picking up. The new advertisements, the mood is switching back to Detroit and our American auto industry," Sue says.

"Yes, I know. I've decided, you're welcome to become general manager. I would help you. Maybe someday you could buy the franchise."

Sue gasps. Wipes her nose with the back of her hand.

"The point is. I wish you well. You need to hear that. I know my father would want you to do well, too." When Jeannie says that her eyes fill. Is she being too generous, ripping away shreds of anger? No. *I have everything, I can afford to be. And it's the truth.*

Beside her, Sue catches a sob, and then mutters, "I miss you. You're so amazing."

They stroll past the hummingbird and butterfly garden, the only place where there are flowers. Orange zinnias and purple coneflowers buzz with flocks of white butterflies. Jeannie misses Sue, too, but there's no going back. Jeannie doesn't need to rub salt in wounds that are scabbed over. Eventually, she'd bleed again. "We're here, back at the concession stand. Let me know what you decide. I'll be calling a meeting of the staff for this Friday. I'd appreciate it if you'd let me make the announcement. I know you're good at keeping secrets. But let me know if you've decided something before the meeting, okay?"

Sue's voice is doting and warm when she says, "You know what I'll decide. Thank you, Jeannie. Thank you for everything," with tears in her eyes.

As Jeannie walks away, she understands the power that money sometimes provides. There's recklessness that can become entitlement, like she displayed with Ricardo, and responsible use of power, like she's doing with the staff of the dealership as she hands it on to its future.

It's time to pick up Sara from her track camp and enjoy a family dinner.   The three of them. Her family.

## Twenty-three

*In China, the Hun dynasty built the great wall with funds from lotteries.*

IT'S AUGUST. JULIET enters the Farmer's Market and is surrounded by the aroma of the earth's richness, the vibrant colors of tomatoes, and peppers and peaches and eggplants. She turns from a display of cherry and is inches from Taylor, a bag of produce topped with a bouquet of zinnias strung over her arm.

"Taylor." Juliet exclaims. "Isn't the market glorious today?"

"Yes."

"I just got back from Naples, visiting Rosie. They have a terrific place right on the beach. And I did some singing again." Taylor's red hair glints from the light.

"That's wonderful." Juliet grins at her friend's happiness.

"Hey, you wanna get a cup of coffee?"

"Sure."

Once they settle into table in the patio, the leaves of a tree shading them, Juliet asks, "Any news on Rick? When'll the hearing be?"

"I went to see him."

Juliet's eyes widen. "What? You did *what*? In Connecticut?"

"On the way to Florida, after I dropped off the kids at camp." Taylor leans across the small table. "Don't tell anyone. Especially not Rosie. I can imagine what she and Kevin would say. 'It'll seem like you're pursuing him, threatening him, stalking him, interfering with his current life. He could file a Personal Protection Order against you. All that will hurt your case. Stay away and let us and the courts be your weapon.'" Taylor uses Kevin's authoritarian tones, but, with a shrug, switches back to her own. "The courts might not be a weapon against him, you know?" Taylor stops for a breath.

"Yes. I do," Juliet says and slightly turns her lips down.

"I couldn't stop thinking about all the things he stole from me. He used me up and spit me out. Bastard. I had fantasies of killing him. Over and over again. All different kinds of ways," Taylor shudders. "And then he wanted my lottery money.

"I found his house, a standard grey ranch. No flowers that litter when they drop petals. The lawn precisely cut and maintained. Whatever is necessary for appearances. But only that. No joy. No beauty. Just like his music. Perfect notes, but no attention to the emotions sound creates." Taylor's words bubble to tell Juliet the story.

Juliet's fingers are wrapped around the paper cup. Her eyes big as she listens to Taylor.

"Then I saw him. He had jowls under his chin. His neck has thickened and sagged. The bald spot on the top of his head is meeting his receding hairline." Taylor's shakes her head, eyebrows lifted. "He's a pathetic dweeb. There's *no way* I'd be attracted to him now, there's *no way* I'd even bother with him."

"That's all you did is *see* him?" Juliet leans forward, realizing the depth of Taylor's emotion and how quickly rage can get out of hand. "It sounds dangerous."

"Then I saw Natsumi, the woman he left me for, driving my old brown Honda Civic!"

"Did        they        see        you?"

"They didn't recognize me. And you know the weird thing, Natsumi used to be beautiful, with long hair, baby face, push up bra, pouty red lips, and long lashes. Sexy. Now she's thin and drab."

246

"You're so much better off without him. Even if you have to give him half the lottery money."

"That's what I learned. Natsumi was behind him, trotting for him. He didn't turn. Didn't greet her, this woman he left us for. He acted as though she was nonexistent." Taylor turns to Juliet, "Unbelievable. Sometimes you don't even realize how bad things are until they're over, you know what I mean?"

"Yes, I do." Juliet sips her coffee and thinks about Tom and Dan and how much she had to go through to deal with the past so it could stay the past.

"So she kept reaching for him." Taylor's eyes are wide. "Her forefinger touching the side of his palm." Taylor strokes her own palm with her finger. "But all he did is shrug her away and quicken his pace. She toddled behind him, struggling to catch up. God, Juliet. That gesture was so recognizable. How many times had I trotted behind Rick, trying to get his attention, trying to tell him something, trying to kiss him only to be discounted, shrugged away, ignored? Then I realized Rick's behavior had nothing to do with me. Nothing. It's who Rick is."

Taylor leans back in her seat. "And you know what? I was free. Just like that. Finally." She snaps her fingers.

"At last." Juliet touches Taylor's hand.

"But there's more. In Natsumi's rush to reach him, her purse bounced against a trash basket. I could hear the clang standing across the street under a tree. But Rick paid no attention. Her keys fell to the ground. But Natsumi kept running after him. So I picked up the keys and tapped Natsumi on her shoulder."

"You stopped her? Did she recognize you then?"

"No. Remember? I was just as bland when she last saw me as she is now. I'm back to being who I was before Rick." Taylor chuckles. "She and I have switched places."

247

"That's right. You've gone from Miss Rock 'n Roll to Mrs. Housewife and back again."

"I guess it's Rick's M.O. to hook up with a vibrant woman and turn her drab. So I gave her the keys. And said, 'You deserve so much more, so much more than running after a man who is indifferent, who doesn't see your beauty.' I didn't even know I was going to say it 'til the words popped out of my mouth. 'You're worth more.'"

"I think you were telling yourself as much as you were telling her," Juliet says.

"Yep."

"What did she do?"

"She resumed chasing him. And then," Taylor leans forward. "She stopped, looked at the keys. She threw the keys in her purse, turned around, and marched back to the office."

"That's incredible. You tried to help her out. What a generous thing you did."

"You know what I learned? Even when I was poor, I was better off without Rick. I'm grateful he left me so that I can see this. I no longer run after him. I'm no longer his unwanted shadow."

"You think winning the lottery helped you realize that?" Juliet asks.

Just then Jeannie crosses the patio, a bag from a clothing store looped over her arm. "Hey guys. Look at the cute outfit I bought Sara." She pulls out a bright colored tunic, and leggings.

"Pull up a chair and join us." Juliet says.

Jeannie grabs an empty chair and jerks it across the brick patio.

"We were just talking about how lottery changed us."

"Yep." Taylor says. "I learned how much I gave up for Rick. I'm richer without him even if we never won. But

248

it made it easier." Her eyes move to the sky.  "Brought everything to a head." Taylor stops a minute and then says, "Hostility and hatred are addictive.  The more cavernous my hatred, the more I required Rick to release me. And when he didn't, the more my fury amplified until it became the only sound I heard."

*Unless you switch the hatred to something else. Or spend all your energy repressing it,* Juliet thinks.  *That's what I did.*

Jeannie's head tilts. "You're so right, Taylor. Maybe we expect the people who have wronged us to somehow release us from the pain they caused. But they can't do that."

"Only we can do that ourselves. Using our own courage," Juliet says.

Taylor continues, "The joy of winning, and the cruise reminded me of happiness. *I had forgotten happy.*" Taylor's voice amplifies. "Before then, I believed I *needed* him to free me. But then I knew I had to free myself. No matter what happens, I'll be who I want to be."

"Me, too." Juliet says. "That's what winning the lottery has done for me.  It resolved my feelings about being so different.  About growing up poor."

Jeannie says, "You know, me too. In some way I needed the magic of winning to help me figure out what I wanted to do for me. To quit being so stuck on the whole crap about my dad and Sue and Rosie. Did you guys hear? Sue is going to manage the dealership. I feel so free," Jeannie says.

"I didn't know. So generous. And forgiving."

"It's what's best for the dealership. I don't need revenge."

"Me either. Ohmigod, you can't imagine how often I fantasized killing him. How many different ways I fantasized murdering him," Taylor shakes her head.

"He's so not worth that blot on your soul," Juliet's lips make a round oh. "And revenge isn't so sweet." She's thinking of Joey and Stainface.

Taylor crosses her legs and sips the coffee, now lukewarm. "Well, either way I'm okay. More than okay. I have two great kids, wonderful friends, and I'm rid of him. Oh, and a seven figure sum in the bank, even if he takes half ….who would have thought that?...Life was so hard then, in one day everything in changed." Taylor snaps her fingers again, her rings sparkle. "I was single and rich. Then," she shrugs. "It seemed it vanished and I was his victim again. Now I realize what I have. I'm ready, finally, to start a new life."

Juliet reaches out to squeeze Taylor's hand. "Yes, all of us, but you most of all have been on a roller coaster." Then she turns to Jeannie. "And you. With your dad's stroke the same week. How do you deal with tragedy and elation simultaneously?"

"It's been crazy. It's that rollercoaster of life. But I'm off that ride now."

Taylor says to Juliet, "I can only imagine what this money means to you and your family. For most of us, we have a chance to live dreams. But for the three of us, the money has helped us, or forced us, to resolve some things." Taylor tilts her head.

"Yes." Juliet says. Then she touches the base of her throat, assured the chain is not there. "It's too bad we required a spectacular event to do what we really want and need for ourselves."

"Too bad money makes such a difference," Taylor says.

## Twenty-four

*People who have a hard time making decisions, felt helpless, and were passive were more likely to be taken advantage of after winning the lottery.*

*In 1978, a study found that lottery winners scored below accident victims who were partially or wholly paralyzed in the pleasure of day-to-day events.*

MARNIE BOUGHT A Ferrari on a deal for $160,000. The purchase was full of delight, as impulsive, and crazy as she'd ever been. Black and sleek with the surprising flirt of purple leather interior. Part of the excitement, the motivation was imagining the joy on Jim's face, his toothy grin, his ecstasy driving it.

But when she told Jim, he said, "Are you a dude in a mid life crisis? You bought an overpriced convertible? An extremely expensive one?" He shakes his head and inhales through his teeth. "Didn't even discuss it with me."

"I can afford it," she leans back.

"Yes. *You* can," he almost shouts the word *you*. "What exactly am I? Some sort of pudgy boy toy?"

Marnie laughs. "Sorry, Charlie. You're too old for a boy toy. I think they're in their twenties, or maybe early thirties." She laughs at her joke, but instead his face reddens with anger. Any other night, he would have chuckled with her. "What? I don't get what's going on. If you don't want to drive my new Ferrari, I'll take Sky."

"Fine." He stands, turns to walk out, but then swivels his head, and spits, "I assume you can cover the bill."

THE NEXT MORNING, Jim calls. "I shouldn't have walked out like that. Yeah, I'd love to take a ride in your new

Ferrari. It's a wonderful day, how 'bout we take a spin across the state? Still early enough to do that and, if we want, stay overnight in Saugatuck."

She recognizes the size of his apology. "I shouldn't have made that crack about the boy toy," she replies softly.

"How 'bout I come by in a half an hour?"

"Sure."

As she anticipated when she bought it, Jim thrills at the car's sleek handling. They play with the car, the road, the cool waters of the lake in the burning sun, and, finally, refreshing air conditioning of a Victorian Bed and Breakfast that welcomes them for the night.

A few weeks later, Marnie sells her house for exactly what she bought it for ten years before, but that doesn't take into consideration the money she invested remodeling her bathroom, painting, carpeting, putting in a new deck and landscaping with shrubs and perennials. Nor the new furnace, new hot water heater, or remodeled basement. Luckily, her hard work and fabulous decorating eye provide an instant sale. "It's a different time than when you bought it," her real estate agent says, lips curled downward. "Then, we thought real estate could only go up and every house in a good neighborhood was a great investment. But it's beginning to pick back up."

THE OFFER JIM receives for his ranch is below what he owes. "I can't afford to lose money, and I don't have the extra savings to pay off my mortgage with cash."

"It doesn't matter, darling," Marnie squeezes his hand. "The lottery changes all that."

"You and the cookie bitches won."

"How are we going to solve this?" They continued having fun together ignoring the fight about the car and the disagreement about a new house as though the issues would simply melt away in the summer heat. Marnie hoped with time he'd realize the downside of her having the lottery money is much smaller than the upside.  Those ideas of masculinity are so old fashioned, aren't they?

Now, they're in the Ferrari gliding to the grocery store to make dinner for Jim's sons, Sky and Rachel. It's a quiet Sunday morning, they have just heard a sermon on the importance of gratitude and generosity, especially in stormy times.

"I appreciate your generosity, Marnie."

"I'm not being generous," The beginning of her sentence is harsh, but when she remembers the argument, she softens it. "I love you. I want us to move to the next step. Money can make things easier for us. Isn't that what you want, too?"

Jim slams the brakes as a burgundy SUV cuts in front him, squealing to the green arrow in the left turn lane. "Jeez." He shakes his head and then glances at Marnie. "Yes, but I don't feel comfortable taking a loss, giving up my house, and living in yours."

"Ours. It'll be ours."

"Not really."

"Are you using this economic issue as a way out of a bigger commitment?"

"It's how you're handing it."

"We both want to live together, right? You're not going to stop loving me, wanting to share a life with me 'cause I'm rich. What would you want me to do?"

Jim makes the left turn onto Stadium Drive passing the high school that Marnie attended. The carnival is in the parking lot, a Ferris wheel, merry go round, and roller coaster motionless except for day-glow flags twirling in the breeze. "I don't know what to tell you."

"How 'bout you rent your house and move in with me? Does that seem comfortable to you?"

"I considered suggesting that, but it means that house will never really be *ours*, not financially. I won't have anything in it."

"I don't care. You know that, right?"

"We've both been through break-up wars that resulted in financial calamity. We don't need to repeat past mistakes."

"We don't have children together. And it's not likely we will." They both laugh.

As they drive through town, heavy green branches bowing over them, Marnie struggles with scenarios. Finally, she asks, "Do you *want* us to figure out a solution? Or is this really a red herring?"

He hesitates.

Marnie's mouth is skewed by bewilderment. Then she remembers his quip about being a kept man. "You're uncomfortable by the money differences? It's a gender thing, right? If the situation were reversed…." Marnie's voice trails off. "I'm not trying to control you."

He exploits weaving in and out of lazy Sunday traffic to consider a reply and then turns into a neighborhood where the fresh cinnamon scents of cut grass and Sweet William welcome them. "Hmmm. I want a predetermined fall-out position if things don't work. We're not kids anymore."

She surveys the swaths of lawns, set to welcome guests, but also keep strangers at a distance. "How 'bout you rent your house, move in with me, and, when it sells, you buy into our house? Or use the rent to buy into our house? Or we figure out some kind of agreement for sweat equity because you know I'll have a *honey do* list. Or all of the above." She chuckles to soften the seriousness of their conversation.

"Sort of a non-marriage pre-nup?"

"Great idea. A contract between us...how's that? And it will include estate planning, too. I mean if one of us dies first the other has sole ownership of the house, I guess. And then it's split between our kids." She shrugs. "And meanwhile we'll have it figured out so you won't feel that the lottery money or I control you. Except how you want it to."

"If we decide to marry?" He smiles at her and touches her arm.

"Then it'll serve as a pre-nup. Hey, if lawyers can figure out the complicated stuff with the lottery, this will be a snap. They'll help us anticipate situations we'd never think of. Meanwhile, you'll have all the advantages of living rich, and being with me." She winks at him, but he misses it studying the street. "Because I saw a house for us, right on Silver Lake with fabulous views, an atrium for plants in the center, forest on three sides, four bedrooms which means an office for each of us, and a guest room. *And* the dock is ready to go. I can hardly wait for you to see it, because I bet you'll fall in love too." She widens her eyes, her voice going up in excitement, "The owner is so motivated he'll throw in a Cocktail boat, and a paddle boat. We'd have so much *fun.*"

Marnie puts her hand on this thigh and he turns to her. "I so hate bucket seats. Why did they ever become popular?" she asks.

IN AUGUST, JIM sells his house for his asking price. "You know what did it? I bought a St. Joseph statue and buried it upside down in my yard right before the last open house. And sure enough, a couple came in and offered a purchase agreement that night."

"St. Joseph statue?"

"A friend told me it worked for his family, and I saw one near the checkout lane at Ace Hardware and remembered what he said. Figured, what the hell, might as well try."

"Wow. We have the luck to win the lottery and you have the magic to sell a house for the asking price."

Jim laughs.

"So does this solve the money and house issue?"

"You'll still be putting in twice as much for the down payment. But it helps. So does the agreement we made."

ON LABOR DAY, they celebrate their new house and the holiday with a party. *Guess what! It's going to be catered. Just bring a bathing suit, towel, kids, and lots of picnic spirit!!* Her email announces to their families and friends. *Can't wait to see you and play in the lake!!*

As usual, Rosie is the first to arrive with Kevin, and Ben who totes a backpack of toys. Jeannie, Mark, and Sara arrive next, and Sara instantly takes over Ben. Levy runs in with water wings and a slide, Disney at his heels skipping with excitement. "Look what we got for everybody," he squeals, shaking a water slide. Sissy and Aaron are right behind him lugging a playpen. Tara walks slowly carrying Hannah, almost three months old, fastened to Tara's chest with a Snugli. One hand cups her baby's back, the other the strap of a diaper bag. Hannah looks around, capturing the rustling leaves, the dazzle of the zinnias, and the faces of the people, her forefinger in her mouth. Marnie kisses Tara on her cheek, slides Hannah out of the Snugli, and then grins, laughs, coos to her while Hannah watches her grandmother's shifting features with wide eyes and then chuckles a song of such thrilling merriment that Marnie laughs, too.

Rosie hears the baby and is right next to Marnie. "She's soooo gorgeous. Let me hold her," she says as she commandeers the child from Marnie's arms. "You get her all the time." Rosie has not yet announced her pregnancy.

"Look at all that hair. All those great black curls and gigantic eyes."

"Yeah. She's our wild child," Tara laughs.

Sky and Rachel enter, and Rosie reluctantly hands Hannah to her Aunt Sky. "Let's see if you got Mom's smile, too," Sky says.

"Nope. She got Daddy's," Levy giggles. "Granma didn't share her smile twice. Just gave it to me."

The baby wraps her fingers around Sky's index. Sky opens the tiny hand, and kisses the palm, inhales the infant's milky sweet smell. "Looks like you got her beautiful hands."

Chandra's hair, loosened from its usual bun, almost reaches her waist. Juliet and Dan arrive with Taylor, Buzz and Nicole. Then Tracy, Silver and Allie. The picnic table, spread with a red and white checked cloth, is laden with cheese, crackers, colorful vegetables, and dips. Casually dressed servers wander the lawn with trays of fizzing champagne flutes, platters of phyllo dough appetizers. The house and lawn are jammed with friends, and family talking, laughing, the eating and drinking. The colors of summer are echoed in clothing of pastels or vivid hues matching purple and yellow flowers and twinning morning glories, barrels of pink and lavender impatiens, baskets of which also hang from a dogwood tree. The lake flashes glints under a deep blue sky. The multi-hued rich greens of trees and lawns created by the abundant rain and humidity fill the very air they breathe. Sounds of happy chatter, giggles, the lake lapping quietly, the aroma of barbeque and mesquite float in breezes.

It's one of those scenes that you want to freeze. Not an ordinary day that is special because everything is right and the magic exists in that wonder of the mundane. But a day of celebration, because nothing has been average or common since they won the lottery. Maybe in the future, some year, it will be.  But for now, the lottery win is like the sun throwing everything into sharp relief and sending sparkles of light.  Marnie's blue eyes reflect the cerulean sky, her children are happy, she has three beautiful grandchildren, a man who loves her. Her friends are here. Life is good.

"There's nothing like a Midwest summer day. Perfect like this one," Jim says, brushes her with a kiss, grilled chicken breast on his plate.

Jeannie, wearing a purple tank bikini top, and a multicolored sarong, asks Marnie, "Where's Vera?"

"Maybe she's just late. She just finished her last round of chemo and radiation on Friday. She said she'd be here."

Marnie doesn't tell her that Vera hasn't been able to work.  The week before, Marnie learned their hot water heater died and they didn't have money to replace it.  Vera heated water on the stove to give herself birdbaths for three months.  Marnie bought her a new heater.  Marnie had most of her money tucked away in various annuities, a conservative asset allocation of stocks and laddered bonds. Her children were taken care of.  She had bought her dream car and her dream house.  $25,879.34 was what Vera owed on charge cards. *Vera doesn't owe that much,* Marnie thought as she wrote the checks.  Then she remembered how much, just six months ago, her debt strangled her and it was less than $25,000.  And now, 26 thousand didn't seem like a lot of money.

How quickly we adjust.  How quickly our attitudes change.  Chills creep up her arms as she enumerates that she shops in different stores, buys more expensive clothes, thinks nothing of having a mani and pedi and massage and facial all in the same week, pampering herself. She spent

$160,000 on a car. That was equal to three years income just a few months ago.

*I can't have whatever I want though. I can't buy a Lear jet, or a five million dollar house on the ocean. But I'm thinking like that. Amazing. But other people, the people who have billions, think my two hundred dollar jeans are cheap, my new house a steal.*

"I don't want your charity," Vera said. Her collarbones appeared pointed and her veins stood out sharply forming a blue roadmap on her arms and chest. She wasn't wearing her wig revealing a short cap of white hair that made her eyes startling. *Like a baby's,* Marnie thought.

"It's not charity. Besides, I'll tell you another secret." She meets Vera's eyes.

"I'll keep it. I won't even tell Flynn. Promise," and Vera crosses her fingers.

"Well, we're contributing, some of us, anonymously, to a fund to be divided among you, Alice, Tracy, Allie, and Charlene. In October, we'll distribute it." Marnie wags her finger, "Don't get your hopes up 'cause everyone has other obligations, too. Meanwhile, this will solve a few months of worry." She resumes writing the check. "And next time I come, I'm bringing cookies. You need to eat, girlfriend."


"AND ALICE? WHERE'S she?" Jeannie continues.

"They're in California this month."

"Hmmm," is all Jeannie says and her eyes search out Rosie, playing with Hannah and Ben, Taylor and her children, Nicole and Buzz, taking turns with Rachel on Levy's water slide. Disney laps at the water, and tries to bite the splashes.

Marnie watches Jeannie stride to the group. Jeannie says something to Rosie and then places her palm on

259

Rosie's shoulder. Then the two of them, heads down in conversation, wander to the paddleboat, get in and push off from the dock. *Their friendship is healed. I wonder if Rosie has told her about the pregnancy.* Marnie has been sworn to secrecy. Marnie was surprised Rosie's marriage survived the first pregnancy, but somehow she quelled Kevin's anxiety about the conflicts between freedom and parenthood by giving him all the attention he wanted and juggling Ben, their office, and her marriage. What did Barbara Walters say? Something like, *You can have a career, be a great mother, and have a happy marriage. But you can only do two at once.* Rosie manages to do all three. And now another baby. Yet, though Kevin is here, he and Rosie haven't spent time together. Marnie notices Rosie's slight swell. The baby is beginning to show.

Marnie smiles as she watches Rosie and Jeannie skirt the edges of the water, their legs moving in synchronistic circles, a large floppy hat on Jeannie's head. Their faces turned to each other.

A game of croquet is set up and Juliet, Tracy, Chandra, Marnie, Sky, and Sissy play.

"How'd you get so good?" Tracy asks Chandra who beats everyone. Chandra, hair swinging with each motion, just chuckles.

"You've been practicing in your backyard or something?" Sissy asks.

"It's all physics. I just know the angles."

"Oh like blackjack, and what's it called, options?" Sissy says.

"Yeah, how's that going? You still making yourself richer and richer?" Marnie asks.

Chandra studies the line between her red ball and the hoop she must slide it through. "I've had some bad luck," Her eyes measure the distance. "Not luck, it's never really luck. I had a good-sized option and it was going up and up.  But I had a hairdresser appointment, put a stop on it, and left. Figured it would be okay and the option fell way below my stop before it sold, at a huge loss, and then bounced right back up again. But by then the money was gone." She straightens up and leans on her mallet, shaking her head. "If I'd been there to see the charts, I might have been able to save it. I lost all the extra I've made."

"All of it? Over 80,000?" Tracy asks in alarm.

Chandra twists her mouth and shrugs as though it's no big deal. "A hundred and forty, but I've reworked my strategy. You know, found money, like the lottery, is money for nothing."

"Are you saying earned money is more valuable and we enjoy more what we've worked for while lottery money is squandered?" Marnie considers Jim's reaction to the Ferrari.

Chandra leans on her stick. "With the souped-up lightning fast computers capturing the tiniest indications of upticks, the small guy is at a disadvantage. The market swings hundreds of points in a few minutes. And those computers are actually manipulating the market to a company's advantage."  She inhales through her teeth. "I've made new rules and restudied the Fibonacci curves. I'm only playing when I'm watching the screens. Easy ins and outs. I'm going to spend some time nearer to the big computers, and buy a faster computer myself, since now the tiniest increments of a second counts."

"You're being careful aren't you?" Sissy asks. "What if you lose your internet? You have most of the money put away so that nothing can touch it, right? In equities, bonds, annuities, and cd's that you can't touch?"

"It should be good from here on out."  Chandra straightens and puts her hand on her waist then taps the ball; the white stripe wobbles through the wicket. "Just like that," she nods and winks.  Marnie turns her head slowly with slightly narrowed eyes, a sidelong glance, and pursed lips that says, *You're sure? You're taking care of yourself, right?*

"You get another shot," Sky says. "Once it's your turn the rest of us just watch you win."

A caterer wanders by with a plate of raspberry cake slices and Sky takes one.

"I'm trying to go for a croquet. Sometimes I win." Chandra's laugh has an edge.

Marnie can't quite place it, but she senses desperation. "Options aren't as easy as croquet?"

"Not by a long shot," Chandra snorts back.

"Tour of the lake in the pontoon boat in fifteen minutes," Jim calls. "All aboard who're going aboard."

A group fills the boat, cans of beer or soda in hand. Jim pulls away from the dock and begins circling the lake. Houses surround the water, which is busier than usual with a variety of boats. On the marshy side, Allie spots a blue heron, and they notice a few fish jumping to catch dragonflies. Behind the houses is a maple forest, the leaves the black green of late summer.

Juliet and Dan hold hands. Watching them, Marnie senses a comfort and joy that she's not witnessed between them in years, as if they've fallen in love all over again. Juliet seems softer. Then, she giggles at a remark Dan whispers, mirth without any force or artifice. Unplanned and spontaneous. Is it winning the lottery? Juliet, secure at last, can let love in? Juliet turns and Marnie notices the gold chain has vanished from her neck. Has she lost it? No. *She's ended her relationship with Tom.*

Juliet senses Marnie's gaze and meets her eyes.

Marnie touches her throat, tilts her head, and mouths, *What happened?*

Juliet forms a phone with her hand and mouths back, *I'll call. We need a looooonnnng lunch,* and then grins.

"Hey," Aaron says, "Look whose following us." Disney's curly black head bobs in the water, his droopy ears dangle on the surface while his paws churn to reach the boat.

"He's doing a dog paddle," Sara jokes. "For real!"

Jim cuts the motor, lets the dog reach the pontoon, and Aaron pulls him in. When he's safely on the boat, he sits, his pink tongue ready for licks. And then shakes his fur.

"Gross," Sara shudders, "Dog juice." Sara huddles her arms together and pulls away. She has her father's hair, but the long limbs of her mom. She's a woman now, Marnie thinks. She's wearing purple, just like Jeannie, too.

And then Allie says, "Oh, no." and points to a small figure with bright pink water wings swimming from the shore. "Guess who joined Disney."

Rachel, her head well above the water buoyed by water wings, paddles her arms. She flashes a smile, and shouts out, "Look what I can do. I can swim across the lake."

Allie jumps in the water and does a smooth crawl toward her, the boat's occupants watch the swimmers. Jim turns the boat around and heads toward Rachel.

Sky holds her breath, and then whispers, "I thought Rosie was watching her."

"Allie, Allie, I've almost reached the boat!" Rachel's pink plastic pillows circle in the dark water.

"I'm coming with you," Allie shouts.

Then Allie reaches out her hand and touches Rachel's. "OK. Let's swim to the boat and see your Mom."

"Mommy, Mommy. Look what I can do! I'm wearing my water wings."

"Thank God," Sky whispers.

Everyone watches the small girl and the woman approach the boat, Allie now doing a breaststroke instead

263

of a crawl so that she can view Rachel while the boat slowly narrows the gap.

"That kid believes she can do anything," Jeannie remarks.

"Tara would have done something like that as a child," Marnie says and searches for her daughter's eyes.

"She's still doing stuff like that," Aaron smiles. "But so am I." He glances at Levy whose arms are wrapped around Disney's neck.

"Can we get a dog, Dad? Please."

"Right now a new sister is enough," Aaron laughs.

On cue, Hannah starts crying, Tara kisses her and then shifts to nurse her so the two of them have a private view of the lake.

By then, Allie and Rachel have reached the boat and Dan and Silver lift her up. "I did it, Mommy," Rachel sings. "Swam almost aaaalllll across the lake."

Sky hugs her. "Yep. Next year you're going to join a swim team, how's that?"

"Yippee!"

Allie says, "Looks like she'll be a long distance swimmer. She sure loves the water." And then in a more serious voice says, "And has to keep an eye on you."

"I wish I had my camera to take a photo of the dog and the girl swimming across the lake," Dan laughs. "An image of perseverance, determination, and comradeship galore." And then he meets Juliet's eyes, puts his arm on her shoulder, brings her closer, as his hand slides down her back and he pats her butt.

"Jeez, you two. Get a room," Silver jokes.

Jeannie notices Juliet drinking champagne and studying the lake, ignoring the wind whipping her hair. Jeannie grabs a glass and stands next to her. "Beautiful, isn't it? The sun's last ribbons of light on the water."

"I was thinking how lucky we all are."

"Yes, and you seem to have fallen in love with Dan all over again." Jeannie thought that Dan and Juliet were unconnected as though they went through motions of life together. But then, no one knows what goes on in anyone else's marriage.

Juliet laughs. "Yes. Maybe completely for the first time."

"That's great. Since winning the lottery, you seem more, I don't know, relaxed. Comfortable."

Juliet nods and places her arm around Jeannie's shoulder. "You, too. Marnie told me you figured out what to do with the dealership."

"At last, uh? Sue'll run it. I'm finally free of my anger at her and Rosie. What a relief," Jeannie giggles. "Amazing isn't it? I never would have predicted so many changes. I never would have thought that money would do what it's done. I've known you, since when, high school, and this is the first time you didn't need to have everything, all perfect."

"I was trying to compensate for that trailer park."

Marnie comes up and the conversation stops. "Hey, did I interrupt?"

"You? Never?" Juliet says.

"We were just talking about how long we've known each other."

Marnie says, "Yeah. You two are my oldest friends." She puts one arm on Juliet and says, "I met you in middle school," puts the other arm on Jeannie and says, "I met you in ninth grade."

"In band. God that was fun."

Marnie hugs them all. "I love you guys so damn much."

"Me, too."

"And look," Marnie says, nodding at Silver and Tracy, Taylor and Rosie, and Allie and Vera and Flynn laughing over a comment one of them made, "It looks like that rift between the winners and the non-players is smoothed out."

"Yes. We're back to being the cookie bitches all together again," Jeannie laughs.

"Thank God for girlfriends," Juliet says.


NIGHT TIPTOES IN slowly, first launching a few fireflies to dance across the lake, their glows reflected in the black water. The sun sinks behind the forest, blinking its last ember. The caterers distribute sparklers and the group waves circles, infinity signs, and names while flickering stars burst from the wands. They stroll with small glasses of colorful liquors. The caterers put the tablecloths in the laundry, tie up garbage bags with separate burdens of paper, plastic, and cans, stack plates and cutlery in the dishwasher swishing it spotless. One by one, the guests, family, and loved ones drift away to drive to their own homes through the starry night.

Jeannie hugs Marnie before she leaves and says, "It's a wonderful house and fabulous party."

Marnie leans close and says, "Yeah, but I missed your orange and walnut salad, and Rosie's Brie, the familiar delicious foods our friends make."

This day is over. The celebration finished for now.

Marnie and Jim ease into their bed, the skylight above divulges a crescent moon. "How do you like living together so far?" She snuggles close to him.

"I love it."

"There're advantages in being rich, uh."

He laughs.

"Look, darling. The moon smiles at us."

Jim softly draws her to him so her head is on his shoulder and inhales her lavender scent. "I'm as happy as I've ever been. Right here. This night. With you."

266

## Twenty-five

*"Money, not morality, is the principle commerce of civilized nations."* Thomas Jefferson.

*THERE'S PEACE IN my life now,* Jeannie thinks as she drives from Vera's through bowing yellow and red branches of fall. Fall is the beginning of a new school year so Jeannie reevaluates the completed one to start the next year fresh. This year seems more pressing, the evaluation more necessary as Sara is going into middle school, on the verge of the excitement and terror of being a woman. Now its makeup and nail polish. In a half dozen more years, it'll be sex and leaving home. They go by so quickly, these years, each one marked by secular rituals signaling a turn around the sun: the start of school, Halloween, Thanksgiving, the cookie club party, making a snowman, the crocuses popping up, the top of the park, the art fair, and then it begins all over again.

*But this year? The highs and lows happened the same week. And they could be the highs and lows of my life: my father's stroke, the lottery win, my realization of Sara's growing confidence and womanhood when I saw her acting.*

Joy and sorrow eat away from the other.

Jeannie gives Vera private yoga lessons once a week. Mostly it's an excuse to visit. She's lost so much weight, reduced to translucent skin and bulging tendons, her pink scalp with only slight fuzz.

Jeannie isn't sure Vera will make another fall. A vase held red and yellow maple leaves, preserved with glycerin, she said.  She collected them on a walk.  Her smile was like a child's as she touched one of the bright leaves, her finger absent of polish.  A few years ago, she was glamorous with perfectly blond coiffed hair, red or purple nails, voluptuous figure, always fully made up.

Today they did restorative poses: legs up the wall, child's pose, reclining bound angle pose, *Savasana*.  Vera made tea. Jeannie brought her chocolate cookies and fresh raspberries to tempt her appetite.  She nibbled at the cookie and ate one berry as she huddled under a soft afghan.

"You should get some marijuana.  Maybe you'd eat more and feel better."

Vera's laughter was creaky rather than bubbles of joy.  "Working on it."

Later she said, "Something like this puts life in perspective, uh?"

"Yes," but Jeannie was thinking of Dad.

As if she knew where Jeannie's mind went, she asks, "How's your Dad?"

"He's walking with a cane, now. One of those tripod ones, but it's better than that walker. Finally, he can dress himself, feed himself, and talk. Slowly, but surely."

"How much we endure and recover," Vera said, but not to Jeannie.  A few minutes later she added, "You have a plate full, don't you." Her eyes, the blue almost faded away, stared at the curtain hiding the sun, the outside. Vera tilted her head, turned those almost white eyes toward Jeannie. "Who said money solves everything? Or is it that we want *something* to solve everything? So money becomes a god. And if you have money, then it's proof of God's blessing. This happened all together. All at once. My cancer, the lottery, your dad, Marnie moving in with Jim, Taylor being sued by Rick, Sissy's foundation, Money..." Vera jerked her head, closed her eyes, and let the word

268

drift away with the exhaustion of her breath. It was as if she didn't know how to finish her own sentence. Then she whispered, "It escalates everything whether you have too much to know what to do with or not enough. Otherwise, money's just another part of the messiness of life."

So it's with those words ringing in Jeannie's head, that sense of so much, too much cluttered together that she drives back through the city, the tips of the leaves at the edges of the trees the colors of the last fire of summer.

Snow will soon be upon us.

After being with Vera, Jeannie has started a routine of walking through the park, as though birds singing, and ducks sailing on the river, cart away the burden of her friend's illness. In truth, death could swamp her. Or maybe the chemo and radiation are so difficult that death seems easier. The doctors remain optimistic, or at least that's what Vera says. She doesn't put on a game face anymore.

Jeannie wraps a shawl sweater, one of those cardigans that are so long, you can tie the front, or wrap it. This one is a winey purple that she hopes dramatizes her bland coloring and features.

Fallen leaves crunch under her feet. The pecking of a woodpecker in a nearby tree sets a rhythm like the typewriter she heard as a child. Consistent. Serious. Inevitable. Jeannie makes the loop around the river. Then takes the path into the forest.

She enjoys the moment. The empty park. No people walking their dogs. Too late or too early for fishermen. Just the sound of her own shoes, the birds, the rustle of the leaves when a wind buffets them. She studies a solitary leaf sail to the earth and nestle with his brothers. And realizes she's in the now. No longer trying to figure out what she's going to do about Sue, Rosie, Dad. Ricardo. The restless whirring of her mind, struggling to form a comprehensive understanding, a pattern has stopped.

She's pleased with her decisions; they're right for her. Everything is resolved, or as settled and peaceful as it can be.

Jeannie rejoices for the gift of life. The air that her lungs take in, use, and release, the tide of it as her feet set up their rhythm. She coasts into that, the blessedness of this one moment that is, after all, an infinity. That's the biggest luck of all. Being born. Having a life.

Off in the distance, there's the sound of another walker. Moving fast. Not with the loopy, fluid constancy of a jogger, but this person runs from something. Or for something. She looks back, but doesn't see anyone. The steps are heavy, staccato.

Someone running in boots.

It stops.

She continues the peaceful walk. A pheasant camouflaged by its fall colors flies from the leaves to land a few feet away. She's never seen one before.

Steps start again and come closer, almost like a ghost.

Closer.

Her heart quickens as the running, crashing through the forest, tromping on the crisp leaves become insistent, rolling echoes. Pervasive. Surrounding her so she can't distinguish its direction.

Once again, silence.

She turns again, and this time before she has a chance to twist away, she's grabbed from behind.

Hard arms, rough jacket.

Hot breath in her ear. He pinches her breast hard, twists it.

"So my little beauty I've caught you at last." He rips her shawl sweater with one hand, twists it around Jeannie's neck.

She pounds his chest, his face. Tries to kick him.

"Isn't this just so handy. For whatever I want to do, almost like you knew I was coming." He growls and tightens the wrap around shirt. He smells sweet, a musk that is stomach turning, a plethora of flowery musky cologne. His breath is hot and sour on her neck, scalp, as she struggles, coiling, bending.

Jeannie hits him.

He grabs her hand, turns her own sweater into a straight jacket. He flashes a knife that catches a bitter diamond from the sun, glinting viciously.

Jeannie screams with all her breath.

"My little beauty, we can make this hard or easy," he hisses as he shoves her down on the ground, his elbow over her throat so that the shriek is blunted to gurgles.

Jeannie kicks. Bucks him off.

But his forearm presses her neck. His other hand thrusts down on her chest, pushing ribs, sternum into the earth.

"That's better, my strong little beauty. Now you'll be a good girl, right?" He grins.

Jeannie's heart crashes in her throat, around her skull. She shoves him away with all her strength.

He hits her with his fist.

She falls. Her head hits something hard and she sees stars. Yep. Didn't know that actually happens, but there're bright flashes behind her eyes. Red and white like exploding fireworks.

She passes out and next thing she knows her pants are down.

He kneels on her and unzips his fly. This man with bushy hair, and ruddy skin. This man with a plaid flannel even in the warm weather.

Behind him, she sees another man.

*Oh, no. Not two.*

271

But then the man, with a flock of soft curls, a piece of the sun behind him highlighting his hair, puts his finger on his lips, and points up to the sky and nods.

Jeannie looks up for an instant as though there is an answer, a savior there.

The man on top of her has his cock out.

He slams Jeannie again. He wants her unconscious. Limp.  Why would a man want a woman who doesn't move?

Dark swallows the flashing lights.

The blackness clears.  The second man, blond man, is strangling him, pulls him away.

The first man kicks her in the ribs. Black cascades again like a curtain. From somewhere far away, there are the slaps of blows and muffles of kicks. Groans. Churning of dead leaves.

Boots clapping on the trail.

A soft voice asks,  "You okay?" his face is inches, just inches from hers.

Jeannie groans, and must pass out again.  Her sense of smell is changed, a funny taste in her mouth that's like as wet cement. *How can I taste wet cement? There's no cement.  Where am I?* A buzzing whirrs in her head like a broken machine. She rolls to the right, tries to rise to her feet, but her knees are weak. She's nauseous, about to throw up. She sinks back to the ground.

The man helps her up. "We need to get you to the hospital," he says.  "Can you walk?"

She takes a step, but nausea and dizziness swamp her. Then she tries another step.

"You're about a half mile to my car. Can you make it? I don't want to leave you." His words are louder than the whining drone in Jeannie's head.

He has hazel eyes, a halo of curly hair, dishwater blond.  He's nondescript, the kind of man you'd never

272

notice in a crowd. He pays as little attention to himself as others do. Forgettable.

Jeannie takes a step and then another. He holds tight under her arm with one hand, her elbow with the other. Maybe she can walk back to her car and drive herself. Sharply afraid of him, this man who after all rescued her. He senses her wariness and says, "You're going to be okay. I'm the protector of the forests," he chuckles almost musical.

Slowly they shuffle down the wood chipped trail littered with the fallen leaves.

They get into his car, a brand new red Malibu, Jeannie can't help but notice the sticker of her father's dealership on it. She wants to tell him that and ask which salesman sold him the car, all that polite and excited small talk people make to keep the flow of community, but the wooziness, the strange taste of cement and puke prevent her.

"You have a phone?" he asks.

"It's in my car."

He hands Jeannie his, "Figure there might be someone you want to call."

When she tries to focus on the numbers to call Mark, a wave of queasiness hits her again. "I don't want to mess up your new car." She puts her hand on her forehead.

"It's not even a mile to the hospital."

Then she remembers. "Thank you. For preventing my rape."

"It's what I do. My job. Like I said, I'm the protector of the forests."

*Is this guy crazy?*

"I'm Joey," he says.

"Jeannie." She looks out the window at the road into the emergency entrance. "I'm lucky you happened to be there." Then a curtain of blackness falls.

JEANNIE IS ABLE to give her name to the triage nurse. And birth date and address. No her insurance hasn't changed. She's in the system at U Hospital. She uses Joey's phone to call Mark. "Someone tried to rape me and this man prevented it and brought me here."

"This man? Who?" He's suspicious.

"Joey, his name is. This is his phone. He just happened to be in the forest and had the courage to intervene. I was so lucky. Hey, I have to go. I'm not supposed to use a cell. I can't wait to see you."

"I'm on my way." She hears his fear.

Jeannie lies on a bed in a cubicle, white curtains pulled around her. Joey is with her. "Is your husband coming?" he asks, the light behind him tips his curly hair with radiance.

Jeannie nods.

"My sister works here. I'll see if she's in today." He walks out of the cubicle.

Her eye hurts, she can't seem to open the lid. Maybe that's why everything is so dark. She touches it, and realizes it's swollen.

A nurse enters and takes her blood pressure and temperature. "The doctor will be here in a moment." Then she shifts awkwardly. "We've called the police. They'll want to talk with you, too. Are we going to need a rape kit?"

"Joey prevented the rape. He saved me."

Juliet's name is called on the loud speaker. "Ah, that's my friend," Jeannie says, but the nurse doesn't answer or seem to hear.

"You have some bad bruises on your neck. Looks like that eye is going to be colorful, too. I'll get some ice to bring down the swelling." She puts the clipboard under her arm and sashays through the white curtains.

The smell of ammonia covers the stench of illness. It smells like her father now and her eyes fill. *I can't cry. It'll make my eye worse.* The nurse returns with a bag of ice that she plops onto Jeannie's eye. "This should help. You're lucky. Your friend saved you from being raped. Maybe more. These bruises, well he was serious and violent. We have to check for a closed head injury."

*Aren't all rapes violent? How much more violent if I had been raped, too?*

When Jeannie holds the ice to her eye, she realizes her arm is sore. Sure enough a bruise starts its course. She tries to breathe, concentrate on the now, exhaling longer than she inhales to relieve stress. Her nose swells, clogged with dried blood, she opens her mouth.

"The doctor is on his way and the police want to talk with you after that."

Then Joey comes in the cubicle followed by Juliet wearing scrubs.

"Juliet?"

"Jeannie?" her voice is surprised and startled.

Jeannie starts crying then, and Juliet hugs her whispering, patting her shoulder, while Jeannie cries into her, both afraid, and aware of how woozy she feels, the world spinning and going in and out of focus and how much her neck hurts, her arm, eye, breast.

"You guys know each other?" Joey asks.

"Jeannie is my good friend. I've known her forever. She's in the cookie club." Juliet turns to him and then she meets Jeannie's eyes. "Joey is my brother."

"Your brother?" Jeannie looks back and forth between them and sees the resemblance in the curly dishwater blond hair, a firmness of chin, and lanky limbs. "He just saved my life. He prevented me from being raped. He's a hero."

Jeannie shuts her eyes, the lights are so blinding. "This is crazy. Just crazy. Some fucking asshole tries to rape me. A Good Samaritan prevents it and he turns out to be your brother. Your brother?" She swallows, which is difficult since her muscles and tendons don't cooperate. *We win the lottery. The damn lottery. With my numbers, the numbers I made up from my family's birthdates, magical numbers. And Vera struggles for her life. And my father. Sue. Rosie....*Jeannie thinks all this, but all she can say is, "It's a crazy life."

The doctor enters, glances at Juliet and frowns, and introduces himself, Dr. Tom something or other. "Juliet?" His voice rises in surprise and something more Jeannie can't pinpoint.

Juliet explains how they know each other and Jeannie tells him what happened.

"So you weren't raped?"

"He was seconds, inches away, but no. I wasn't." She laughs at her joke, but no one gets it.

JULIET STAYS FOR the exam which is mostly the doctor asking questions like what day it is, wanting to hear what happened. He looks into Jeannie's eyes. Feels the bridge of her nose. Checks her arms and neck. She touches her nose and then forefingers while standing with eyes closed. It makes her dizzy to stand, her head starts pounding. She starts to faint, but catches herself. The whirr in her ears is now a hum. She accomplishes the task even though she's always trying to improve her balance in yoga. He checks through her hair to see if there are any cuts, but there aren't.

But the back of Jeannie's head is swelling. Her eye, nose, neck and arm are swollen and turning colors. She's not bleeding. Well, her nose was but it's stopped. Nothing is cut. No stitches needed. He asks Jeannie to tell him what happened again. He asks her to tell him how she knows Juliet. He asks her to tell him about Joey and how she got to the hospital. When she answers all his questions, he nods. "You've had a concussion."

Joey is outside talking to the police.

"We'll run an IV, just in case. Your nose isn't broken. We'll put you on a regiment of pain relievers and anti-inflammatory agents for the swelling. I'll look in on you in a few hours." He slides his pen into his lab coat pocket.

"Good seeing you," he jerks a nod to Juliet before he leaves.

"So weird your brother saved me."

"My brother is the avenging angel," Juliet replies, but Jeannie doesn't understand what she means and Juliet says it more to herself than to Jeannie, her voice brimming with whimsy and awe.

The police question Jeannie. They ask her to tell them the entire story. Twice. Just like the doctor. They ask for a description, she tells them how he smelled like a bottle of cologne, but she doesn't have the words to describe it. He was average height and weight. His nose was red. Oh, he had a unibrow. They ask her to tell them again, and then tell her that someone will be by her house to take her to the station tomorrow. When she's feeling better. Maybe she'll be able to recognize him from one of their photos.

"You're one of the women who won the lottery?" an officer asks, the tall one.

"Yes. Me and my friends."

"You're a lucky lady all around. Lucky Joe was in the woods today, too."

Then Mark, who waited outside during this interview, enters. His face pale, his eyes dark with concern. He holds Jeannie, rocks her, loves her. She inhales his sweet familiar scent -- soap and coffee.

"Ah, my poor sweetheart." He softly touches her swollen eye and nose. "You're so beautiful, still beautiful." he whispers after she tells him the whole story. Then Joey tells him the story. He thanks Joey and looks back and forth from Juliet to him, shaking his head. "It's a small world," Mark says. "Such a coincidence. Thank God she's okay," he tenderly smoothes Jeannie's hair from her forehead and kisses her swollen purple eye.

She feels warm with his love.

*I'll be all right. I'm lucky. So lucky. Have been all my life.*

## Twenty-six

*To fulfill a dream, to be allowed to sweat over lonely labor, to be given a chance to create is the meat and potatoes of life. The money is the gravy.*
*Bette Davis*

EVEN THOUGH THE planet continues its inevitable surge around the sun, it has stopped for Jeannie. Mark wakes with her quiet beside him. "Hey, sleeping beauty. How're you feeling this morning?" His voice, if she could hear it, runs over with love and concern.

She doesn't respond.

"Still tired from yesterday?" He pushes himself up, leans over her, his weight on his arms. She lays, in a fetal position, on her right side, her back toward him. She doesn't roll toward him, throw her leg over his and put her head on his shoulder. She doesn't sigh. She's inert.

His heart quickens. He gives her a gentle tug, but she doesn't stir. Hand on her shoulder, he moves her toward him and tenderly shoves her away. He knows.

How did this happen? She was fine. The doctor said she was fine when he brought her home from the hospital.

He can't think of what to do. Mark, the attorney who has answers to everything, who knows the procedures for everything.

He bites his finger, the base of his forefinger. He doesn't know why he does this as he kneels in the bed beside her static body, biting himself and rocking as though pain in his hand will quench his sorrow and confusion.

Then, his back shakes with sobs. His throat raw with moans. He pushes her again, gently, but it's obvious.

His howls cascade around the room and around Jeannie, lying there, as she usually did every morning through all these years.

All was well. She smiled at him. She laughed with him. She fell asleep cuddling with him, just like always. Saying that Joey was an angel. How lucky she was. How lucky they were. Perfect lucky life.

Then she drifted off. Seemed like it was right in the midst of a sentence, but she was tired. And now? He woke her, like he was supposed to. At least twice. She answered his questions, just like she was supposed to. Everything was good. Seemed fine.

And now?

Now.

Everything is gone.

He can't think, still can't think of what to do, so he calls 911. Tears stream down his face, dribble from his nose. As the phone rings, he wonders if Jeannie knew when she had her last breath. Did she know it was her last, or did she sleep through it? He's not sure what he wishes for her. She talked about how amazing the simple act of breathing really is. We never honor it enough, it's so easy, automatic, but crucial. We take it for granted. He wonders what he wants for her. Then he knows the answer: He wants her to know it was her last breath. He wants her to know she died.

He listens to the phone ring, his face tilted to the ceiling, weeping, doesn't know what else to do. Sara is staying overnight at a girlfriend's. He'll call her later, after things are settled. He's glad she's not here, not witnessing this.

Finally, someone picks up.

"I need an ambulance, but I think, I'm pretty sure my wife died in her sleep last night." Sobs interrupt each word.

## Twenty-seven

*The 6 Wal-Mart heirs are worth as much as the bottom 41% of households put together. The top 1% own assets worth more than the entire bottom 90%.*

IT'S ALMOST THANKSGIVNG. Juliet and Joey are the first to arrive and stand close to each other, hands almost touching.

Slowly, stunned friends and family appear for Jeannie's memorial, uncertain what to say. They don't quote platitudes like *time heals all wounds*, or *in a few years this will all be behind you*. The cookie club ladies are here, even Alice has flown in at the last moment from California. All unnerved by a sudden death, a death that takes place early. All unnerved by the attempted rape, the reminder of violence against women, and the reminder that wealth guarantees nothing except a defense against poverty. Being a good person doesn't guarantee long life or happiness. How do they reconcile this tragedy into a sensible view of the world so they can continue to comfortably live?

Juliet and Joey know better. They have since they were children when their fantasies of a just order were destroyed.

But Juliet knows how people think. And for her friends, as they get older, the age at which death is fitting gets pushed back. When they were twenty, sixty seemed old. At forty, eighty seems old. And probably at sixty, ninety plus seems sufficient. Old enough to die means

281

squeezing the last drop of living from a long productive life span.

It's still inconceivable, a shock they can't get their wits around. They have not yet consumed and integrated that this is the way their lives will be. No more Jeannie's bright smile and purple clothes. No more Jeannie at the cookie party. No more Jeannie reminding them about yoga classes, how important it is to maintain flexibility, core strength, and balance. Metaphors, really, for arranging life.

How is someone fully present and alive, and then snapped away?

It could happen to any of them. An attack. Rape. Was it just a few months ago they talked about it as a fear they all shared, a fear that structured how, when, where they went? The biggest fear: rape. The biggest wish: winning the lottery. How had both occurred in the same few months to Jeannie who picked the winning numbers?

No answers to these questions.

They had to pass through a phalanx of reporters with mikes, and cameras hunting for someone to stop and say something. But what? The irony of winning the lottery and then dying? Was her attack a result of rage or jealousy for winning the lottery? How much everyone, her husband, her daughter, her parents, her friends, her students, the staff at the dealership will miss her? What a wonderful person she *was*? In the past tense?

Can't possibly be.

The tragedy doesn't rise beyond a sound bite as reporters mine emotions.

That's it. They want videos of crying so the audience will feel *their* lives are lucky even though *they* didn't win the lottery.

At least they're still alive.

Jeannie's death is a reminder of something that everyone knows, should know. Death is the great equalizer. And life is a gift, borrowed from the universe... It has no price.

"IT WAS JEANNIE'S numbers that won the lottery." Rosie dabs a tissue on red eyes then fishes in her purse for a new one. "Magical numbers she devised from her family's birth dates." Rosie rocks on her heels in the entry to the chapel.

The wainscoting is old mahogany. Bouquets of flowers flanked by burning candles top tables with memorial books for visitors to sign and write messages. Pens wait beside the closed books. No one writes anything.

"I still can't believe this. Can't believe Jeannie is dead. Just like that. Like a snap of the fingers. Out of the blue." Taylor shakes her head, her arms crossed, her palms gripping the inside of her elbows.

"The probabilities are low, but not as low as you might think. Higher than being the victim of a terrorist, say," Chandra's hair is knotted in a stiff bun. She wears no make-up. No one even looks at her, no one wants to hear her drone on about statistics. "Actually dying after you have a concussion is more likely than winning the lottery. Way more." She jerks her head in a fast nod.

"This isn't about statistics. We'll never again see her." Rosie's tears stream down her face.

"Probabilities don't matter. It was a hundred percent likely for Jeannie," Sissy says sadly, listening from the side.

A stained glass window emits a miserable light. The cobalt triangle settles on the floor, muted by the brown stone tiles fitting the somber occasion.

They glance surreptitiously at her father looking so frail, and pale. His scaffold of bones props the flimsy tissue of muscle and inadequate flesh. He leans on a tripod cane whose metal support seems to be the only factor preventing him from tipping over, or crumbling in a heap on the ground. Purple circles his eyes, blue veins knot up

283

his hands and disappear under the white shirt and requisite jacket sleeves. He looks around as though uncertain where he is, why he is here, looking for someone to flash a wan smile of recognition.

Jeannie's mom, Frances, stands next to him, glances up repeatedly at him, all her worry and concerns focused on him. She nods and smiles when people speak to her, thanking them for their condolences and well wishes.

"I am so sorry. So sad. So unfair," Rosie says.

"Yes," Frances says.

"If there's anything I can do let me know."

But of course there's nothing anyone can do.

Marnie kisses Jack, but he blinks at her, not sure who she is, then wraps her arms around Frances.

"It's heartbreaking," Marnie relaxes in Jeannie's mom's arms. They cry into each other's shoulders. "I'll always miss her," Marnie says. "Always."

Frances nods.

Marnie helps them find a seat in the small chapel and sits with them. The wood seats, with high backs and fixed arms become a shelter. Their palms fold on over each other on their laps as they stare at the podium and mike waiting for the next thing to happen. Narrow windows let in eerie light through the dusk. The colors of the glass, red and blue and green and yellow, splay across the pews, the faces of people already seated.

This is where Sarah was christened.

This is where Jeannie and Mark married.

A bouquet of white lilies, festooned with a gold banner, stands on the floor and reaches the mike in front of the podium. They emit no scent.

People slowly file into the chapel. Joey and Jeannie sit in the second pew across from Marnie and Jeannie's parents. Kevin slips in next to Jeannie.

Mark and Sara arrive last as though they can't stand to be there, don't want to come.  There is nothing the gathered friends and family can say, nothing anyone can say. Mark holds himself stiffly, he's lost weight in the last few weeks.  A few of Sara's friends are there, huddling together, looking unaccustomed to the drab dresses they wear, the conservative hairstyles and shoes.  They wave to Sara and she walks to them.

"Are you okay?" her best friend, Katie, asks, her eyes darting.  What Katie is really asking is, *How do you survive your mother dying, just as you are about to enter middle school? Maybe you don't really need parents any more, you have your friends.* Who knows when they haven't, not any of them, done it yet? They realize if they ask an adult he will tell him how important parents are. But maybe that's because they don't want to relinquish control.

Sara looks down and hugs her purse closer.

Katie says, "You have us, your friends. You have me. I love you." Her eyes puddle with tears. As soon as she says it, she grasps that a friend doesn't make up for a mother.

Then they file in, take the program that an usher hands him, Mark's arm around Sara's shoulder. A hush fills the chapel as they walk down the aisle.

Everyone stares into their faces, examining them for visible signs of grief, swollen red eyes, puffy circles, and sunken cheeks. Yet they walk. They are together.  They slide in the pew next to Jeannie's parents.

The service is a Protestant ritual.  There is comfort, perhaps, in reciting the customary words, the shadow of death, ashes to ashes, give us this day, fear no evil.  The minister reviews her life, her journey now to be with God, to continue on in the universe in some way.  Certainly she remains in all their hearts and minds for the goodness she has done, for the beauty of her soul.  He has little words of

285

comfort for Mark and Sara. Even he does not believe that telling them simply she is with God, or time makes things easier, or she will exist in their hearts will ease their pain. Maybe only the stonewalls of the chapel, the familiarity of ritual and the soothing music will help. Mark holds Sara's hand. Her palm cool. He's not sure yet how he'll go on, but he knows he will because he must.

After the service, people mill in the entry before being ushered into a reception room. The sun is lower and no blue glow flows from the windows. Sissy writes in the memorial book, as do Charlene and Allie. Jeannie's yoga friends surround Mark, he has met them, but they are almost unrecognizable with their hair flowing free on their shoulders instead of pulled in the necessary ponytails or buns. They sign the memorial book. The entire staff of the dealership,-- salesmen, accountants, mechanics and cleanup crew-- attend. Only Sue is absent. The dealership is closed for the day. They cluster around Jeannie's father, Jack, who squints and then grins with recognition. He toddles into the reception room, Frances at his side, and sits down at a table. His salesmen, Jay and Kurt, immediately flank him.

Chandra starts to leave, but Sissy stops her. "Aren't you coming with us to the reception?"

There's a tightness to Chandra's mouth as she smoothes her already slicked hair.

No one but the two of them are in the entryway, the others have strolled into the reception room. The burning candles and shallow light from a chandelier that is mostly brass filigree create a dim intimacy. Sissy puts her hand on Chandra's arm, "What's wrong?"

"I lost it." Chandra's eyes fill.

"Lost it? Lost what?" And then Sissy realizes she means the money. Her eyes widen. "All of it?"

"Yes. And my retirement."

Sissy shakes her head sadly.

"I thought it was all perfect. I had almost doubled the money. Almost doubled it. Riding high and confident. Then this day, this one damn day, the Fibonacci lines, predicting the ebbs and flows of the universe, were saying just what was going to happen. The probabilities all lined up. It was the most perfect trade ever. A sure thing. So I set up the trades, a bunch of options, and put in the stops. I placed the order. And damn if there wasn't a crazy fall in the market that blew right through the stops, right through them, and I lost a seven figure sum. Seven figure!" Chandra's words are fast, but whispered, like water tumbling over stones that smoothes them only slightly. "The irony is it bounced right back up, just like it was supposed to. But my trades, my money was out of the game. So I figured, okay, that was those superfast computer trades that screwed me up, the big institutional players. I need a faster computer, and to be closer to Wall Street so I can compete with their speeds. So I actually did that. Bought a faster computer and went to New York for a week and checked into a hotel. I knew what I was up against. But they're trading billions and I'm not big enough, and it all went. I sat there for a week working the math, the math was right. I went into my retirement account, certain I could regain that fire and win. Then I started playing puts on shorts, and calls on the ultra shorts trying to get it back. But" She shrugs, raises her eyebrows. Turns her palms up, fingers spread. "It's gone. All gone. I couldn't stop it. And now...."

They stand looking at each other. Sissy puts her hands on Chandra's shoulders. "Now what?"

"I'm alive." Chandra snorts bitterly and shuts her eyes.

"Do you want a job?" Sissy asks.

Chandra tilts her head.

"We sure could use a numbers cruncher to help with the grant proposals, and fund raising. It's not full time. But the foundation is doing great, our promotions are really working. Talk to Allie, she's doing the grant writing and reports."

"Thank you, Sissy," she says as if she's apologizing.

"Hey. We need the help, and it's not full time or high wages. But you'll be putting your talents to a good use." Sissy starts walking into the reception room. "Come on. We need you there." Chandra follows.

ROSIE ARRANGED PLATTERS of sliced meats, salads, breadbaskets, cheese platters, fruits and veggies delivered. Now she makes plates for Jeannie's parents.

People sit at long tables covered in white, pastel silk flowers in bud vases. Jeannie's cookie friends and spouses cluster together at the end of one table and, following an uncomfortable silence interspersed with comments that it was a nice service, begin talking about their lives.

Funerals are for the living.

The group eats the sliced meats and potato salad. Drinks the ice tea and soda. The muffled shuffles of utensils on the paper plates, the brush of waxed glasses on the cloth are the only sounds that, for a few minutes, seem to reverberate.

Sara sits with her friends at the end of another table. Mark is pleased that she has this chance to be with people other than him, he's been so laden with sorrow.

"So, Taylor, did you tell everyone the good news?" Rosie asks. "We need it."

Taylor swallows a bite of turkey. "All the shock and sadness about Jeannie has made it seem, I don't know, inappropriate? Unimportant?"

Sissy shakes her head, "Now is when we need good news."

"Tell us," Marnie encourages.

"I could use some." Vera spent the last shred of her energy to come to Jeannie's funeral. The chemotherapy and final radiation have left her weak. Flynn sits close, a protective arm on her shoulder.

"Well, the judge has made his decision about Rick wanting half of my lottery money." Taylor stops.

"And…."

"He decided in my favor."

"Yeah!" Marnie says.

"Yes." Rose pumps her fist in the air proud of her and Kevin's success. "He agreed that the lottery ticket was not part of marital property when Rick made his settlement offer or when Taylor signed the divorce decree."

"She had it." Taylor jerks her head to Rosie.

"Sooo, it wasn't part of marital property. There was no way that Taylor knew she won money when she signed the agreement. Rick is *not* entitled to half," Rosie's voice thrills, as she pushes the food around with her fork and then grins at Kevin. "Yeah for us," she says and then amends it, "All three of us! And your kids, too."

"The best part, the very best part, is that the judge told Rick he should thank his lucky stars that I won the lottery, because he scanned the figures of Rick's and my earnings for the last five years, and he owed me a multiple of a six figure sum. He *strongly* advised Rick, and wiggled his eyebrows for emphasis, to leave well enough alone."

"How long have you known?"

"Several weeks, but I didn't believe it. It was right after Jeannie…" Taylor shakes her head and her glossy red hair glints in the fluorescent lights. "I couldn't believe that I actually beat Rick. Finally. I'm still not convinced."

"You did. But really, Rick defeated himself. The judge was very distressed by Rick's refusal to contact his children or pay reasonable support." Kevin nods, "He isn't

289

going to reward a dead beat dad with your lucky break. This is a judge who is usually dispassionate, but Rick's selfishness and lack of compassion about his own children upset him."

"Sometimes there's justice," Sissy says.

"I'm sorry I made it worse," Vera says. "I'm sorry I let the cat out of the bag and you had that anxiety. And all this publicity." She glances at each of them and points to the door where the reporters wait.

"Turned out to be for the best. Now I know Rick can't take any money from me."

"He sure can't." Rosie waves her fingers, brushing Rick's very existence away.

"But now, here, none of that seems important," Taylor looks down.

Everyone seems reluctant to enter the chill of the fall night air, the clusters of impatient reporters, photographers, and cameras. Blowing puffs of breath into the cold. Shifting from foot to foot. Drinking hot coffee. After all, this is exciting news: the death of a woman after an attempted rape, a woman who won the lottery eight months, only eight months, previous. The sweep from millionaire to murder victim. The irony of winning the lottery and then being killed not for money, but for sex. If rape is indeed sex. The additional coincidence of the hero being her friend's brother who just happened to be in the forest that day. This is a human-interest story that has captured the nations' imagination. Big enough that it was reported on the nightly news of ABC, NBC, CBS and Fox. Big enough that it's been the headliner of the *Detroit News* for weeks. The reporters have pestered all of them for additional tidbits, photos, or sound bites.

Reporters have hounded Joey, the working class, semi-employed hero. His trailer surrounded until he finally talked, giving them only the information the police agreed was wise.

Dalton O'Neil, the blogger who broke the news of their win, is at the forefront, writing daily about Jeannie's murder, teasing out week-long stories from tiny scraps of information. The fact that Jeannie was wearing a wrap cardigan provoked an entire series into their recent popularity and investigation of their safety. Of course, he delved into the possibility of medical error, but then followed with an examination of concussions and closed head injuries. Then there was an in depth look at the trailer park where Iggy Pop grew up, where Joey and Juliet grew up. The fascinating information that Juliet's mother refused the opportunity to move inspired a week- long series, plus a vital internet community discussion, on the meaning of community in spite of poverty. Pictures of Juliet, Joey, Larry, and their Mom flashed on the Internet, the TV, and YouTube. The history of the dealership and the fact that Jeannie was running it following her father's stroke was front-page news. *This is a death that touches the entire community,* Dalton wrote. *Replete with the best and worst in our state. Our hopes and dreams. How quickly tragedy can bring down any of us. A Midwestern story that is a tale of dreams, generosity, friendship, crime and riches.* Dalton's readership has grown into the millions, both advertisers and Huffington Post recruiting him. Dalton's luck is being Vera's hairdresser's husband. And being tenacious.

To avoid the crush of reporters, to avoid being turned into a flash-in-the-pan celebrity object, people remain in the reception room, hesitant to greet the intrusive media.

Juliet and Joey rise from the table of cookie ladies to leave. Joey knows these reporters now and has become adept at brushing them away. Mark sees their coats draped over their arms and strides to them. He feels, somehow, he doesn't understand why, less anguished when he sees Joey. Comforted by his presence. Joey wears a suit that is baggy in the torso as though he's recently lost weight, or has shrunk. The two men embrace.

Joey presses his lips together, and shakes his head. "I'm so sorry I didn't save her, didn't get there earlier. Just a few minutes earlier, maybe I could have prevented him from hitting her."

"You were a hero. She died feeling lucky. Better that than being a rape victim, too."

Juliet looks away, then turns back. She grabs her brother's hand, and says, "Yes. Absolutely." She says it with such determination and conviction that Mark gains a new understanding of Juliet and of Joey's need to be the protector of the forest. He nods at them.

"I've quit my job to work with rape and child sexual abuse survivors as a crisis counselor." She stares into his eyes as she says it, and he witnesses the long ago but still haunting sadness in her gaze.

Joey puts his arm on her shoulder, looks down at her from his height.

They stand with a blank white wall at their backs.

Mark shifts his weight. "What's happening with the investigation?" He looks at Joey.

"I was able to pick out his photo, turns out he's wanted in Ohio, Indiana and Illinois for rape, and rape murder. There's a nationwide search for him. They've managed to keep his other crimes out of the press. But, in a few days, the reporters will have his picture and the publicity will help find him."

Juliet doesn't know why she does it, but tells Mark the story of her rape. Not in detail. Just the headlines. When she and Joey were kids they played in the forest near the trailer park and one day, three teenagers tied Joey to a tree and took turns raping her. She was 8 or maybe 9. Joey was 6 or 7. "Babies really," she said. Her voice wavers. It's still unfamiliar to tell the narrative, even shortened.

Juliet learns from her telling, hearing her own story each time. Now, she can tell it. There are many women like her, like Jeannie. 100,000 women are raped every year. 20% of adult women were sexually abused as children. A chill goes through her. Juliet knows what she'll do next.

"You might not want to hear this today, on a day like today. Who wants to hear more pain?"

"It puts it in perspective. We, most of us, deal with tragedy and go on. I don't know how, but it gives Jeannie's death more sense. A part a history that ends up forming a circle of meaning, if only a terrible one."

Joey says, "Now that he's wanted for Jeannie's murder, a task force is on the case. With all this publicity." He jerks his head to the exit doors and the barrage of reporters waiting for them. "Eventually we'll find him."

"You know," Mark looks away from them, shifts slightly as though to make sure he means what he's about to say with all its implications. "I don't really care what happens to him. I just care that Jeannie is dead and nothing can bring her back."

"He needs to stop damaging women and children," Juliet says. "We need to do something. Sissy has the right idea." Juliet stops, nods her head and grins. "I've just decided where I'm going to put my money. How 'bout we form The Jeannie Jeffries Foundation set up to stop violence against women and children, linking up with Phoenix and Take Back the Night. Who better than Joey and me? Want to join us?"

Mark nods. "But I have no fantasies of revenge, or retribution. But maybe, something good can come from this tragedy."

"You're a more generous, compassionate man than I am," Joey says.

"It's one of the benefits from living with Jeannie, I guess." Mark's eyes fill with tears.

## Twenty-eight

*Appreciate the magic of the ordinary.*
Jeannie

*I WATCH AS they make them, my beloved Sara and Mark.*

*They're so bleary-eyed since my death that this one thing should be happy, or at least bittersweet, as they redo my most difficult cookie, the fortune cookies. I don't know why exactly they decided to do this one. Or did they not realize what they were getting into?*

*Once again they try to invent the fortunes. What will they wish my beloved girlfriends for their futures? When they've won everything that everyone else wants? All of them still stunned and shaken. Moving as though through quicksand.*

*Sara asking, "I don't get it, I still don't get it. Tell me again how she died."*

*My stainless steel bowl is full of liquidy batter.*

*Mark patiently repeats the facts. She had a concussion. We can't see into anyone's brain, there's a mystery there in spite of CAT scans and MRIs. Everything seemed normal. But it wasn't. Something deep inside her brain started bleeding and killed her.*

*"I still don't get it," Sara says. "It doesn't make sense."*

*"No," Mark agrees. "It doesn't. Not really."*

*Shit. I agree. It doesn't make sense. But it is what it is. Sometimes it really pisses me off, everything was finally settled, everything was good, but I can't do anything about it.*

*"Life is meaningless. How can you die when everything is fine and you're healthy and happy? And young. Still young?"*

*"I don't know," Mark shrugs.*

295

Mark pulls out the sheet of pancake-like cookies. The aroma of cooked sugar and vanilla fill the air. How I love that smell.

Now the hard part comes. I'm warning you guys. This is the hard part. Don't burn your fingers.

Their fingers are incased in dishtowels so they don't burn. A spatula releases the cookie from the sheet. They try to insert the fortune, fold the cookies, and then curl them into the muffin tins, or over glass lips.

I want to see the fortunes they have devised for my beloved cookie bitches. Each of them still as shocked as I am that this happened. All of us still so surprised.

But I didn't have anything to do with it.

It was so long ago when I made those fortune cookies. It was when I started doing yoga. Back when I thought the biggest tragedy of my life would be that Rosie and Sue kept a secret from me. I was right in a way, because that secret and the transgression it contained wound its way into my father's stroke, wound into him now, looking bleak and bent, struggling to talk, unable yet to do buttons. At least he can pull on his pants, slide his arms in his shirt. Mom patiently, lovingly does his buttons.

Now Sue runs the dealership. There're ironies in that... a mockery which a few years ago would have made me twist and collapse in a crumbling terminal sense of betrayal and abandonment. But now, the irony is in how fitting it is, truly is. It absolutely should be that Sue would be general manager and his other salesman, Jay and Kurt, would be helping, paying my mother rent for the building and a percentage for the franchise. Sue thinks about my father, she must, every day she enters the dealership, and sits at his old desk (I wonder if they made love on that desk, that very desk, but even from my exalted state, I'm not privy to that kind of information or visions of the time when I was alive.)

296

*Sometimes Dad gets confused and asks my mother why I haven't visited him. It seems like it's been so long. She has to tell him all over again. His face crumbles, his eyes wet, his lower lip quivers. His head shakes as he pushes away the thoughts, the memories once again.*

*I get to float around like this, spying on people for a while.*

*Now, I return to my kitchen, peaking on my husband and daughter as they struggle with the fortune cookies. I should have warned them how hard they are to make. So hard. And to make 156 is a time consuming, finger-burning task for even the most experienced baker.*

*They are together. Heads bent toward the task. I never noticed how alike the whirls at the top of their heads are. Working as a team, this father and daughter. Mark congratulates Sara on how smoothly they do it, and their fingers work as one as they fold a fortune into the warm dough and drape it over the edge of a glass.*

*Hey. They're pretty good at this. I want to tell them. I kiss those wonderful whirls at the top of their heads, and Sara touches her head. She reaches me for a split second and I feel her warmth and turn over inside myself. Mark just revolves his head on his neck, his hands busy with folding cookies.*

*What I really want to see is their fortunes, their wishes for themselves and my friends.*

**Celebrate life!**
**Love your own breath.**
**Live each day as though it is the last, because it may be.**
**Exercise and stretch**
**Laugh every day**
**Remember gratitude**
**Follow your bliss but consider others**

*Make it matter*
*Honor before popularity*
*Cultivate kindness and compassion*
*Appreciate the magic of the ordinary*
*Don't say no to something you're able to do*

     *Cookies are curved over glasses, cups, muffin tins, bowls, everything they find. All those morsels of wishes drape over assorted utensils covering our dining room table. The aroma of vanilla and almond, the cooked sweet smell of sugar fills the room.*

     *Ah, my wonders, both of you.*

*SO THIS WILL be my last cookie party and I get to lurk around it. Marnie has not filled my spot with another cookie bitch, she knows that Mark and Sara will stop by with fortune cookies, already bundled in tissue and folded into bags.*

     *Marnie's house is decorated as it always is. A new house, but the same tree, with its cluster of teddy bears at the base, the same wooden Santas grace the same tables. It feels like another home to me, even though I've been to this house, with the dark lake now quiet and beginning to freeze, the boats put away, and the dock pulled in, only a few times. The dining room table is already crowded with Brie en Croute, pear salad with walnuts and goat cheese, quiche. Marnie's tomato soup simmers on her stove. I think Marnie decided our potluck was yummier than catered! It smells like it always does, though people are more somber than usual. I see the slower movements, the hesitation, and the dark mood.*

     *Come on everyone! It's the best party of the year! Time to celebrate life. That's the gift of my death. Maybe I won the lottery so you would learn. Time is important. How you spend your time, not how much money you spend.*

*We have it all backwards. We think money is important because we exhaust so much time working for it. And yes, for most of us, our jobs are only for money. But, in truth, money is merely a stand-in for our way to stay alive and, because our lives are precious, we imbue money --the gathering of it, saving it, relishing it --with the same quickened passion. Of course our capitalist culture and the media work in harmony to make us think money defines us. But we got it backwards.*

*I say it again: It's how we spend our lives, our time, that's important. And yes, we have to spend some of it, too much, on gathering money. So we hate money and love it both.*

*I blow in Rosie's ear, and she giggles. I tickle Sissy under her chin, and she laughs. My friends begin to loosen up.*

*They take their wine glasses and plates into the living room. There is an empty chair. On the seat is a burning candle. That must be my chair, in remembrance of me.*

*Thank you, Marnie. I see this and I thank you.*

*Rosie stops in front of it and nods. I was once her best friend. Her pregnancy softens her, her glow lets me know Kevin continues supporting and loving her. Vera looks at the flame and a tear rolls from the corner of her eye. She's wearing her wig, but it seems too big, too flamboyant for her. She's beginning to get her weight back. She'll be okay for a while. Maybe a long while. Vera shakes her head, and places her fingertips on her chest and bows her head. Each of them files past my chair.*

*Okay, good. Now I'm out of the way and the fun is at hand!*

*Allie has already passed out her cookies (Extra-chunky peanut butter dipped in dark chocolate) (I can* smell them, but can't taste. But smell is almost delicious enough.) Then Sara and Mark arrive.

They smile, wan smiles, not giving over their entire faces to the motion, wave, and Mark says, "We brought Jeannie's fortune cookies. We know how much she would want to be here...and...well...I guess it's our way to have her a bit longer...."

Marnie looks down, purses her mouth together.

Come on, Marnie. You're never without words. It's your party. You're the head cookie bitch.

Juliet says, "Well, you're going to stay and pass out the cookies, and tell your story aren't you?"

"You already know the story," Mark says.

"No, we don't," Allie stands, her voice is soft. "We don't know your story." She says this looking into Sara's eyes. "We'd love to hear your story."

"You can stay for the whole party if you want..." Rosie says.

"Go, Mark. I'll see that she gets home," Marnie says.

Ah, this worked out even better than I hoped.

Sara looks back and forth between her father and Marnie wondering if this is really okay.

He tilts his head in an unasked question.

Sara shrugs halfheartedly.

"Okay then. Have fun."

SARA GOES LAST. By then she's eaten soup, and tasted the appetizers. By then Rosie has told everyone that she and Kevin are going to sell their practice and buy a boat to go with the condo. After their baby is born, they'll float around the Caribbean.

Taylor has announced that she and the kids will be spending the summer in Naples, too. Sounds like a new branch of the cookie club will be forming in Florida.

The lottery players have pooled money for the non-players. There's a six-figure sum for each of them. Taylor stands with the envelopes in her hand. "This is for you, our wonderful cookie bitches. We each contributed and then divided it equally between you. I can't begin to tell you how much I love you guys. How much I appreciate that you've been there for me even though I've been a bitch and a half. Not a sweet cookie bitch but a Cruella DaVille bitch. None of you ever deserved it. All you did was love me and try to help me. You were always there for me. Took me and my kids in when I would have been homeless." She meets Allie's eyes and both their eyes fill. "Tried to help me find jobs. Gave me encouragement and great advice, which I knew was right, but I couldn't figure out how to follow. It took a loooonng time to sink in." She jerks her head for an exclamation point. "Soooooo, as Rosie would say," Taylor grins at Rosie, "This is for you. Each of you." And she hands an envelope to Allie, Vera, Alice, Tracy, and Charlene.

They won't know it, but Taylor contributed the most.

Sara has her own bag stuffed with beautifully wrapped cookies: pecan butter balls, and truffles, gingerbread ladies, double chocolate, Pennsylvania dunkers. Kisses. Her favorite. The ones she ate up as soon as I arrived home with them.

She stands, this little girl of mine, almost a woman, I guess she is a woman now. "You know my story. It's yours too. My mama died in a crazy way. I still don't get it. Not really."

"None of us do," Vera says.

"But I guess Dad and me wanted to do this one last thing for her. Almost a way to be her, doing what she did. What she would do. I decided making up fortunes would be fun. But it's hard. I thought making these cookies would be fun, but chocolate chip are much easier. Hmmm. maybe yummier, too. But, well, here they are." She hands a bundle to Taylor sitting next to her and it's passed around the circle.

I notice again how much she looks like Mark, though she has Mom's eyes.

"I still don't get it though. It seems unfair."

"It is," Sissy says.

Rosie immediately cracks a cookie open, "Cultivate Kindness and Compassion", she reads. "I'm working on that one." She tastes the cookie. "Oh, and they're yummy as well as cute and communicative." She lifts her wine glass and sips.

"Remember Gratitude." Vera tilts her head, and looks at Sara, "I don't know if you know that I've been sick, and your Mom came over and helped me by doing yoga with me. She was with me the morning that she died. Do you know that?"

Sara's eyes wet and she shakes her head, no.

"Now, whenever I do those poses, and I do, legs up the wall is my favorite, it's as though she's there, and I hear again her words of encouragement and peace. She helped heal me. I'm grateful that I knew her. And I miss her terribly."

Ah, Vera. I miss you, too.

'We all miss her. We all loved her," Allie says.

"I guess that's my story," Sara says, shrugs, and plops herself down on the chair. A gesture that is so the typical teenager, my friends can't help but grin or giggle.

Then Juliet rises. "I have, well Sissy and I have, another surprise. Some of you know about this," Juliet glances at Allie and Charlene. "Your dad knows, too," she says to Sara. "It's our way of honoring Jeannie and trying to prevent what happened to her from happening to others. Many others. Including me. We're forming the Jeannie Jeffries Memorial Foundation to prevent rape and violence against women. It'll be connected to Sissy's foundation."

*"Can I help?"* Rosie asks and wipes her eyes with the back of her hand. *"I so would like to do something to carry on Jeannie's spirit."*

*"Of course. You'll have a computer on that boat, right? I remember what a great marketer you are. And you can contribute money, too."* Juliet laughs.

*"Count me in,"* Marnie says.

*"Charlene and I will be helping out Jeannie's foundation, also,"* Allie says.

*"Tomorrow night, we're announcing it."* Sissy adds. *"Vera, you can make sure your buddy Dalton attends. And his wife."* All my friends laugh. *"Take Back the Night will be there and we'll march through the city and make the announcement at the Federal Building."*

*"Can I come?"* Sara asks.

*"Yes. Invite all your friends! We need young women to get involved."*

*I don't know how I feel about this. It's hard to be happy since I had to die to get a memorial foundation in my name. But still…. If I had to die I guess this is an honor.*

*I'm loved.*

*My wonderful cookie bitches and husband can help change the culture of rape. If anyone can do it, they can. Positive change will result from my death. And my life.*

*Thank you, I whisper in Juliet and Sissy's ears.*

*"You forgot to eat your cookie,"* Rosie says to Sara. *"What's your fortune?"*

*Yeah, I want to know, too.*

Sara cracks open one of her fortune cookies. *"Know the magic of the ordinary,"* she reads.

*"That's so Jeannie,"* Charlene and Marnie say, almost in chorus.

*Sara giggles.*

*I give my daughter a butterfly kiss, so lightly she only feels a sense of love. I am proud of the woman she is becoming. And wish her contentment and clarity.*

*Ah, but alas. We're programmed to want more of everything.*

*More beauty, more sex, more money.*

*More of the ordinary.*

*And most of all….*

*More life.*

*The End*

## Acknowledgements

Though we write alone, I have a team that brings the dictation I receive from the universe (sometimes as chaotic and surprising as the world often appears) to fruition. This novel is no exception. So my heartfelt thanks first go to: Tim Kornegay, Elizabeth Hinton, Ruth Behar who are so relied on, so appreciated, and so loved. Added to this are: Amina Henry, Pavarti Tyler, and Keith Ferrell whose suggestions and edits are crucial to the final form of this story. Luckily, Elaine Clayman's eagle eyes picked out additional errors. Thank you all.

*The Lottery* would not see the light of day without the work of many people. My literary agent, Peter Miller, believed in it, and treasured it as he has each of the novels in *The Christmas Cookie Club* series. The White Glove staff, specifically Katy Ardens and Nathan Rosenbaum, made sure it was available and known.

In doing research for this book, I want to thank the party store close to where I live where I bought my lottery tickets and the clerk who patiently walked me through my various betting options. I read several books which informed this novel: Shayne Jones, *Lottery-winners' Guide, Aunt Sally's Policy Players' Dream Book,* Professor Jones, *The Basics of Winning Lotto/Lottery,* Don Catlin, *the Lottery Book,* and Richard Sennet and Jonathan Cobb, *The Hidden injuries of Class.* For the years I worked on this novel, I trolled for information on the lottery, day trading, gambling, wealth, inequality and other aspects of the plot in movies, newspapers, magazines, and museums. Information from all that gleaning is woven in the novel.

## About Ann Pearlman

Ann Pearlman has been passionate about writing since the eighth grade. A Pulitzer Prize and National Book Award Nominee and international bestselling author, she's the author of *Keep the Home Fires Burning, Infidelity: A Memoir, Inside the Crips, The Christmas Cookie Cookbook.* An illustrated short story, *Other Lives,* combined her love of art with writing, and she followed that up with *Angels,* for adults. *His Eyes Is On the Sparrow* is part of the launch of the new publishing company, Shebooks.

    *The Christmas Cookie Club,* Ann's first novel, was translated into six languages and became an international and national bestseller. It was followed by widely praised and loved, *A Gift For my Sister.* *The Lottery* is the third novel in *The Christmas Cookie Club* series. Check out annpearlman.net to learn more.

Made in the USA
Middletown, DE
01 December 2021